SHATTER CITY

SCOTT WESTERFELD

■SCHOLASTIC

Published in the UK by Scholastic Children's Books, 2019
Euston House, 24 Eversholt Street, London, NW1 1DB, UK
A division of Scholastic Limited.

London – New York – Toronto – Sydney – Auckland
Mexico City – New Delhi – Hong Kong

SCHOLASTIC and associated logos are trademarks and/or
registered trademarks of Scholastic Inc.

First published in the US by Scholastic Inc, 2019

Text © Scott Westerfeld, 2019

The right of Scott Westerfeld to be identified as the author of this work has
been asserted by them under the Copyright, Designs and Patents Act 1988.

ISBN 978 1407 18828 7

Printed by CPI Group (UK) Ltd, Croydon, CR0 4YY
Papers used by Scholastic Children's Books are made
from wood grown in sustainable forests.

1 3 5 7 9 10 8 6 4 2

This is a work of fiction. Names, characters, places, incidents
and dialogues are products of the author's imagination or are used
fictitiously. Any resemblance to actual people, living or dead,
events or locales is entirely coincidental.

www.scholastic.co.uk

To everyone searching
for family.

PART 1

DRESS
TO MOVE

Everyone sees what you appear to be,

few know what you really are.

—Niccolò Machiavelli

EVERYTHING

My engagement bash is the talk of the feeds.

It should be.

My dress is spectacular—an azure sheath orbited by hovering metal shards. My publicity team designed it, using crowd metrics and flash polls. It was big news, Rafia of Shreve letting randoms choose her outfit.

But the dress is nothing compared to my fiancé: Col Palafox, the first son of Victoria. The leader of a guerrilla army, until a month ago, when he attacked my father's city and lost everything.

Our families are at war, you see. Col is our prisoner as well as my betrothed. Engagements don't get much better than this.

The feeds love it. They're calling us the most logic-missing couple of the mind-rain. The scandal of the season.

Wait till they watch me kill my father on my wedding day.

Wait till they find out that I was never really me.

"Rafia?" my room asks. "Dona Oliver is here to see you."

Rafia isn't my name, but I answer, "Let her in."

The door slides open. My father's secretary wears a distracted look, her eyes glinting with data. All those details swirling around the party, like the hovercams around this tower, waiting for luminaries to arrive.

"We've added something to tomorrow's schedule," Dona says. "A public appearance, just the two of you."

I try not to flinch. "Dad and me?"

She shakes her head. "You and Col, so the citizens of Shreve can see you together. Give them your *best* smile, he said."

"This one?" My lips curl, a perfect imitation of my twin sister.

But the smile doesn't impress Dona. Her eyes clear of data, and she lowers herself into the chair where I used to sit and watch Rafi do her makeup.

I keep my gaze on the mirror, letting a drone layer my foundation in smooth strokes. Dona stares at me, a little uncertain.

Maybe because Rafi would never allow a machine to do her makeup.

"It'll be okay," Dona finally says.

She's wrong.

I'm a prisoner in this tower, just like Col. There's a bomb collar around my neck, like the one around his. Spy dust watches my every move, tracks my every glance. Sooner or later, I'll choose the wrong

4

dress or make the wrong joke and someone will realize I'm not my big sister, Rafia.

She's out in the wild. Free at last, but hunted by my father's forces. They think she's me, and have orders to kill her on sight.

Everything is a long way from okay.

"We'll have a dozen guards around you," Dona goes on. "A hundred security drones overhead. You'll be just as safe as when Frey was here to take your place."

That's almost funny. Dona thinks I'm scared of a crowd of randoms, because I don't have a body double anymore. But it was *me* in front of those crowds.

I was born to be sniper bait. My body resists sitting here motionless, letting a drone spray on my makeup. Dodging bullets was better.

And I miss my sister. Rafi deciding on our makeup, our hair. Telling me the gossip from a party the night before, trying to give me a life.

Living in her shadow wasn't so bad. Pretending to be her is a hundred times more lonely. In this whole city, only Col knows who I really am.

I hope Rafi's okay out there in the wild.

"I'm not afraid of crowds," I say.

"Maybe something else is making you nervous." Dona's voice goes soft, as if the spy dust won't hear. "Like marrying a boy you hardly know?"

Wrong again—Col and I love each other. We fought a war together. He was the first outsider to know my secret. I was there when his world crumbled.

Here in my father's tower, we see each other only at formal dinners and publicity events, never alone. Me playing the haughty Rafia, him the humbled prisoner. But the air still sparks between us.

I've fooled everyone else; he recognized me in the first five minutes.

It was worth it, staying here to save him.

"He really does seem to like you," Dona says. "That's more than we could hope for . . . given everything."

I give her one of Rafi's sidelong looks. *Everything* includes my father's missiles destroying Col's home and family. The army of Shreve occupying his city. Our forces still hunting his younger brother.

My publicity team was worried that our engagement would look like a sham, a spectacle to make the world forget my father's crimes. But it turns out people *live* for stories about lovers whose families are at war.

"Col's not a problem," I say.

"You hardly know him, Rafia. And marriage is serious."

"So is war. Allying our houses will end this one. Maybe the world will start to forgive us for invading Victoria."

"I know you're doing the strategic thing," Dona says. "But that doesn't always make it easy. This must be scary."

I put on my sister's imperious voice. "I'm not afraid of some *boy*."

"You've changed," Dona says gently.

Those words freeze me. I stare at the mirror, watching the drone sculpt my face with artful lines.

I am Rafia of Shreve.

I am always watched, but I am never seen.

"It's no wonder, of course," Dona continues. "Your home was invaded. You were forced to admit your oldest secret in front of everyone."

She means my speech with Rafi, the night Col was captured. We sisters stood together in front of the hovercams, revealing at last that there were two of us—the heir and the body double. Explaining that our father used his own daughter as a decoy for snipers and kidnappers.

That speech was supposed to make the city rise up against him. But speeches don't win wars, it turns out.

"What does that have to do with Col?" I ask.

"He came along just as all your certainties vanished. When you felt most exposed."

I laugh. "You think I have a *crush* on him?"

"You persuaded him to accept your hand in marriage. That took some work."

"Hardly." One of Rafi's shrugs. "Dad would've executed him. Col's lucky he's more useful as a son-in-law than a corpse."

"But you still had to convince him, and your father, and the rest of the world that you wanted to be together. Maybe you convinced your-self too."

I close my eyes, letting the drone work on my lashes while my heart settles in my chest.

Dona has seen the way I feel about Col.

She was always the most thoughtful of my father's staff. Not just a

7

thug. I will need her on my side in the all-important seconds after he's dead. For now, she needs to think that Rafi remains as selfish as always.

"I have plans for that boy."

"I'm sure you do," she says. "You've worked hard on your part of the bargain."

She means my deal with my father—I get to marry Col, to keep him alive, as long as I'm the perfect daughter. Go to my classes. Do what Publicity tells me. No public mention of Frey.

"But sometimes the heart makes its own plans," Dona says. "You've fallen for him."

I keep my eyes closed, letting the drone work. She must have watched us in those early days—Col pretending to resist my offer of marriage, like a defeated, sullen captive. At first, we insulted each other, then we argued the merits of an alliance, only letting ourselves flirt a little at the end.

It made my skin hum, keeping a secret together while the spy dust watched.

But something true must have slipped out, caught by Dona's sharp eyes.

"Believe what you want," I say. "That boy is a means to an end."

"Of course, Rafia. Sorry to presume." She stands up, adding lightly, "By the way, he wanted to see you before the bash. He's waiting on the eighth-floor terrace. Alone."

I open my eyes too quickly, and the drone pings its disapproval.

My eye shadow is smeared, just a touch. Brain-missing of me, but the promise of a private moment with Col makes me want to run to the stairs.

Dona smiles, noticing everything. "Don't do your hair yet. It's windy out."

Spy dust doesn't work well in the breeze. But I stay in character— cursing softly, flicking the drone aside to inspect its work.

"Tell Col I'll be there in forty minutes."

STEADFAST

On my way to see Col, I step across the red line like it's nothing.

Growing up, only our tutors and a few of my father's closest advisors knew there were two of us. I stayed hidden in the secure part of the tower, my world bounded by colored markings on the floor. I was trained to walk and talk like Rafi, to stay in her shadow, to kill. A deadly secret in the shape of a girl.

But now that I've taken my sister's place, I can go anywhere. The staff looks down at the floor as I pass, clearing my way with small backward steps. They remember Rafi's temper tantrums, her rage at being the first daughter of Shreve—*his* daughter. Or maybe they sense something nervous-making about me now, the killer inside.

I've changed from an invisible girl into someone dangerous to look at.

When we were little, Rafi was always beside me, telling me what to wear, which rules we could break. She knew the servants' names, and how to stand up to our father.

She always promised that after he was gone, she'd reveal me to the world. That was all I wanted back then—to walk freely in my own home.

But not like this, alone.

Without Rafi, I don't belong here anymore.

I only see her on the feeds now. Out there in the wild, with the rebels and what remains of Col's army, Rafi records herself every few days. She calls on the world to punish our father's crimes, telling them to boycott everything Shreve makes.

Pretending to be me.

The impersonation is uncanny. Like she's been practicing all along.

Watching her is dizzy-making, like leaving my own body and seeing myself from the outside. All those years of me copying her walk, her stance, the way she raises her eyebrows—that whole time she was watching me too.

And I have to ask myself . . .

Was it this unnerving for Rafi, watching *me* impersonating *her*?

Col waits on a high stone terrace that overlooks the gardens. We're on the private side of my father's tower, where newscams aren't allowed to fly. The late-winter sky is pale blue. No clouds, just spirals of birds coiling up from the forest.

Col isn't dressed up yet—tonight he'll be in a silver knee-length suit, its threads programmed to reflect the colors of my dress. But he looks beautiful in his rust linen jacket and . . .

When did I start paying attention to clothes? I used to only care about improvised weapons and my enemies' weaknesses.

Maybe after a month of pretending to be Rafi, I'm turning into her. Studying for interviews, trying to impress my tutors, taking on every duty my father asks of me. Sometimes in bed at night, my muscles ache from standing like her all day.

But it's worth it to keep Col alive.

"You look lovely," he says, taking my hand.

He plays his role well, enthralled by me reluctantly, someone who's fallen for an enemy's daughter. We have to stay in character, even out here in the breeze. Security can still listen through the walls, the windows, the smart fibers of our clothes.

"Thank you." I push my hair behind my ears. "But they'll all be staring at you tonight."

"Don't be silly, Rafia. You're the belle of this ball."

I keep my eyes fixed on the horizon. I want to look at him, kiss him. But the real Rafi wouldn't give Dona the satisfaction.

And every time we kiss, my father might be watching.

"The people of Shreve have always been fond of me," I say. "But now that they know about Frey, what if it's her they love?"

"Maybe it doesn't matter."

A frown crosses my face. "Are you saying we're *interchangeable*?"

"Hardly. Frey isn't like anyone else."

"She had an unsual upbringing." I try to sound flippant. "Strange hobbies as a child."

"I know. We fought a war together. Your father should be afraid of her."

"He is." My laughter sounds like a bubblehead's. "But Frey won't bother us."

"Don't be so sure. She's as fierce as she is beautiful."

Fierce. One of our words, like *steadfast.* I flush under my party makeup, trying to think what Rafi would say.

"Are you trying to make me jealous, Col?"

He shrugs. "You're more like her than you realize."

"We're opposites. She's a warrior. I've never even punched anyone!"

He gently curls my fingers into a fist. "There's plenty of time to learn."

His touch makes me shiver, and I watch the military hovercraft circling overhead, just to have something to look at. I want him to keep saying these things about me, so I tell myself it's what Rafi would want too.

"I've always meant to ask . . ." I give him one of Rafi's dramatic pauses. "When you two were playing soldier together, were you ever more than just comrades-in-arms?"

Col hesitates, glances at the tower behind us.

"Not that it matters," I add. "It wouldn't be the most awkward thing in our past. The point of this wedding is to get beyond all that."

I come to a halt, flustered by how the words *all that* compare to my father's crimes. Rafi is never flustered.

"Your sister and I were allies," Col says.

13

Such a neutral word. Anyone listening would think we weren't even friends. But that was our first promise to each other—to be allies.

"I've been meaning to apologize," he says. "I laughed when you proposed to me. That was rude."

I shrug. "Under the circumstances, it must have sounded odd."

"It took a while to understand." He takes my hand again, firmly this time. "You weren't just saving me from execution. You really do like me."

Rafi would look away, so I do. "It's a sin to waste good breeding."

He nods. "I'm just saying, I see you for who you are. You aren't your sister."

I turn to him. "Col."

His lips barely move, mouthing my name.

Frey.

I have to look away again. It's madness, playing games like this, hoping the dust won't catch it.

But something tightly wound inside me loosens a little.

I am seen.

The scars of war spread out beneath us—gouges in the earth where invading Victorian craft fell during our attack on Shreve. The hedges where my own hovercar crashed still haven't regrown.

We almost won, almost ousted my father from power, only to fail and wind up here. Two prisoners.

But at least we showed the citizens of Shreve that my father isn't invincible. We infected his surveillance dust that night—the system still crashes once a week or so, giving the citizens of Shreve a few precious hours of privacy.

My plan hinges on my father being weaker now. And, of course, on everyone thinking that I'm the spoiled Rafia, not the trained killer, Frey.

"About our appearance tomorrow," Col says lightly.

"Yes. Dona just told me about it."

"We should wear something special."

I'm not sure what he means. My staff always chooses Col's clothes, walking the fine line of making him desirable without anyone forgetting that he's our prisoner.

But then he glances at my necklace—the bomb collar.

He wears one too, a thick gray ring of metal around his neck. If we try to escape this tower, the collars will detonate, turning us into a fine mist of blood and meat. Now that I have no body double, my father likes to be certain that no one can ever steal me away.

But there's something he doesn't know. On the night of the attack, we cracked the code that unlocks the collar. The key is hidden in the trophy room.

Col doesn't know about the key either. So why is he staring at my neck?

"Something less formal?" I suggest.

"Exactly—I don't want to look stuffy."

I nod, still uncertain of what he's trying to say.

Then he steps forward, as if hugging me good-bye, and murmurs so softly that the wind takes it away . . .

"Dress to move."

CLICK

"Entrance in ten minutes," Dona says. "Are you ready?"

"Me or them?" I ask.

There are five people fussing around me—sewing the bottom of my dress, adjusting my jewelry, checking the batteries on my lifters, fixing my hair.

No one answers.

The party thrums the floor beneath our feet, shakes the walls around us. Light pulses through the slim gap between the double doors waiting to let me in.

I get that tickle in my stomach. All those eyes on me, just like in my nightmares. Will they see through my act and finally realize that I'm Frey?

"Ready," someone finally says. One by one, the others repeat the word and take a step back.

"Final dress check," Dona says. "Spin it up."

Maltia, my sister's fashion mistress, waves a hand, and I feel my arm hairs start to tingle. The magnetic lifters woven into the fibers of my dress are coming to life.

A small galaxy of metal shards detaches from the hem, rising into the air. At first it's shiny chaos, but soon the shards find their proper orbits. I'm standing at the center of an intricate mechanism, as if a solar system has formed around me.

Dona takes a moment to drink it in before she speaks again.

"Proximity check?"

Maltia steps closer, inside the orbiting metal. The shards sense her and react, slipping from their paths to envelop her as well. For a moment, we're together inside our own private celestial clock. It's oddly intimate, but Maltia doesn't meet my eye.

As she steps out again, my satellites artfully avoid her.

"Perfect," Dona says, and they all clap for me, as if I had anything to do with this dress. "Entrance in four minutes."

I look around. "Where's Col?"

It comes out too eager—Dona gives me a look. She'll be watching us tonight. But I have a plan to convince her that my feelings for Col are purely mercenary.

"On his way," Dona says. "Which reminds me, one last jewelry check."

At these words, the others lower their eyes.

Dona steps forward, parting the orbiting metal around me. She holds up a wafer of flat circuitry, presses it against my neck.

The bomb collar makes a soft *click*.

I stand there, stunned, as Dona pulls the collar open. Its weight lifts from my shoulders, my heart, my future.

But the feeling only lasts a moment—then another *click*.

When I look in the mirror, I see that she's slipped on a jewel that matches my dress. As if the collar was decoration.

Col comes in, flanked by two bodyguards. They look like soldiers stuffed into formal wear, but Col was born to dress this way. The morning suit and tie are a dull gray at first, but the threads turn reflective as he draws near. The color of my dress glints along his body.

He hesitates, wary of the satellites in orbit around me. But when he reaches for my hand, the shards adjust, taking up stations around his arm.

Col glances at the jewel around my neck and smiles.

"Lovely necklace," he says.

"Thanks. It's the same old thing, though. Just a new stone."

"Entrance in one minute!" Dona calls.

Col adjusts his cuffs, his eyes on my collar again. "You aren't bored of it?"

"A family heirloom. I don't go anywhere without it."

He takes my arm in his, straightening to make our entrance.

"Family is important," he says.

Dress to move, he whispered on the terrace.

Is he planning an escape tomorrow?

There'll be soldiers, security drones, half the Shreve military on standby. Neither of us is armed with so much as a pulse knife, and the collars will kill us on command.

That's why I've given up on running away. There will never be any freedom while my father still breathes. The only solution is for me to end him with the whole world watching, and then declare myself and my sister rulers of—

"Smile, you two," Dona says. "Entrance in five, four, three . . ."

The doors swing open, and a wave of sound rushes over us, a galaxy of light, an ocean of eyes and hovercams.

I barely have time to put on Rafi's smile.

BASH

After a moment of applause from the crowd, my sister's friends swarm us. Their possessive bubble surrounds me, a human version of my metal satellites.

"You're so beautiful, Rafia!"

"I *love* that dress."

"So brilliant—letting the randoms vote on your outfit!"

"Can I touch one of your little planets?"

I've studied Rafi's friends my whole life, so I'd know who to wave to in a crowd. But before this month, I never really talked to them. As part of my deal with my father, my presence is required at all their parties.

I used to envy my sister for her friends, but every minute with them is full of terror that I'll say the wrong thing.

I know their faces, their names. But they're strangers to me.

Their eyes shift from me to Col.

"So *this* is the boy you've been hiding," one says—Katya, who changes her face once a week. For this party, her little finger has been surged into a tiny snake.

"I can see why," Demeter says. "He looks even better in person."

"Rebel boys are so rugged," Sirius says, his flash tattoos spinning. "Should I get one too?"

They all go silent, waiting for me to respond with something cutting. To remind them that they're just rich kids, while I am the first daughter of Shreve.

The attention freezes me, like when my father expects Rafia's wit from my mouth. But then Col pulls me close, and the metal shards take up orbit around us both.

"Did you say *rebel*?" he asks. "I'm the first son of Victoria."

Sirius frowns at him. "So?"

"Rebels don't have cities," I tell him. "Col, these are my friends. Apologies that they're so manners-missing."

I wave my hand. Suddenly polite and obedient, they step forward one by one to introduce themselves.

"So this is *real* between you two?" Sirius asks. His dark eyes are full of glitter implants. "That's what everyone's asking."

"Of course it is." I idly brush one of my satellites aside. "As real as having my own city."

This takes a moment to click. It's Demeter, whose mother commands the Shreve police force, who speaks up first.

"You're moving to Victoria after you're married?"

"We're going to *rule* Victoria," I say.

Katya's eyes glisten with sudden tears. "You're leaving us!"

I shrug. "Who says you can't come along?"

Demeter sputters, then grins an apology at Col. "Sorry. But that place is so culture-missing."

"When we're done with it, Victoria will be the envy of Shreve." I wave my hand at the party—the safety fireworks, the fountains of bubbly, the hoverdancers over our heads. "None of this matters when the whole world hates us."

Now my sister's friends are scandalized. A little nervous, even, uncertain if I'm setting a trap. Maybe they're checking to see if the dust has crashed again.

It hasn't, but Katya decides to be brave. "Raffles is right. My school in Paris won't accept Shreve trade credits anymore. They make us pay tuition in gold, like smugglers!"

"We can't buy decent caviar anymore," Demeter says. "No one wants to sell to us!"

"I wasn't invited to the London Equestrian Ball this year!"

"My publicist told me to stay home tonight! She said coming to this bash wasn't worth the reputational—" Sirius freezes, his flash tattoos spinning with terror.

I ignore the insult, taking Col's hand.

"We're going to rebuild Victoria, make it the *best* city. The rest of the world will adore us for it."

There is a moment of cautious silence. Then Katya starts clapping, her eyes brimming again. "I *knew* you'd fix this, Raffles! I'll follow you anywhere!"

The others join in the applause.

Of course, I'm saying all this for the dust, for Dona, not these bubble-heads. But some of it is even true. We're going to rebuild everything in Victoria that my father destroyed. After we've destroyed my father.

"Won't living in a foreign city be nervous-making?" Demeter asks. "Is it even safe?"

"With Col beside me? Victorians *love* him."

"Not them." She leans forward to mock whisper. "Your *sister*."

Another hush comes over our little bubble—Rafi's friends remembering that there were always two of us. One sister invited them to dinner, gave tasteful birthday presents, let them bask in her fame and power. The other, they only brushed shoulders with on the dance floor . . . but she was a killer.

And none of them ever noticed.

"Frey would never hurt me," I say firmly.

Hearing my name entrances them. At all those parties, we've never really talked about me. My father's publicity machine has spread the rumor that the whole speech was faked. That Rafi was drugged, and Frey was a Victorian agent with impostor surge.

No one close to him believes it.

"What was it like, having an extra *you*?" Katya asks.

"I wish my parents had made me a secret twin," Demeter says. "Someone to take my exams!"

"She'd probably fail them. Remember that speech? Frey was so *dirty*."

"Still, if you needed a kidney transplant—no waiting for one to grow!"

23

It's my turn to say something bubbly, but I can't. After everything our father has done to us, they still see Frey as an accessory. A spare.

Suddenly I need to leave.

I manage a smile. "We have to mingle now, bubbleheads. Don't be strangers."

"*You* should talk, Raffles! You went missing for the whole war!"

"You're so much better now."

"Love the dress!"

I guide us out of the VIP area, my fingernails in Col's arm.

My heart gradually settles. It's more crowded out here, but no one knows my sister personally. People offer their congratulations without swarming us.

"Your friends seem nice," Col says.

"Sorry."

He shrugs. "I'm used to awkward conversations with your crowd, Rafia. But it's even stranger now that . . ."

His voice trails away. *Now that I'm the captive of my family's murderers. And engaged to their daughter.*

"They're just bubbleheads," I say.

That's what Rafi always called them when she got home from parties. I thought she was just trying to make me feel better for having no friends of my own. But she was right.

The whole time we were growing up, I never saw that she was as lonely as me.

Does Rafi have new friends now? Somehow I can't imagine her enjoying the company of rebels and Victorian resistance fighters.

"I'll get used to them," Col says.

"Don't bother. None of them are brave enough to follow us to Victoria."

"Maybe Victoria will come to them." He gestures at someone approaching us. They're wearing a dress almost as magnificent as mine. It's built from whorls of high-res flatscreen fabric that shows clouds rolling across a dark sky, a human-shaped storm blowing straight at me.

It takes a moment to recognize them—the last time I saw Yandre, they were wearing a sneak suit and body armor.

A rebel commando is here at my party.

CRASHER

I try not to freeze.

Yandre was one of the rebels who stormed this tower with me during our attack on Shreve. A mortal enemy of my father—yet here they are at my bash, undisguised.

"Let me introduce an old friend," Col says. "Yandre Marin."

Yandre extends a hand. "A pleasure, Rafia. Though I feel like we've already met."

I try to look confused. "Have I seen you on the feeds?"

"I was at your welcome bash in Victoria. But that wasn't really *you*, was it?"

"Right, you met my sister! I was watching that night, and saw you three together. I looked you up—your father is a . . . novelist?"

"You have a good memory."

"You made an impression." Actually, I can't remember what *novelist* means, only that Yandre's father is a famous one. Famous

26

enough to wrangle his child an invitation to my engagement bash, it seems.

We disabled my father's spy dust the night of the attack, and Yandre's rebel allegiance was a secret. Even Col didn't know until the war began.

But why take the risk of coming here?

"It's lovely to meet the real you at last." Yandre steps closer, and my metal satellites drift outward to surround us.

I expect a whispered message, some explanation for this act of daring. But Yandre simply looks me up and down and says, "You and Frey really are alike."

"Genetically identical," I say. "But different in every other way."

A knowing smile. "Except taste in men?"

"Not according to Col." I give him a look. "He says he and Frey were just allies."

Col shrugs. "I never said *just* allies."

I turn back to Yandre. "The plot thickens!"

"With Col, it always does."

We keep up this bubble-talk, me trying to figure out why Yandre isn't out in the wild with the other rebels and the last free Victorians— and my sister.

My heart stutters a little. Maybe they've brought me word from Rafi.

Col didn't miss a beat when Yandre appeared. Like he *knew* they were coming . . . which is impossible. Security watches him every second. There's no way anyone could sneak him a message.

I take a risk: "Will you be joining us tomorrow?"

Yandre blinks. "Tomorrow?"

"Col and I are appearing in public, to show everyone how in love we are. It might be persuasive to have one of his old friends with us."

Both Col and Yandre hesitate—the silence lasts a split second too long.

Then Yandre says, "Sorry, but I'm expected home. I've been traveling since the war began. Haven't seen my parents in *ages*."

"Of course," I say. So Yandre is headed back out to the wild to rejoin the rebels.

Or maybe the rebels will be here tomorrow in force. Coming to save me.

For a moment, my heart swells.

But it's too soon to run. I have to kill my father first.

"Don't go to any trouble on our account," I add lightly. "Please."

Yandre nods. Do they understand what I'm saying?

I don't need your help. I have my own plans.

"May I?" Yandre reaches toward me. "You have a hair out of place."

"How awful. Yes, please."

We stand there inside the clockwork of my dress, its shards glittering in the party lights around us, as Yandre smooths my hair.

My skin sparkles at their touch.

"Did you feel that?" Yandre asks. "Must be the magnetics in your dress. How many lifters do you suppose you're wearing?"

I shrug. "A dozen?"

"No, more than that! It'd take at least a hundred to get this dress to move."

Eyes alight, they step back from me, parting a dozen orbits.

My ears echo with those last three words—*dress to move*.

Something is definitely happening tomorrow.

FATHER

After the bash, my father summons me to his study.

"I'm tired, Daddy."

"This won't take long," the bedroom says in his voice.

I let out a dramatic sigh. My head is spinning from the party, and I have to be ready for whatever Yandre and the rebels are planning for tomorrow's event.

I need sleep, not a conversation with my father.

So I do what Rafi would—ignore him, sitting here letting nanos clean the pores of my face.

A minute later, all the lights in my bedroom snap on, brighter than daylight. Just like during her tantrums in the old days—the room won't darken again until my father gets his way.

"Fine, I'm coming." I start wiping nanos off my face. But the lights don't dim.

He must be watching, so instead of changing into real clothes I throw a coat over my pajamas. I head to the secure elevator, looking like a vagabond.

Bright lights turn on in the corridor, leading me all the way.

"You were exquisite tonight," my father says. "Preparation, execution, all of it."

I don't answer. I'm still not used to this. Being alone with him was one duty I never had to perform as Frey.

His study is at the tower's apex, just beneath the hoverpad. Curved windows look out across the dark horizon. The fireplace burns real wood, hissing wet and angry.

As Rafi, I've learned that our father's firewood is flown in from a special source in the Amazon. The leather in these chairs isn't vat grown, but made from real animals, raised and slaughtered for this sole purpose. The gently curving windows were ground by a master telescope maker in Japan.

So much care put into all of his possessions. But there he sits, unhappy, glowering into the flames.

I stay standing, wearing Rafi's best sulk face.

"The metrics were better than expected," he says. "At the peak, three million viewers."

"Hate-watchers? Or did they like us?"

He shrugs, still looking at the fire. "Who cares? The numbers ticked up every time you two were on-screen together."

31

I feel Rafi's smirk on my face. "And you thought no one would believe us as a couple."

"I said that?" My father waves away my answer. "Didn't think you could pull it off. After your meltdown during the war, it looked like you were gone for good. But you're hitting all your marks. You've kept your part of the bargain. Clever girl."

An unwelcome trickle of pride rills me. After sixteen years of my father pretending I don't exist, some small part of me still craves his approval.

I tell myself that it's just the pleasure of my plan working. I need him to trust me, to depend on me.

He doesn't look up from the flames. "But maybe not as clever as you think. I know what you're up to."

I manage not to flinch. My father's rooms are full of sensors, ways of telling if guests are nervous or upset.

"I'm up to something? Enlighten me."

"You told your friends you're moving to Victoria. Did you think we weren't listening?"

I shrug off my relief. "It's the best use of Col."

"You can't have it." My father is always blunt in argument, to knock people off their guard. But tonight I am steadfast and prepared.

"Neither can you."

He turns from the fire, looking at me for the first time. "Why not?"

"As long as we hold it by force, the city's worthless." I sit down in the chair across from him, making us equals. "We have to exercise control by other means. That's the whole point of this marriage."

"I don't care about Victoria. Only the ruins mattered."

The ruins, of course, are how this all started. Col's family controlled an ancient Rusty city full of metal. My father offered to help them secure it from the rebels, for a cut. In the end, he took everything—their ruins, their home city, the life of Col's mother, Aribella Palafox, and thousands of others.

"If you don't care about Victoria," I say, "then give it to me and Col."

My father shakes his head. "That city will always have a stain on it. I don't want people looking at you and remembering those missiles."

For a moment, it's almost like he's taking responsibility for turning the world against us. But the bomb collar around my neck reminds me otherwise.

"This isn't about my reputation, Daddy. What are you really up to?"

Firelight gleams against his bared teeth. "I've found a better home for you and Col—the city of Paz."

"Paz?" I shake my head in disbelief.

It's a city with no spy dust, where everyone indulges in the wild freedoms of the mind-rain. Everyone has their own feed, and they keep themselves happy by touching a button on their wrist. It's everything my father hates.

I've always wanted to go there.

"The Pazx have been helping that little runt Teo Palafox," he says. "And your sister's last feed rant was recorded on a city street there. It was obvious where she was!"

I frown, wondering how Rafi could've made such a simple mistake.

"You're still worried about Frey?" I ask.

"Of course I am. She's the only person who's ever come close to hurting me since Seanan was taken."

That freezes me for a moment. It's the first time I've heard anyone but Rafi say our older brother's name. He was kidnapped before we were born, but Seanan is all around us, in everything my father does. My very existence is a testament to him.

"Yes," I manage. "Frey is dangerous."

"She should be—I made her that way. The Palafoxes are dead-weight, but if ever she comes at us alone . . ." He turns away again, his face going pale.

A question rises up in me.

"Daddy. If you're so scared of Frey, why did you make an enemy of her?"

"Because she wore that red jacket." He looks up. "That was *your* idea, testing her like that. Seeing if she'd fallen in love with Col. Have you forgotten?"

I have to look away.

When I was in Victoria, my sister asked if the rumors about me and Col were true. She said to wear red if I was falling for him, white if it was just gossip.

34

I wore red, and my father destroyed House Palafox that very night.

But that test of my loyalty was Rafi's idea? She must not have realized . . .

"Every day Frey is out there weakens us," he goes on.

"You want me to look for her in Paz?"

"I want you to *destroy* her." My father smiles. "Then you can have the city. A wedding present."

I have to hold myself steady as the oldest, strongest part of me takes over—the need to protect my sister. The bomb collar around my neck is all that stops me from killing him now.

His forces are hunting her, of course, but to ask *me* . . .

"This plan won't work, Daddy," I say in a calm, cold voice. "You can't take over another city."

"We have to destroy everyone who helps your sister. They're all our enemies."

I clench my fists, letting my rage flow into one of Rafi's tantrums. "You're worried about enemies? We'll have a hundred more cities against us if you go to war again! I'm marrying this *boy* to help your reputation, and you're going to wreck it all, just to hurt Frey? Why are you so *brain-missing*?"

My father's face shows nothing but amusement.

"I won't be invading Paz."

"You think *I'm* going to do this for you?"

"Never you, my dear." He stretches his hands toward the fire and cracks his knuckles. The little pops sound like the wood stirring as it burns. "Have you ever wondered why I went to all that trouble for the

Palafoxes' ruins? Did you really think I'd set the whole world against us for some *metal*?"

I shake my head. "You did it to show the world how dangerous you are. That you'd risk your own daughter to win."

"That was just a bonus." The leather of his chair creaks as he leans back. "Let me tell you some ancient history, dearest. The Palafoxes' ruined city was once the site of a research center, a bunker deep in the ground where the Rusties designed weapons. Devices that were never used, as powerful as forces of nature."

I stare at him.

When I was a littlie, my military history tutors never tired of talking about the Rusties. They lived three centuries ago and almost destroyed the world with their endless wars. They could set the air on fire, make their own diseases, obliterate whole cities with a single bomb.

I speak very clearly. "After what we did to Victoria, the other first families won't allow it. If you hit Paz with a city-killer, they'll burn Shreve to the ground."

"They won't know it was us," he says. "They won't know it was anyone at all."

"What are you *talking about*?"

"We're going to break Paz, leaving no evidence of how it was done. And then, my dearest, you will take their city from them so gently, they'll hardy know it's yours. Your sister will have one less place to hide."

My fists tighten again, fingernails in my flesh. There's no choice but to scream at him until he understands.

But as I open my mouth, Dona's voice interrupts us over the comms.

"Sir, the dust has crashed."

"Again?" My father stands, swearing. "Get some drones out over the city, right away. Rafia, go to your room."

"Daddy, this argument isn't over. Your plan is—"

"Go to your room," he says.

My first instinct is to keep arguing, but then it falls into place in my head.

The dust has crashed. My sister is in danger. And the rebels are coming tomorrow.

There's something I need to do tonight.

TROPHIES

I storm out of my father's study, knowing exactly where to go.

The cleaning staff is out in the halls this late, but they scatter at my approach. In a long coat and pajamas, muttering under my breath, I must look sense-missing.

Since I was a littlie I've had to control my reactions, watch my every word. But Rafi got to show her anger. Throwing tantrums was one thing I always envied her.

Spilling over with emotion feels glorious, but also like I'm unraveling inside.

Col's attack on Shreve was my idea, and it was a disaster. What was left of the Victorian army was destroyed, Col and I were captured, hundreds lost their lives. Only one good thing came out of it: my father learning that he isn't invulnerable, that he might lose everything if he goes too far.

But now he's forgotten again.

Does he really think that if a mysterious attack strikes happy, freedom-loving Paz, the world won't guess who was behind it?

He's going to plunge the world into a war like the Rusties used to have. City-killers and synthetic plagues. Weather patterns lethally disrupted. Whole nations wiped away.

And all because he thinks Frey is there. He's that afraid of me.

He should be.

I head down through the heart of the tower, remembering the night of the attack. I fought my way up these stairs with rebel commandoes and Victorian techs. Ready to rescue my sister and reveal our truth to the world. Ready to make things right again.

But we lost.

I scream once in the stairwell, letting the echoes wrap themselves around me. It doesn't help.

Rage doesn't fix anything. It only feeds the beast inside me.

I push open a door and come to a halt, checking my comms again. Security is still yelling about the dust being down.

I'm in my father's trophy room. I should have come here weeks ago, but it still sends panic creeping down my spine.

The walls are covered with paintings of his defeated enemies. Former business partners, leaders of Shreve, enemy commanders. Some of them are nobodies now, some are in exile. Most simply vanished.

This is the room where I last saw my sister, as the attack on Shreve was failing. We were all about to escape, but then we heard that Col had been captured. When the rest of them ran, I stayed and put on Rafi's dress . . .

And her bomb collar.

The key to that collar is hidden here. If the rebels are really coming tomorrow, I need it in my hands.

The dust is down, but there must be cams in here. So I walk aimlessly among the paintings, like a daughter calming down after a fight with her father. Staring up at the faces, contemplating his victories.

When I reach the painting of Col's mother, I pause.

Aribella Palafox looks down at me, so regal and certain of herself. She appears invincible, but she and her mother were killed in the first minutes of the war. Col and I watched the missiles hit from the outskirts of Victoria.

I hold her gaze, freezing in place. I've tested this in other rooms, waiting for the motion sensors to turn the light off, and it always works.

Counting silently, I feel my muscles start to burn. Like when Naya, my fighting master, used to make me hold a fencing pose for ten minutes straight.

The thought of Naya makes me queasy. She was the closest thing to a friend I had besides my sister. But on the night of our attack, she was the last person standing between me and Rafi.

And she wouldn't get out of the way.

I hear the buzz of that pulse knife in my ears. She barely put up a fight.

After long minutes of silence, the motion detectors decide no one's here and turn off the lights. There are no windows in this room of murdered enemies, so the darkness is absolute.

Barely breathing, I move slowly, below the detectors' perception. Reaching behind the painting of Col's mother, I search for the handset I hid a month ago.

My fingers push into emptiness.

I shut my eyes against the darkness, edging a little farther.

Where *is* it?

The lights flick on.

I jerk my hand back, open my eyes to gaze at the painting, heart pounding. I must have moved too much.

Do I dare try again?

"Looking for this?" asks a familiar voice.

DONA OLIVER

I turn, keeping my expression under control.

Dona Oliver holds the handset with the codes to my collar. My mind spins for a lie that has any chance of working.

All I've got is what Rafi would say: "That's mine."

Dona smiles. "I'm certain of that now."

"What are you doing with it?"

"Repair workers found it here, after the attack." She thumbs the handset on. "The encryption was impressive. Took us weeks to crack."

Not letting myself panic, I offer Dona a piece of the truth.

"The rebels gave that to me before they escaped. It unlocks this stupid collar."

"That was obvious. We also know it's already been used once."

I give her a shrug. "They showed me how it worked. They wanted me to run off with them, but this is my home. So I decided to stay and help Daddy rebuild."

"We're grateful for that. You've helped a great deal." Dona looks at the handset. "That's why I haven't told your father about this."

A trickle of relief starts inside me. She still thinks I'm Rafi, and that I'm on my father's side. But how did she know I'd be down here tonight?

Then it comes to me.

"*You* crashed the dust. You wanted to catch me here."

"I wanted to test you," Dona says. "And to provide a gentle reminder for tomorrow's event—I'm always watching. If you want me to keep your secrets, you need to keep playing the good daughter."

Her smug expression makes my muscles tighten again.

"That's why you haven't told him about the key? So you can blackmail me?"

She shakes her head. "The question is, why haven't *you* told him? He'd be pleased that you put that collar back on willingly. The first daughter wanting to help her father, to make up for being a basket case during the war. But you also wanted a way out, in case he didn't forgive you for that speech. And you were being such a good little Rafia, I tried to believe you . . . but you were being *too* good."

My body is flexing for a fight. I have to stay calm.

"What do you mean?"

"Since the attack, you've arrived at every one of your classes on time." Dona's eyes are steady and piercing. "You let the randoms choose your outfits, like Publicity has always wanted. You study for interviews, hit every talking point."

"I've always been spectacular at interviews."

"Yes, but Rafia was good in spite of herself. She always pushed back, just to prove she mattered." Dona steps a little closer. "You, Frey, are *trying* to be useful."

The sound of my own name rings in my ears. The world starts to tip beneath my feet.

"*What* did you just call me?" I demand.

"The saddest part is that your father hasn't recognized you. I suppose he never thought of you as real. And why would he ever suspect a switch? Because *why would Frey put her sister's collar on?*"

I stare at her. She already knows—she told me this morning.

"You're really in love with him, aren't you?" she asks softly.

My heart tears in my chest. I am seen.

I'll never get Col out of here. I'll never strike my father down.

But I can't give up.

"Love?" I say, letting Rafi's sarcasm flood me. "Don't be so dramatic, Dona. It's what you said before—everything went wrong after Frey left. And when Col showed up, he was just a way to fix Daddy's mistakes. Yes, I've started to like him. But he's just a boy!"

She stands there, unmoved. "I know it's you, Frey."

"Then why haven't you locked me up?"

"Because if it wasn't for you, your father's regime would have fallen already."

The floor shifts again. Gravity is breaking.

"What?"

"The war made him look weak," Dona says. "The guerrilla attacks, the boycott, Shreve itself invaded. Then you and Rafia made

44

that speech, turning him into a *monster*." She shakes her head. "We've studied the metrics—the whole city was ready to rise up. By the time the dust was back in the air, the schools were shut, the workers striking, and the police were going to stand by and let it all happen. Even the army would've turned against him soon enough."

My heart slows. "So what happened?"

"You did. After everything he'd done to you and your sister, *you stood by him*. Going on the feeds, assuring them that it was all okay. At that crucial moment, you made them doubt what they'd seen with their own eyes."

"But that's not what . . ." My voice breaks. The deal I made to save Col's life.

I thought the revolution had fizzled on its own.

Because that's what my father told me.

"It didn't make sense, you switching sides again." Dona smiles again, this time sadly. "Until I saw the way you look at Col and realized that you were Frey, here to save your sad little first love. The real Rafia would never have made a mistake like that."

I try to swallow, but I can't.

I'm to blame for keeping my father in power.

"You almost won." Dona leans closer, like I'm an insect she's studying. "But you threw it away for a *boy*."

I know a hundred ways to kill her. Lunge forward, drive my hand into her throat. A kick to the temple. A strike to the eyes to blind her and then—

She lifts up a small remote. "Stay calm, Frey. I need you to keep your head."

A warning sizzles through the collar. Like a slap of heat through my whole nervous system.

It's all I can do to stay on my feet.

"Everything's going to be better from now on," Dona says in a soothing voice. "This is what Shreve has always needed—a Rafia who'll do what she's told. I should have put a collar on that girl when she was five years old."

I gather myself. "My sister would rather die. So would I."

"Oh, Frey, I know you're not afraid of death. We *made* you that way." Dona stares lovingly at the remote. "But you're not the only one wearing a collar, are you?"

For a moment, I can't breathe. She means Col.

This is the woman who I thought would help me take control of Shreve after I killed my father. Who was always a curb on his impulses.

What if she's *worse* than him?

"Repeat after me, my shiny new Rafia: 'I will be the perfect daughter.'"

"You won't kill Col," I say. "If he dies, the world will blame my father. It'll all start to fall apart again."

"Not all of these buttons kill, my dear. Some do small, annoying things, like an itch that never stops. Some do incurable, dreadful things."

I can't hide the shudder that goes through me.

"So say it just once, in your sister's voice. *'I will be the perfect daughter.'*"

"Say it yourself. You need me to help control my father."

"All I need is this." She lifts up the remote, one finger lightly on a button. "I can set Col Palafox's nerves on fire, so they can't ever be turned off. So promise me. *Now.*"

Every fiber of me wants to attack, or to let her kill me. But being a prisoner in my father's house has taught me one thing most of all: patience.

Tomorrow will come.

"Okay," I say in Rafi's voice. "I'll be the perfect daughter."

Dona lets out a low laugh, like someone having the happiest day of their life. Like someone who's finally grasped all the power they've ever wanted.

Like someone who doesn't know the rebels are on their way.

47

APPEARANCE

The weather sours the next morning.

The sky is a gunmetal lid on the world. It's going to rain, and the collar around my neck feels like iron.

Getting ready for this appearance feels like when I was a littlie—those first times in front of a crowd, posing as my older sister. The tight muscles in my arms. The pinpoint fires burning in my stomach.

Dona knows I'm Frey. She'll never let me leave this place.

This rescue attempt today is my only hope.

For once, I know exactly what to wear. The problem is, Rafi wouldn't deign to own body armor, and my publicity team won't let me dress myself. They've color-coordinated the whole event, and I don't have the energy to argue with them. I have to save my strength.

I wonder how the rebels will come in. From the air? Hidden in camo suits? Disguised as randoms in the crowd?

My staff has decided to outfit me in scarlet and fiddly laced sleeves. Easy to spot in a crowd—at least my own guards won't shoot me by accident. That's a plus.

My objective today is for exactly one person to get hurt, and it's not me.

I put on a training singlet and shorts under the scarlet dress. Ignoring the shoes they've chosen for me, I put on ballet slippers with grippy soles.

My pockets stay empty. The dust is working again, and Dona will be watching closer than ever. I'll have to grab a weapon from a guard at the last second.

My own plan is still the best one—wait till my wedding day and end this all in one stroke. It's the only lasting solution to the problem of my father. But the rebels may not give me a choice.

And, of course, I have another problem now, which makes today's rescue attempt useful.

In all the confusion, Dona Oliver is going to have an accident.

"You look stunning," she says an hour later. "The crowd will love you."

"They always do."

"Of course, Rafi."

Dona smiles to make sure that I noticed—she called me *Rafi* instead of *Rafia*. A little reminder of the power she holds.

We're standing on the hoverpad atop my father's tower, my hair whipping free in a stiff breeze that smells like pine needles and rain. A limo is idling, waiting to carry us to the event.

Today's schedule trembles in an airscreen in front of me, a second-by-second plan for the event. Pretending to ignore it, I memorize every detail.

"Where's Col? Why am I always waiting for him?"

Dona doesn't have to look at the schedule. "Three minutes."

"Time to straighten these brain-missing sleeves, I guess." But when Maltia steps forward, I wave her off. "You do it, Dona."

Dona's smile goes tight. But she can't disobey me in front of my own security detail. As promised, a dozen guards are with us. Enough to need their own hovercar.

I stretch my hands out, palms up. Dona flicks her scarf over her shoulder and starts to work, tidying the mesh of lace along my arms. Let her think I'm being petty in defeat—it will keep her distracted till the excitement begins.

Her assistant looks on, a little confused. I wonder if Dona has told anybody else my secret. Not that it matters—once she's dead, no one will dare tell my father that they helped hide the truth from him.

Staring out at the city, I can almost see the Bossier Fountain, where today's event is taking place. In the center of Shreve, its array of a thousand sprayers creates a watery globe spinning slowly on its axis. The fountain shows the world that my father can waste resources with all the arrogance of the Rusties.

As Dona finishes my sleeves, Col and his guards emerge from the elevator. He squints in the daylight, looking out at the city below us.

"Quite a view."

I shrug, trying not to look at his bomb collar. "Daddy likes looking down on things."

"Beautiful." Col takes my hand. "As long as you don't fall."

I search his eyes—suddenly uncertain whether this rescue attempt is really happening, or if I'm imagining it all. It seems impossible that Col could've stayed in touch with the rebels all this time.

But Yandre risked everything to be here, and both of them said *dress to move.*

Col's face reveals nothing. He straightens his clothes, a dutiful fiancé on his way to a bash. They've put him in bright colors, easy to see from the back of the crowd—a mint-green shirt, a rose jacket. The two of us are like candy in our wrappers.

"Ready for takeoff," Dona calls.

Inside the limo, Col and I share a look—this car is identical to the limo his little brother used to find us in the first days of the war.

I miss those weeks of danger and freedom. Me, Col, and a handful of Victorian soldiers out in the wild. No bomb collars. No dust listening as we shared our secrets. No reason to measure our words. The thrill that ran through me every time he said my real name.

Maybe it's worth running away with him today, whether I kill my father or not. Col and me free together, and my sister with us at last.

But Dona has that remote, and her warnings from last night ring in my ears.

I can set Col Palafox's nerves on fire so they can't ever be turned off.

The roof drops out from under us, and we make a sweeping turn out over the void. The limo's right-side windows fill with grass and gardens, the left side with gray sky.

An escort of military hovercraft drops into formation around us. Taking a groundcar into town would be safer, but my father has to show he isn't afraid of an ambush. Besides, arrivals from above are always more dramatic.

I watch Col closely, wondering if the rebels are going to hit us here in midair. He smiles blandly back at me.

Exactly four minutes later, we're descending, the towers of Shreve slicing the sky around us. We drop straight through the fountain, the limo's windows blurring with condensation.

I can hear the crowd now, a dull roar beneath the hum of our lifting fans. A prickle of nerves hits me again—all those staring eyes. Pretending to be Rafi was easier back when no one knew there were two of us. No one was looking for a slipup back then. But these days, anyone with a feed can point out my mistakes.

My hand aches for a pulse knife. The guard next to me has a sidearm, a shock wand, and a few stun grenades for crowd control.

The limo lands softly, music building around us. The bass kicks hard and fast, designed to push heartbeats, to make the crowd roar.

The people of Shreve really do love my sister—and me too, I guess. Maybe they love us more than ever, now that they know what our father did to us.

But what if Dona is right? What if my staying here was the only thing that stopped the revolution?

They should be jeering me.

Col sees my expression and takes my hand as the limo doors swing open. We look out into the glare, the great sphere of Bossier Fountain overhead, spotlights carving a hundred rainbows in the spray. The spectators are phantasms behind walls of mist. A resistance field sparkles overhead, keeping us dry. Our bodyguards fall into a protective ring.

"You ready?" Col asks.

I hesitate a moment, looking into his eyes. I'm used to making the plans, worrying over every detail. He's asking me to leap into darkness.

With him.

"Of course," I say.

We step from the car.

The music builds to a climax, and all at once the sprayers shut off. The watery globe falls like a curtain with cut strings, splashing down around us as the music ends.

The air clears—everyone can see me and Col at last, and we can see them. Twenty thousand people, all given time off from work and school. All provided with extra rations in colored packages that match our outfits. All prepped by meticulously crafted feed specials about how Col and I fell in love.

53

They cheer for us as the fireworks begin.

Col leans closer. "So . . . what are we supposed to do here, exactly?"

"This is it, pretty much," I say through my smile. "Keep waving."

This is my father's favorite kind of rally. The schedule listed no speeches, no announcements. Just music and giveaways and pyrotechnics. An ecstatic display of nothingness.

"Well, then," Col says. "We might as well give them something to cheer about."

"What do you—" Before I can finish, his arms are around me, and he's looking straight into my eyes.

The roar of the crowd redoubles.

For weeks, I've wanted to kiss him this way, without reservation, my whole body screaming for it every time we've been together. But *here*, in front of a hundred hovercams? It feels like all my lies will tumble into the open if our lips meet.

"Col. Is this a good idea?"

"It's perfect," he whispers in my ear. "And it's the signal. Be ready to hold your breath."

I don't stop him. His lips are on mine, pressure and softness, melting and tangling. Our breath hot in our mouths, the thrum of my blood matching the roar of the crowd.

The fountain hisses back to life, and as we pull apart, I see a fluttering fill the air—countless white butterflies.

Dona, over by the limo, is shouting into her wrist.

Butterflies weren't on the schedule.

A cool spray settles on us from above. The water smells sweet and heavy, like desert flowers after a hard rain. My head is spinning, not only from being in Col's arms . . .

"Don't breathe."

The mist isn't just water. I hold my breath.

A series of small explosions rattles the air—sharper than fireworks.

The rebel attack has begun.

ESCAPE

Col catches me when I stagger.

My lungs are screaming for air, and darkness tinges the edges of my vision. I'm still dizzy—half from the knockout mist, half from holding my breath.

Suddenly the white butterflies are swarming us, and Col grabs one from the air. He shoves it onto my face—its wings wrap around my mouth and nose.

"Breathe!" he gasps, snatching at another butterfly.

When I suck in air, the heavy smell is gone. The world steadies, and I feel warm slivers of smart plastic securing the mask to my head.

Half my bodyguards are on the ground, the rebreathers in their helmets activating too late. Dona, her scarf over her mouth, is crawling toward the armored limo.

I run at her, trying to look like a panicking Rafi. If this all goes wrong, Security will dissect everything that happens here. Even if

56

the rebels have crashed the surveillance dust, there are still my guards' bodycams and the limo's sensors.

I see Dona pull something from her pocket . . .

No.

My foot kicks at her hand as I pass, sending the remote flying into the open limo doors.

I follow, scrambling for it on my hands and knees.

My fingers close on the remote. It feels like nothing, a wafer of plastic and nanocircuits. It crumbles in my hand.

Dona's flat on the ground just short of the limo, succumbed to the gas now. I need to kill her while I can and hope the attackers have crashed the dust. If we're caught again, they can't know I'm Frey.

The door swings down across my view.

"Limo, open up!" I shout through the mask.

"Emergency protocol," it says. "You will be taken to a safe—"

"Override!" I start kicking at the window, wishing I was in boots instead of ballet slippers. "Let a guard in!"

The limo hesitates, probably asking Security for clarification. But twenty thousand people are panicking outside, and rebel hoverboards dot the sky. With Dona unconscious, my father's staff is overwhelmed.

And they have no idea how dangerous I am.

"Order accepted," the limo says.

The door swings open. A guard waits outside, ready to help.

I grab her arm and pull hard, banging her helmet askew against the doorframe. I hold her till the gas crumples her in my arms, then tear her bodycam free and smash it. I unholster her sidearm and belt, push her out.

Col steps over her, the white butterfly clasped across his nose and mouth.

Maybe if I destroy the limo's AI, what I'm about to do will be erased.

I point the gun at Dona's head.

"What are you doing?" Col asks.

I shake my head. "She knows who I am."

"That won't matter once we're gone!"

"But I had a plan. To wait till the wedding and—"

"Frey," he says.

My name freezes me, and he steps in front of the barrel of my gun.

"Our friends are here, Frey. We can leave *now*."

"But my father has to die! He's going after another city soon! We'll never be safe while he's alive!"

I'm screaming, but the voice in my ears doesn't sound like mine. It sounds like Rafi's—incandescent rage, pure and imperious. Nothing but the best plan, *her* plan, absolute and final.

Something shifts inside me. I can run away and be with Col, right now.

I can be Frey again.

Most of my bodyguards have managed to get their rebreathers in. They ring the limo, facing outward, sidearms lowered at the roiling crowd. The rebels are keeping their distance—no one's shooting yet.

Col and I have to make the next move.

"Okay," I say. "What's next?"

"They couldn't tell me much. I guess we improvise."

"Improvise?" As I start swearing at brain-missing rebels, a body-guard turns to look at me, staring at the pistol in my hand. I shoot him in the knee and pull Col inside.

"Limo, get us out of here."

This time there's no argument. The door swings closed again, and we lurch into the gray sky.

Both of us are still wearing collars.

FLIGHT CONTROL

"Going to top speed," the limo says. "We'll reach the tower in three minutes."

I'm tired of arguing with this limo. I grab the shock wand from the ejected guard's belt, climb into the front seat of the limo, and thrust the wand into the AI casing.

Sparks fly and smoke fills the cabin. We drop sickeningly.

"Whoa!" Col says. "What are you—"

"Improvising!" I grab for the flight stick.

Some safety measure in the limo's lizard brain stops us from hitting the ground. But the stick isn't responding yet.

Our military escort appears again, dropping into place around us, four big hovercraft bristling with weapons. They still think we need guarding from this rebel attack.

A slender white strand arcs through the air—rebel antiaircraft fire. It strikes the escort in front of us. Tendrils of smart plastic spread out, wrapping around the car until they tangle one of its lifting fans. The spinning blades jam, then shatter in a burst of smoke, sending fragments in all directions.

With a deafening *smack*, the limo's bulletproof front window is spiderwebbed with cracks.

The rebels are shooting at our escorts—we have to give them room.

The flight stick in my hand finally starts working. Banking hard, I try to slip past the hovercar to our right. We collide with a glancing blow—the limo slews, losing more altitude.

The spire of a building passes beneath us. A few spindly antennae shatter in our wake.

Col climbs into the front seat beside me. "The rebels are in the north, I think."

"You *think*?"

He shrugs. "They were using Victorian hostage code, key words hidden in Rafi's speeches. But I only caught snatches of them."

"Clever." I wrestle the limo level again, wondering if Rafi put any messages in there for me too. "I'll head north, draw these escorts into the antiaircraft."

"Won't they shoot us if we make a run for it?"

"Not if they still think I'm the first daughter." I point at the cracked front window. "It'll look like our flight controls are damaged."

Col glances at the smoking AI. "They *are*."

"Yeah, but not like this." I pull the flight stick hard to the left and set a weaving, shaky course northward.

The three remaining escorts follow, staying in a protective

formation around us. They must be wondering why the limo AI and comms are out.

My fingers go to the bomb collar at my throat.

"Col, I'm not sure what happens when we leave city limits. These collars might be programmed to stop us."

"It'll be okay. Yandre has a key ready."

It takes me a moment to figure it out. "At the party?"

"That dress was one big scanner. We just have to get to them."

Of course—that tingle I felt when Yandre stood close to me. And when the two of them danced, they were scanning Col's collar.

Another white tendril streaks past the front window. A miss—I can't even tell who the rebels were aiming at.

"Are they trying to hit *us*?"

"Who knows?" Col crawls into the back again. "I'll look for bungee jackets."

Great. The rebels have already shot me down once. I thought being on their side would keep it from happening again.

A crunch rattles through the limo, sending us swerving.

One of our escorts looms in the side window. It's nudging us back toward my father's tower. The escorts are bigger than us, with heavy armor and massive engines.

Half the Shreve fleet must be in the air by now. For a moment, I wonder if the rebels really have a plan. Or was this all just to make my father look weak?

I have to believe that Yandre wouldn't put us in danger without a way to get us out. And my sister was part of it too.

"Did those coded messages tell you *anything* else?" I yell to Col.

"All I got was a few key words—*north, gas attack, collar scan,* and something about a snake."

"A *snake?*"

Then I see it below us, stretched out across the farm belt . . .

The Cobra mag-lev line.

It used to be Shreve's main trade route, until the rest of the world started its boycott against us. Now the train shoots past the city every morning, never stopping at our fancy new station, ignoring my father's wealth at three hundred klicks an hour.

Faster than an armored hovercraft.

Another crunch rings through the cabin—one of our escorts giving us another shove. The limo slews beneath me until I wrestle it back under control.

We don't have long. The mag-lev train is there in the distance, right on schedule.

"Col!" I shout. "Did you ever find those bungee jackets?"

JOLT

A third arc of white shoots into the sky, striking another of the escort craft.

The tendrils burst across its airframe, and soon its engines are jammed and smoking, the car falling. We're almost free, but flashes fill the northern sky in front of us—my father's fleet going after the rebels.

We can't count on more help from them. And it won't be long before more Shreve hovercraft are on us.

I jam the flight stick hard, heading east toward the approaching mag-lev train. Our escorts stay in close pursuit, but the two still flying aren't enough to hem me in.

Col crawls back into the front seats, wearing a bungee jacket, holding another for me. I let go of the stick long enough to shrug it on.

"Where do we jump?" he asks.

I grab the flight stick again, pointing with my free hand.

"That train line's called the Cobra. You're the nature expert—that's a kind of snake, right?"

64

"Um, yeah." He tightens his straps. "But jumping onto a mag-lev . . . is that a thing people do?"

"Not really." I've heard of people jumping onto trains from hoverboards, but never from the air. "Are you *sure* Yandre likes you?"

Col sighs. "They have an exaggerated notion of my courage."

"The trick to bravery is not having a choice," I say. We reach the rail line, and I bring us around, lining up over the tracks. Our escorts take the turn slower, their armored frames making them sluggish.

My maneuver is too clean, though. It's only a matter of time before someone realizes that we aren't really out of control.

I don't know what happens then. Would my father really give an order to shoot Rafi down? Or does he detonate our collars and pretend it was an accident?

"I'll see if I can get a door open," Col says.

"Open both!" At top speed, this limo's going to spin if we try to fly with the doors open.

Again, I wonder if this is just a rebel plan to create chaos.

But then I see it—

Toward the end of the mag-lev train, some kind of dish-shaped object is mounted on top of a railcar. Tiny figures crawl around in its lee.

But what *is* it? A magnet strong enough to reel us in?

Whatever their plan is, I'm pretty sure the rebels haven't tested it on actual people.

"Got it!" Col says. "Doors opening in five, four—"

"Wait! Let the train catch up!" I glance at my rearview monitor, making a quick calculation. "Count to fifteen and then—"

A vast agony hits me then, burning though my nerves like a lit fuse. My muscles spasm, spine arching, lungs squeezing a gasp from my lips. Every centimeter of my skin lights up like I'm on fire.

It lasts seconds, or forever, or no time at all. The eternal, perfect, blistering expression of pain.

Just as suddenly, the wave passes.

I gasp. My clenched fingers have sent us skidding off course. I wrestle our flight path back over the tracks.

Over my shoulder, Col's in a shuddering pile, his fingers at his throat.

Of course—the collars.

A warning from my father:

You can never leave me.

I lock the flight stick and scramble over the seat, screaming Col's name. His body goes limp.

"Col!" I turn him over. His eyes are open, but his breath comes in ragged gasps.

"Frey," he manages.

"We have to jump before they hit us again! Can you move?"

He raises himself gingerly, pulls a flash grenade from the guard's belt. "If they think we're dead, they won't shock us again."

"Right. You ready?"

Col's eyes are glazed, but he says, "Let's go."

He pulls open a floor panel marked with an override symbol and yanks a pair of levers inside.

Both doors swing up, sending a gale-force wind through the cabin. Champagne glasses rattle frantically in their racks, then break into fragments that whirl through the air. The limo starts to shudder and roll, the blurred landscape shooting past the yawning doors.

I glimpse the mag-lev track and the engine of the train, just starting to overtake us. Col throws the grenade into the front seat.

The flash burns my eyes, and the limo goes into a hard roll. Land and sky gyrate past the open doors. We're dropping fast enough that the metal shriek of the rails builds above the wind.

Col wraps his arms around me.

We roll out the door into the reeling gray sky.

JUMP

The wind hits like a fist, knocking the air from my lungs. We tumble madly, clutching each other while the world spins around us.

A beeping in my ears—our bungee jackets warning that we're too close to each other. Their magnetics will interfere.

I push Col away, spreading my arms to steady myself in the air.

A *pop* comes from the limo—its windows blowing out, spraying glass in all directions. The machine drops past us, trailing smoke and the smell of burned plastic. It hits the ground before we do, scattering wreckage beside the train.

The roof of each railcar is marked with a coiled snake.

Our bungee jackets take hold, using the tracks below to slow our fall. But I doubt they're designed for jumping out of an aircraft at top speed.

The rebels' plan has to work, or we'll wind up blotches on the landscape.

My jacket stiffens around my torso. Not the jerk of a hoverbounce—something more controlled.

The magnetic dish passes beneath us, and suddenly we're accelerating.

At three hundred klicks an hour, the wind is a hurricane in my face. My eyes are forced almost shut, but I can make out Col just ahead of me. He's rolled into a cannonball to reduce his drag.

Falling faster now, he almost hits the ground, but his bungee jacket hoverbounces him up from the metal tracks.

I try a different strategy—my arms out in front, like a mountain jumper in a wingsuit. Every movement of my body sends me veering, but the magnetic dish pulls me back on course.

I am a descending hawk, inescapable.

I take it all back—the rebels are pretty bubbly sometimes. I let them reel me in.

Long seconds later, both of us are coming in for a landing atop the train. The rebel crew, riding the railcar with crash bracelets and magnetic shoes, grab me and Col. They take us down through a hatch into the dull roar of the car.

It's all luxury furniture down here, tools and electronic parts piled onto the fancy tables. Too many familiar faces to register at once.

My hand goes to my throat. Our collars haven't hit us again.

Maybe word hasn't gotten back to my father yet that we jumped. For a few minutes, he'll think that his precious daughter is dead.

At last I've really hurt him.

"Chica." Yandre's voice is right beside me. "You made it!"

They take my arm, gently sit me down. A handset at my neck—the *click* of my collar opening. It clatters to the floor.

I'm free again.

ALLIANCES

Half an hour later, Col and I are in a private passenger car, drinking bubbly with rebels and Victorians.

The magnetic dish has been dismantled and brought down—its pieces are scattered on the floor. The train's staff has dropped by to yell at us. Apparently, hoisting an unapproved device atop a speeding mag-lev is frowned upon. The wardens in the next city have been notified.

But then the train captain herself comes back, sees me and Col, and realizes what's just happened—an incident that will rock the feeds tomorrow. The rail staff stops bothering us, except to bring more champagne.

The rest of the world still hates my father, it seems.

So many old friends are here—Zura and Dr. Leyva from Victoria, the rebel bosses X and Andrew Simpson Smith. But it's not quite the celebration I expected.

"Rafi isn't here?" I ask.

"Why would she be?" Dr. Leyva says. "She's no commando."

I smile. "What lucky person got to tell her to stay behind?"

Leyva doesn't answer.

Even without my sister, freedom pulses bright in my veins. The missing weight of the collar around my neck is like floating. I'll never have to pretend to be Rafi again.

No one else seems to share my mood. Col still looks shaken from the jolt the collar gave him. He listens gravely as the Victorians brief him on how the war is going.

The news isn't great.

"We've been hacking the Shreve agriculture domes," Dr. Leyva is explaining, speaking in English for my benefit. He's the head of tech for the Victorian resistance, a handsome gray-haired crumbly who used to host a science feed before the war. "Disrupting their food supply, here and there."

Col's grim expression doesn't change. "We can confirm a shortage of caviar."

"Yes, the other cities have stopped selling them luxuries," Leyva says. "No champagne either. But no one wants to starve the citizens."

"A tragedy for Rafi's rich friends," Col says. "But shutting off Shreve's supply of bubbly and truffles isn't going to free Victoria."

Everyone's silent for a moment. Despite this victory, they're still a ragtag guerrilla force, outmatched by the might of Shreve.

The rebels look bored with the discussion. They're used to being insurgents, harassing more powerful enemies.

All the Victorians wear crisp uniforms, fresh from a hole in the wall. But the rebels are in their usual skins and furs, the smell of the wild all over them.

This alliance was never a comfortable one. The rebels want to protect the wild from humanity; Col's people just want their city back.

Luckily, my father excels at uniting his enemies.

Zura, captain of Victorian House Guard, speaks up. She's a Special, optimized by surgery not only for combat, but also terrifying beauty, like an avenging angel.

"Having you back will give our people a huge morale boost, sir."

Col smiles a little. "Is *that* why Teo wanted to rescue me? For my propaganda value?"

Leyva and Zura give each other a look.

Col apparently thinks his fourteen-year-old little brother, the next Palafox in line, has been in charge. Somehow I doubt it's working that way in practice. Teo isn't even here.

Col hasn't accepted that every day my father holds his city, the Palafox name means less and less.

"Teo is safe, back at the base," Zura says diplomatically. "This operation wasn't any one person's plan. After our attack on Shreve, we haven't had a traditional command structure."

No one looks at me, but I feel it in the room—I'm being blamed for their weakness. As a hostage, I was the key to my father's schemes against the Palafoxes. They dropped their guard because they thought he would never risk Rafi's life.

73

Even after I joined them, the disastrous attack on Shreve was my idea. I convinced Col to risk everything, because I wanted to free my sister. And since then, they've all watched me on the feeds, steadying my father's regime. I'm surprised they bothered rescuing me at all.

Dr. Leyva speaks carefully. "We've adapted to the situation."

"So we're just another gang of rebels now," Col says.

Yandre laughs. "Don't say that like it's a *bad* thing! You should have seen Zura convincing everyone to back this operation. She's a natural rebel."

Col looks pained again. The rebels are like pre-Rusty pirates— electing their bosses, voting on every mission. Still, I can imagine Zura convincing a rebel crew to do anything. Whenever she fixes me with her beautiful, blaming stare, I want to fall down and beg her forgiveness.

"Whoever's plan it was, we're free," Col says. "Thank you all for that."

"You should thank Frey too," Yandre says. "We wouldn't have risked it if she hadn't stayed behind with you."

Col gives his old friend a look. "You mean, I'm not worth the trouble?"

"Chico, you never would've jumped out of that limo without a push from Frey. You two are stronger together."

Judging by their expressions, Leyva and Zura don't agree.

Col takes my hand in front of all of them. "Thank you for giving up your freedom, Frey. You saved me. Everyone here knows that."

74

I should say something stirring now—that leaving him behind was never an option. But every time I open my mouth, there's a chance I'll sound like Rafi. I haven't spoken in my own voice for so long.

The awkward silence stretches out.

Then Boss X stands and raises his glass, almost brushing the ceiling. He's taken his rebel love of the wild to an extreme, becoming a surgical cross between a wolf and a man. His voice is a low growl.

"To Frey."

The other rebels take up the toast—they still love me. They thrive on calamity, and that's what I am.

Hearing my real name on all those lips at once is strange and wonderful. When I finish my glass, Boss X refills it, a smile on his wolf-surged face.

"Did you lose anyone?" I ask.

X shakes his head. "Automated launchers up north, and down in the city we never even opened fire."

"We knew you two could make it on your own," Yandre says. "You just needed a diversion."

"Knockout gas, antiaircraft fire, and a passing mag-lev train," Col says. "It was all very diverting."

"It worked." Andrew Simpson Smith raises his glass again. He's the oldest of the rebels, with a massive beard, like a wild man come in from the forest. There are rumors that he fought alongside Tally Youngblood herself. "To freedom."

This time, Leyva and Zura share the toast.

My father is still alive, but my plan to kill him doesn't seem important now. What matters are the collars missing from our necks, and seeing my sister again.

"How long till we get back to base?" I ask. "Rafi must be bored of impersonating me."

Dr. Leyva hesitates, turns from me to Col. "This train will take us to Paz, where the fleet is recharging. We've left the White Mountain. Shreve captured too many of us in the attack. Someone might have spilled the location."

Right. One more thing that's my fault.

"So where are we headed?" Col asks. "Paz won't let us stay, will they?"

"No, sir." Zura looks at me. "We've found a spot farther south, in the deep Amazon. Teo thinks you'll like it there. But there's not much hot water, compared to the volcano."

"Rafi must hate that." I switch to my sister's annoyed voice: "'Camping is why we inventing *buildings*.'"

The rebels laugh at this, but not the Victorians.

Leyva leans back in his chair.

"Actually, Frey, your sister isn't with us anymore. She ran away a week ago."

TRUST

"She came with us to Paz," Leyva begins his explanation. "When we were preparing for this rescue."

"She begged to come along," Zura says. "As you said, Frey, she wasn't one for camping."

"But why would Rafi run away?" I ask. "Someone must've grabbed her!"

Leyva shakes his head. "She left a note: *Don't follow me.*"

I stare at them. This doesn't make sense.

"She was on the feeds just a few days ago," I point out.

"Yes, after she ran away," Leyva says. "But she delivered the code words as scheduled. Rafia still wanted to help your rescue."

I swallow my next words—my father's people spotted that she was on the streets of Paz. Did she simply get sloppy? Or was that deliberate somehow?

Why isn't my sister here to welcome me to freedom?

A low growl comes from Boss X. "Our enemy's daughter, who knew all our plans, ran away? And you didn't tell us?"

"The operation was too important to abort," Zura says.

"You should have let us decide that!" Yandre says.

X snorts in disgust. "You 'Foxes never change."

They keep arguing, but it blurs into the roar of the train.

My sister has run away. She's out there somewhere, all alone for the first time.

Why? We're supposed to be together.

I've studied Rafi my whole life. How she speaks, walks, thinks. Sometimes I know what she's about to say before she opens her mouth.

But this has blindsided me.

"Listen, everyone!" Col shouts, cutting through the bickering. "I wasn't here for this decision, but I apologize on behalf of House Palafox. We won't betray your confidence like this under my command."

"I doubt you'll have the chance," Yandre says.

Col stares at his old friend. The rebel bosses are silent. Dr. Leyva sits back and crosses his arms, annoyed at being second-guessed by Col. Zura's perfect face is unreadable.

"We all have the same goals here," Col says. "We need to trust each other."

There's a tense moment of silence, and then Boss X stands to his full height. He grabs two bottles of bubbly, overturning the ice bucket.

"I'll be in the luggage compartment," he says. "You can trust me to be drunk soon."

The other rebels all follow him, even Yandre. We can only watch them leave.

Col sighs. "An auspicious beginning."

"Sir," Zura says. "If we'd told the rebels Rafia was missing, they would've pulled out. *I* would have aborted the mission, if we'd had any other way to get to you."

"I know. An impossible situation." Col shakes his head. "But here's what I don't understand: Why did you tell them just now, Dr. Leyva?"

Leyva's smile chills me a little.

"We could've kept it from them. But Frey was bound to wonder where her sister was." He turns to me, still smiling. "We felt uncomfortable, asking her to lie to her rebel friends."

I hold his gaze. "Is this a polite way of saying you don't trust me?"

"Not *that* polite."

"Leyva!" Col says. "Is it your intention to insult *all* of our allies today?"

"No, sir. But it was better that the rebels hear the facts from us."

Col lets out a groan, staring down at the spilled ice on the carpet.

"He's right, Col," I say softly. "I wouldn't have kept it from X. But tell me the truth, Doctor—do you know why Rafi ran away?"

Leyva shakes his head. "Your sister can be difficult."

"I'm aware."

"She disliked taking orders," Zura says. "And 'camping,' as you put it. In fact, the only thing she seemed to enjoy was imitating you."

This still seems strange to me, but it brings a smile to my lips. Hardly anyone in Shreve knows the way I talk when I'm being myself. It's almost as if the flawlessness of her impersonation was a message aimed at me.

But I have no idea what she was saying.

Col takes my hand. "We'll find her, Frey."

"We have larger concerns at the moment," Leyva says. "Maybe while the rebels have left us, we can discuss the state of the Victorian army."

"We're down to thirty soldiers," Zura reports. "Three hovercraft. No plasma rifles."

"Hardly an army." Col stares out the window a moment. "Any other good news?"

The other two Victorians exchange a glance.

"We'd prefer to discuss the rest in private," Leyva says.

Col looks around the room. The empty glasses where the rebels were sitting.

"Are you joking?" Col says. "Frey can hear anything you have to say!"

Leyva spreads his hands. "She *just* said that she'd rather not keep things from her rebel friends."

A spark of annoyance goes through me. Leyva knew I'd say that to make things easier on Col—he's orchestrating this whole conversation.

"This isn't up for discussion," Col says. "Frey isn't going anywhere."

Neither of the other two speaks.

Col swears under his breath. "Just to make this clear, I'm *ordering* you to continue with this briefing."

Zura raises her hands. "I've given you my report, sir. This is Leyva's business."

"Doctor?" Col demands.

Dr. Leyva crosses his arms. "I have nothing to say."

"Leyva! If you aren't going to obey orders, then I'll have to—"

"Col," I cut in. "Don't. It's okay."

"It's *not* okay."

"Right, but it's okay *for now*." I stand up and walk across the cabin, their stares heavy on me. At the door, I turn to face them. "You can tell me everything later, Col."

He stares back at me, still angry at Leyva. Still in pain from the collar's jolt. Still needing me beside him.

But the Victorian resistance can't afford to lose more people.

"Okay," Col says at last. "I'll tell you all of it later."

I smile for him.

And then I go away.

X

Out the window of the mag-lev, the world is a blur.

At this speed, the hills rise up and disappear in seconds, rolling waves of scrub and sand. Behind them, the desert changes color at the stately pace of the shifting sun.

My sister is missing. She's out there somewhere—alone.

I'm alone too, waiting for Col in his cabin.

He'll tell me everything, of course, but there's a bigger problem: I'm not sure he's in charge of the Victorian army anymore. Leyva was ready to disobey a direct order.

Maybe that's why my sister ran away—she decided the Palafoxes were a lost cause. Deadweight, as our father said.

But she knew I'd be with her soon . . .

Maybe Rafi's still in Paz, waiting for me to show up. She doesn't know that our father's willing to wreck the whole city just to flush out his wayward, dangerous daughter.

I have to find her before that happens.

"Tell me about our destination," I tell the train's AI.

"Paz is a city of two million on the island of Baja, and is often called the City Where Everyone's Happy."

My father always laughed at that. The train keeps talking.

When they turn sixteen, the citizens of Paz get "feels"—a surgical implant that allows them to control their mental state. They can experience joy, infatuation, contentment—an array of emotions at the press of a finger.

I'm not sure their happiness is real, but part of me has always wanted to visit, just to see it in person. It doesn't hurt that my father and Paz are enemies.

I wonder if the feels are what made Rafi choose this city. Controlling her own emotions has never been her strong point. Did she run off for the promise of happiness, away from the war?

No. She still would have waited for me.

When I check the feeds, they've hardly mentioned our escape. Just some shaky video showing the failure of a "cowardly" rebel attack on the first daughter. According to the official Shreve feeds, I'm safe at home, happily preparing for my wedding day.

Only the *best* publicity—our father's too worried about looking weak to admit he's lost another daughter.

By now his people have searched the wreckage of the limo, so he must know we escaped. He'll understand at last that neither of his daughters is on his side.

I wonder what stories the Shreve feeds will start telling then.

*

When the cabin door opens at last, I spring up from the bed.

But it isn't Col. The huge frame of Boss X fills the corridor.

"Oh, come in," I say. "If you can fit."

"I'm very flexible."

Graceful too—X eases through the door and curls up on the bed, leaving me squished in a corner. He seems right at home.

When we first met, back at the White Mountain, X's inhuman surge was nervous-making. In combat, he's a righteous terror. But there's something comforting about the warmth of his body filling the cabin, his fur shining in the late-afternoon light.

"I thought you might be lonely," he says.

"Yeah. Got kicked out. Col's people don't like me anymore."

"Do you care?"

I shrug. "It helps to be trusted when you're fighting a war together."

He looks disapproving. "The 'Foxes are fighting a different war from ours, Frey. They want to rule again. We want a revolution."

"A revolution? I thought you rebels only cared about saving the wild."

"Same disease," X says. "When you put yourself above other people, you put yourself above the planet too."

I go back to staring out the window. "Right—you think the Palafoxes are part of the problem."

"The powerful always are."

"They live in a forest, X."

"But they still claim a city, like your own family." A look of amusement crosses his face. "Maybe that's why you crave their approval."

I just laugh. "My family life isn't something I want to re-create."

"No, Frey, it's something you want to fix. Maybe part of you wants to join the 'Foxes so you'll have a real family at last."

"I didn't *join* the Palafoxes—I fell in love with Col! I don't care that he's a first son. Why are you being so head-shrinking tonight?"

"I only came to keep you company." X reaches up to stroke the pendant around his neck—a piece of wood on a simple leather strap. "And to remind you to be happy."

"Happy? My sister's missing. My allies don't trust me."

"Some of your allies do." He curls tighter on the bed, like he's settling in for a nap. But his eyes stay wide and alert. "Consider this: You went undercover in your father's house, saved your boy, escaped without a scratch. You should be in the next car with us rebels, drinking all night long. Instead, you're here sulking, letting the 'Foxes blame you for their failures."

"The attack of Shreve was my plan. Col's capture was my fault!"

"There are no guarantees on a battlefield. Col knew that. They all did."

"Sure, Boss. But I keep messing up. This whole time pretending to be Rafi, I've been helping my father keep control."

"That's the best part," X says with a feral grin. "He depended on you, and now you're gone. Sounds like a plan for making someone stumble."

"I dispute your use of the word *plan*. But thanks for trying to make me feel better."

"I'm just reminding you who you are, Frey. Not a 'Fox, or the first daughter of Shreve. You're one of us proles."

"I bet Rafi would know that word. Alas, I don't."

"She'd only know the definition, Frey—you know the *meaning*. You were created as a tool, a means to an end. You owe the world nothing but chaos."

"But my sister—"

"Isn't you," he interrupts. "When you stop pretending to be her, you'll be stronger."

"Are you saying I have identity issues? You got surged to be a wolf!" The words spill out in Rafi's voice, raw and spiteful.

X bares his teeth—in anger or amusement, I can't tell.

It's cringingly rude to make someone justify their surge. But Rafi always gossiped when her friends got new faces or flash tattoos. And since meeting him, I've often wondered how X chose to become something so inhuman.

He's so comfortable with who and what he is now.

"Sorry, Boss." I try to control my voice, to make it my own. "You're right. I just spent a month pretending to be Rafi, twenty-four hours a day. I have no idea who I am."

"Let me help with that." He sits up straighter, setting the wooden pendant on his necklace swaying. "When this train gets to Paz, my crew will go our own way. We don't need the 'Foxes. Neither do you."

I'm staring at the pendant—there's something familiar about the color of the wood. "Maybe I don't need them, but I love Col."

A sigh ripples X's fur. "There's no cure for that. But if you ever need a real family, there's no blood like crew."

I stare at him, realizing what he's offering.

"You think I should be a rebel?"

He gives me a solemn nod. "One of mine."

My throat feels tight, like when the rebels made their toast to me. For a moment, I see myself belonging to something looser and wilder than the Victorian resistance. Something flexible, graceful, free of history, free of regret.

X's hand goes to his pendant again, and I recognize the color at last—it's a piece of wood from the stage in my father's ballroom, worn smooth by his touch. I watched Boss X cut it free during the attack on Shreve.

A fresh wave of guilt hits.

"In the ballroom," I say softly, "you told me about loving a rebel boy."

"You think that undermines my argument?"

"No, it's just . . ."

The young rebel in question was the assassin at my sister's first speech, the first person I ever killed. It was my pulse knife that cut him in half on that stage, and X doesn't know.

A dozen ways to confess spin in my head. But there are no words of my own among them, just things Rafi would say. She'd know exactly how to tearfully apologize. How to artfully admit killing the love of someone's life.

All I've got is "I have to save my sister."

X lets out a low, rumbly laugh. "Rafia of Shreve can take care of herself."

"Maybe. But our father knows she's in Paz. He's planning something."

X's ears prick up. "Sending an assassin?"

"Much bigger than that. He found some kind of ancient weapon in the ruins near Victoria." I recall the exact words. "Like a force of nature. Maybe a city-killer?"

"Interesting. Tell the 'Foxes. We'll see what they do."

I frown. "So you trust them now?"

"I trust them to fail you. I just want you to notice this time."

My eyes close, shielding me from the sting of his words.

The face of Aribella Palafox fills my mind. Not the painting in my father's trophy room—the real woman, on the afternoon she promised to protect me while I was in her home.

She was so formidable, but gentle too, like she really cared for me. A perfect inversion of my father. Maybe she's why I can't blame the Palafoxes for hating me. Maybe I could've saved her somehow.

Great. Boss X has me head-shrinking myself now.

"I'll tell Col tonight," I say. "He'll help."

"He'd better," X growls. "Don't forget, he owes you his life."

PRETEND

The Cobra stops in the city of Vega.

Outside my window, local wardens are swarming, and soldiers too. Lifting drones are carting away pieces of the magnetic dish. Everyone looks tense, like we're about to be kicked off the train.

What if they arrest us? Put us in some local jail until my father can—

The cabin door slides open. It's Col.

I jump up and we throw our arms around each other, like the train is crashing and we don't want to be pulled apart.

For a boundless moment, our embrace is everything. Just us alone—no dust, no cams, no guards. At last I can say anything I want.

But we've played the game of lies for so long, I don't know how to change the rules.

The words are lost inside me.

"Frey," Col murmurs.

"Mostly."

Our lips meet—and suddenly the world is limitless, out here beyond my father's walls. This small train cabin is as vast as the wild, but our kiss fills it, everything warmth and certainty.

At last he's in my arms again, safe from my father.

A thud comes from outside—Col and I turn to the window. A lifting drone has crashed against a column in the station, scraping paint and stone. The wardens look upset.

"Are we in trouble?" I ask.

Col shakes his head. "They just want to make sure we don't leave the train, in case your father's figured out we're aboard. They don't want a firefight in the middle of their city. We have to stay on till Paz."

"Fine with me." That's where I have to start looking for my sister.

"Sorry about Leyva kicking you out."

"The time alone was good." And that talk with Boss X was necessary. He was right—I might love Col, but I'll never be a 'Fox, loyal to his name, serving him blindly.

I'm not even me yet.

Rafi's voice lingers in my mouth. Her ballet stance has settled into my muscles like an ache, and I'm still wearing her clothes. Her expressions come to my face faster than my own.

But I can taste hints of myself on Col's lips.

We kiss again, harder now, desperate to tear away all those false hours in my father's tower. All our pretended distance, the walls and air listening to every word. The two of us slipping hidden meaning into our words, hoping to be heard.

Needing to be seen.

I can taste his hunger too, after a month of calling me by the wrong name. After losing his family, his city, his freedom. There's almost nothing left of him but me.

And there it is—that rawness we had in those first days of the war. In the wild. Under fire. Stripped of everything.

Our bodies meet, and a month of hiding myself begins to fall away at last, scattered by Col's kisses, by his touch. I'm in here somewhere.

We start to find me.

The train is moving again.

We're an hour from Paz. The fields around us are full of white weed, an ancient invasive species of orchid that the Rusties made. It once threatened to choke the world, but now it's under control. More or less.

We'll arrive in the city as the sun sets, through a tunnel beneath the Baja Sea.

I wish we had longer on this train. There's so much we need to talk about, and we've hardly spoken yet.

When my fingers brush Col's bare throat, where the weight of the collar still marks his skin, he doesn't flinch. But his eyes darken.

"Does it still hurt?" I ask.

"There's a buzzing in my head." He frowns. "Didn't they zap you too?"

"You got it worse, I think. Dona said she could light up your nerves for the rest of your life."

Col gently pulls my hand away, kisses my fingertips. "No pain lasts forever. She was trying to scare you."

"It worked."

"The agony wasn't the worst part." He closes his eyes. "It was how everything else disappeared. At the flick of a switch, all of me gone except for the collar."

"She hurt you to punish me." I remember him rigid on the limo floor. "Dona hates me—or Rafi, really. She can't seem to keep us straight."

Col sighs. "Leyva's just as bad."

"Right." I pull away a little, leaving space for awkward subjects. "So what's the big secret? Has he got a brilliant plan to save Victoria?"

Col turns away, staring out the window at the blur of white weed. He's silent for too long.

I feel myself slipping away. Lost again.

"You don't have to tell me," I say softly.

"No, it's just . . . he wanted to talk about you."

I stare at him. "Me?"

And finally it hits—there's only one way Col can retain command of his army.

"Leyva wants you to break up with me," I say.

He looks astonished, but then his face cracks into a smile.

"He wouldn't dare, Frey. But he wanted to talk about how to present us to the rest of the world."

92

"How to present us?" I sit up. "He kicked me out of a *publicity* meeting? Seriously?"

"Well, it's tricky." Col switches to his tour guide voice. "Your father's team spent a lot of effort creating us as a couple. They did a good job of it too—on the feeds, at that party, and not just in Shreve. They bribed kickers all over the world to talk about us. We're a big deal now."

"Yeah, I know, Col—it was *my* idea! People had to think we were real, or my father wouldn't keep you alive."

"But that's the problem—we aren't real. The whole world thinks you're Rafi."

"Right . . ." My brain spins for a moment. "So we have to figure out how to explain to everyone that I've been Frey all along."

"Which means admitting that the rebel Frey on the feeds is really Rafi." Col leans back against the wall of the cabin. "The world *just* found out there's two of you, and we've mixed up who's who. Worse— our side's been lying."

"Lying? Rafi *had* to act like me so our father wouldn't figure out who *I* was."

"Sure. But your father wants people to think that your speech with Rafi was fake. If we admit we've been lying, people might start to believe him. And now that Rafi's not around to prove there's two of you, we only look shadier. It confuses our narrative."

"Our *what*?" I ask.

"The story of you and me. Dr. Leyva tested the real us with a friendly focus group in Paz, and we didn't go over very well."

I shake my head. "He focus-tested . . . *us?*"

"Yeah, and it turns out most people love Col and Rafia—two heirs thrown together by war. Romeo and Juliet. But they see you and me differently."

"Sure," I say. "You might be Romeo, but I'm not Juliet. I'm more like . . . that guy who starts the fight and ruins everything."

"Mercutio."

"People had missing names back then."

"Frey," Col says. "What if you kept being her?"

I stare at him. "What did you just . . ."

"Keep being Rafia. We take everything your father built and use it against him."

The words blur as my heart breaks a little. Col's talking like he expects this to be easy for me.

Like he didn't know we had to put me back together.

This is why Dr. Leyva kicked me out of the room—if I'd been sitting there hearing it, Col would have realized.

I have to make him see.

"It makes our story much simpler," he says.

"Not for *me*." I take both of his hands in mine. "For a month, I've been afraid to talk in my own voice, to stand like myself, to *breathe* like me. How am I supposed to find myself again?"

"By *being* yourself, Frey. We'll be hidden in the Amazon. It won't be like Shreve, pretending every minute. It's just making announcements on the feeds."

"And interviews," I say. "And photo ops, and when we visit other

94

cities to drum up help. I know how it works, Col. I've done this job my whole life!"

"I know. But it's not forever."

"It *is* forever. It's in my bones." I guide his hand to my right wrist. "Like here, where Naya broke me in training. And these ribs here and here. And here above my eye, where Dr. Orteg cut Rafi so she'd have a scar just like mine. It's all *forever*, Col."

When he doesn't say anything, I hear Dona's voice in my head.

You threw it all away for your sad little first love.

No. He'll understand what this means to me.

"I can't be my sister anymore, Col."

He looks away. "In the focus group, people got confused. Some of them thought I'd switched my affections back and forth between you and Rafi. So it was like a trashy soap-op feed. For people to support us, we have to be more like a prince and princess in a fairy tale."

Something heavy falls on me. "And I'm not a fairy princess."

I'm a killer right down to my marrow.

"Frey," he says, my name sour and deliberate in his mouth. "My city's occupied. My people are breathing your father's dust."

"How does my being Rafi help Victoria?"

"By weakening him. You supported your father as Rafi. *She* has to denounce him."

Right. And the real Rafi has run away.

I need her more than ever now. This is *her* world—diplomacy and politics. Charming the world.

"How did freedom get so complicated so fast?" I ask.

"It gets worse," Col says. "The global feeds love our little fairy tale . . . but Victoria is a different matter. Seeing me join your family has hurt morale there. They all knew that a marriage would give your father a legal excuse to keep the city. That's why Leyva didn't risk delaying our rescue. It had to happen before our wedding, or the last spark of resistance in Victoria would've been crushed."

Something deflates inside me. "I was going to kill my father that day."

"My people didn't know that," Col says. "But this isn't your fault, Frey. I said yes to you. I betrayed them to save myself."

Another silence descends on us.

All those hours of planning the wedding, those photo ops beside Col, both of us meticulously dressed. I wasn't just helping my father maintain control of Shreve. I was helping him subjugate Col's city too.

"You've defied your father by escaping," he says softly. "My being with you isn't as bad. We need you to denounce him as Rafi of Shreve—his own heir turned against him."

I lean back against the cabin wall, letting the rhythm of the train find the old fractures in my bones.

Col's in a Victorian uniform, but no one's given me anything to wear. Now I know why—they want me in my sister's red dress forever.

Unless . . .

"What if we found the real Rafi?" I ask.

Col shrugs. "Then you wouldn't have to pretend to be her. But her note said she didn't want to be found."

"She didn't mean me!" I cry. "I'm her protector. She left a clue in her last feed before she disappeared, that she was in Paz. What if she *wants* me to find her?"

Col stares at me, uncertain. "You think she's still there?"

"My father does. He's certain enough that he's going to take the city."

BIG SISTER

I explain everything my father told me—the mysterious weapon recovered from the ruins. The coming attack. His plan for me and Col to rule Paz together

For a while, there's nothing but the sound of the train as Col absorbs it all.

"So conquering my city," he finally says, "destroying my family—it was all to find some Rusty weapon?"

I nod. "My father didn't really care about your ruins. All he wanted was an old research bunker hidden beneath them."

Col's voice almost drops away. "If we'd found it first, my mother might still be alive."

"Maybe. But she also might've used it against the rebels. Or Shreve."

Col looks at me like I'm talking nonsense, but Boss X's words are stuck in my head. What if Aribella Palafox was just a more civilized version of my father?

"We have to warn Paz," I say.

"They won't believe us. It'll sound like we're trying to scare up allies."

"But I heard it straight from . . ." My father, who no one trusts. And, like Col just said, our side has been lying.

Would I tell them as Rafi? Or as Frey? Neither of us is credible now.

"You don't know how this weapon works," Col says. "Or when the attack's coming. We can't help Paz defend itself."

"So what do we do?"

"We tell the world who was behind the attack—after it happens. We make sure your father takes the blame!"

I stare at Col. "You mean let people die, if it helps your cause?"

He doesn't answer. In the window behind him, the last shards of sun are turning the white weed red.

Part of me understands—he has a city to save. He can't afford to let anything else matter as much to him. Not Paz, not my sister, not me.

At the start of this, it was so easy for us to be allies. We were like overlapping waves, carried on each other's crests, made twice as strong.

But waves also cancel each other out.

I try to make it simple. "My sister didn't run away because of some tantrum about camping. Rafi always has a plan. Can't you see that?"

"I never met her. How should I know?" Col shrugs, still looking out the window. "None of it makes sense. Rafi did everything my people asked to help our rescue—but then she just vanished. And that last feed from a few days ago, it almost blew everything."

"Right, the Paz street in the background. Maybe that wasn't an accident."

Col looks at me. "She gave your father our location *on purpose*?"

"It wasn't for him—I think it was for me. It always felt like that, watching her pretend she was Frey. Like she was talking to the whole world, but also just to me."

"Saying what?" he asks.

That question freezes me. I'm still missing part of the puzzle. There's something I don't know about the person I've spent my life pretending to be.

That's why I have to find her.

Col squeezes my hands. "Listen. With her gone, you being Rafi is the easiest way. It solves everything."

I pull away. "But she doesn't know what's coming!"

"No one in Paz does. They're *all* in danger. But at least if your father attacks another city, the world will finally have to deal with him!"

I close my eyes.

Col keeps talking. "I'm playing politics, I know. But for my people right now, politics means *fighting for our right to exist*."

He lets me think about that for a moment. The noise of the train rushes into the space between us. I stare out the window, trying to imagine what it would be like to have a whole city stolen from me.

I've never had that much to lose. I grew up with no friends except my sister. No real possessions, just workout clothes and weapons. Even my name wasn't real, because I was never a legal citizen of Shreve. *Frey* was just something they called me.

I know all about having to fight to exist.

Turning back to him, I say, "Col, what if you and I just—"

A shriek cuts me off, the train lurching beneath us. We both careen forward, everything in the cabin tumbling.

The overhead lights flicker, and the wail of skidding metal fills the cabin for long seconds. Col is pushed up against me, the train's momentum pinning both of us against the forward wall.

We come to a slow, aching halt, till finally everything jolts back into place. Col stumbles, and I grab his hand.

It's silent, except for a distant alarm.

Out the window, red streaks ignite the sky—the glowing heat shields of an orbital drone insertion.

"He's found us," I say.

ORBITALS

My hand goes to where my pulse knife should be.

But I'm unarmed. Unmasked. Definitely underdressed.

Someone must have spotted the rebels in Vega and put it on the feeds, or wondered why that dish was being carted through the station. That's all it took to bring my father down on us.

Col throws on his uniform tunic. "How'd they get here so fast?"

I start on the lacy sleeves. "My father has drones in orbit. All they had to do was drop from the sky."

"He'd attack an intercity mag-lev, out here in the open?"

"He'll just stop the train and arrest us. The feeds are saying the rebels tried to kill his daughter today."

And if my father grabs me now, no one will ever find out that Col and I got away. They'll never know that I was Frey.

This would all be better if we hadn't been rescued. If everyone had waited for my wedding day, when I could—

The cabin door slides open.

It's Zura, already in full camo and body armor.

"Come with me," she says. "Get ready to fly."

A minute later, we're in a crowd of half-dressed rebels and Victorians, waiting to climb out the top hatch of the train.

"A fight in the wild," says Boss X beside me, full of battle fever and bubbly. "No civilians in the way!"

I feel it too—the blood rush of combat kicking in. The ecstasy of all my training making contact with reality.

We aren't all killers. But somewhere, deep down, I am.

"Frey." Boss X ceremoniously hands me a pulse knife. "You might find this useful."

It fills my hand, the weight perfect for me. "Is this yours?"

"A little thing like that? Never." He points to the pulse lance on his belt. "I was going to give it to you earlier. But I hadn't wrapped it yet."

"You . . . wrap presents?"

"Exquisitely. I'm a wolf, not a barbarian."

I squeeze the knife, sending it for a moment into full pulse. It turns fierce and buzzing in my hand, ready to tear the world apart.

"Thank you. I love it."

"Use it well," he says, touching the pendant around his neck.

It's my turn on the ladder. I set the knife to follow me and climb.

The metal rungs grow cooler as I go up—the roof of the train is swept with a chill ocean wind. A small fleet of hoverboards waits on top, lit by the flashes in the sky. Col stands on one already, a large rifle over his shoulder, gesturing for me.

I leap aboard, wrap my hands around his waist.

"Where's your armor?" he asks. Someone's given him baffle camo and body armor, while all I'm wearing is my scarlet dress.

"Priorities," I say. "You're the heir. Just fly."

He swears at his soldiers as we lift into the sky, but what I'm wearing doesn't matter anymore.

In a way, I've missed this even more than freedom—fighting alongside him.

I call Boss X's gift into my hand. Clutch it tight.

As Col wheels us around, I count lights in the sky. Three drones the size of aircars are still hurtling down at us, burning meteoric in their heat shields. Another four are slowing, their drogue chutes like black jellyfish against the sunset.

One drone has landed—it stands sentry at the front of the Cobra to keep the train from continuing on to Paz. Two more fly low at us, their lifting fans rippling the white weed.

I crouch behind Col, hoping his baffle camo will hide me.

He hoists the rifle. "Hold me steady. There's a kick."

I grip his waist harder, spread my feet on the board. The closest drone is halfway up the train—a klick away.

Col fires. The air splits into a burning streak between us and the drone, which shatters into fragments of hot metal.

The *boom* hits a tardy second later, kicking the air around us. Our weight shifts perilously—we'd fall, except for my grippy ballet shoes.

Dress to move.

Col extends his arms, and we steady ourselves again. He's got crash bracelets. I don't.

"Rail gun?" I ask.

"Yes." He drops the rifle. "No reloads."

A thunderclap from another hoverboard lights up the desert below, and a second explosion sets the air trembling again. But more drones are coming down. The roar of lifting fans fills the sky.

Zura's voice is in my ear.

"Split up, everyone. Run your patterns. Radio silence . . . now."

I shut my comms down.

"Do you know what we're supposed to do?" I ask Col.

"Yeah, everyone's scattering across the desert except us." He brings us around again, aiming for the front of the motionless train. "We're headed through the tunnel, straight into Paz!"

"We'll be trapped in there. We aren't even armed!" My knife might slow a heavy battle drone down, but not for long.

"Zura's staying with us. She's got a rail gun."

"Just one?"

Col doesn't answer. He leans forward, driving us faster against the wind. Heading up the tracks like this, our magnetics give us extra speed. The other Victorians, spreading out over fields, have only lifting fans.

They're making themselves slow targets, drawing fire away from us.

The drones take the bait—sprays of hot metal light up the landscape. The horizon, bloody with the sunset, dulls with smoke and churned-up dirt. The Victorians melt into vague, shifting shapes, heat signatures hidden by their baffle camo.

We fly low, just beside the Cobra, hoping the enemy won't risk hitting the train. The drone guarding the tunnel entrance waits just ahead.

We accelerate, hitching a ride on the track's mag-lev flow. Soon we're almost kneeling on the board, the wind in my face diamond-sharp with sand.

I close my eyes and let Col steer, feeling our maneuvers in my body against his, in the shifts of our weight on the board. When we clear the front of the train, we swerve over onto the tracks.

My eyelids creep apart—the drone shoots by too quickly to open fire. But now we're in the clear, the empty tracks like an aiming reticle below us.

And I'm not wearing camo.

Looking back, I see the drone coming around. I squeeze my knife and throw it down hard, set to return to me.

The knife skims the ground, and the drone behind us disappears behind a veil of dirt and swirling orchid petals.

I lean, and we swerve right, then left. When the drone opens fire, more plumes of sand fly up. The shots are falling short.

The drone's AI must be confused—it's shooting at the biggest heat signature, my pulse knife.

A moment later, the knife jumps back into my hand, gritty and scalding. The sandstorm behind us starts to dissipate.

"How far to the tunnel?" I yell.

"Five klicks!"

Three minutes, even at this speed. Long enough for the drone to get in a lucky shot. Maybe I should be in front, letting Col's camo hide me.

Behind us, the drone bursts through the haze, picking up speed, raising its own tail of sand.

I throw my knife at the earth again.

"Where's Zura?"

I feel Col shrug. Another flight of projectiles whistles past us. My knife returns.

This isn't much of an escape plan.

A flash illuminates the smoke behind us, lightning trapped in a cloud. My arms wrap around Col just in time—the shock wave sends us slewing across the fields. We lose the track's magnetics, decelerate into a spin.

Zura's barely visible, back there in the haze. She tosses the expended rail gun aside.

Col hesitates. "Should we wait for—"

"Just fly," I say.

We angle back over the tracks, heading straight for the tunnel.

I see the entrance now, the Baja Sea red and silver beyond it. On the other side is Paz, where we'll be safe from the forces of Shreve.

Until my father invades.

The battle still rages behind us. Above the running lights of the train, the sky is starred with projectile fire, streaked with rail gun bolts. I glimpse the shimmer of a pulse lance—Boss X carving up a combat drone.

Our hoverboard reaches the tunnel after a minute of hard flying. The narrow entrance glows with red caution lights.

As we enter, a booming voice calls to us. But it's in Spanish, and we're moving too fast for me to catch it. I assume it's warning that mag-lev trains will turn us into sticky paste. The tunnel is only one track wide.

Col slows down, just a little.

"The Cobra would stop before it hit us, right?" he says.

"Unless it's going too fast." Over my shoulder, the tunnel's entrance is filled with flashing sky. "But our train was supposed be going through right now. They wouldn't schedule two mag-levs that close to each other, would they?"

"Right. Of course not." Col's muscles tighten. "So what's *that*?"

I turn and peer into the darkness ahead.

A light is coming toward us.

TUNNEL

Col banks to a halt, cutting our lifting fans.

We stand there and listen.

There's no roar of a mag-lev train hurtling at us. No clanging of alarms. Nothing but the hum of a cool wind from the tunnel's depths.

Whatever's headed toward us, it's on magnetics.

"Wardens?" Col asks.

"One sec." My night vision kicks in, and an outline takes form around the approaching light—smaller than a hovercar, spindly with lights and cams. "It's some kind of drone."

"Col!" a shout comes from behind us.

We spin around. It's Zura, her armor pitted with projectile scars. Her camo obscures her silhouette in the dark.

"Are you okay?" Col angles us back toward her. She's covered with sand, armed only with a shock wand.

"Standing, sir. You?"

"Not a scratch." He points back into the tunnel. "But something's coming."

Zura narrows her eyes—her implants are better than mine. "Looks like a maintenance drone."

"Let's get moving, then," Col says. "Don't want to get trapped in here."

Zura glances back at the entrance. "We've technically entered the city, sir. They won't follow, unless Shreve wants a war."

"Don't count on that," I say. "My father has plans for Paz. He can always move them up."

She looks unconvinced, but Col and I lean hard on our board, carrying us deeper into the tunnel.

As we fly, the headwind turns damp. It smells of salt and fish, and the ground angles down beneath us.

I imagine the cold weight of the Baja Sea overhead.

The drone takes form slowly in my night vision. Something's mounted to its undercarriage—a fine mesh of wires. Its running lights point in all directions, like it's checking the walls of the tunnel.

It moves slowly, ignoring us. I crouch behind Col and his baffle camo.

Zura drifts out ahead, her shock wand drawn.

She passes the drone unnoticed, and waves for us to follow.

As we drift by, I hear a scurrying sound. Squinting at the wire mesh beneath the drone, I see tiny creatures trapped inside.

What—

A tendril lashes out at us, fast as a snake.

It strikes Col's arm with a *zap*. He cries out, sags into my arms.

Zura tips her hoverboard at the drone. But another tendril whips out at her. A flash lights the tunnel for an instant—she reels backward.

The drone comes at me and Col, looming over us. Three metal tentacles extrude from it, reaching for him.

I cover his body with mine and draw my knife, bringing it full pulse. The tunnel fills with the hum of danger.

The tentacles freeze.

"Disculpe," the drone says. *"¿Ustedes son humanos?"*

"What?" I slash at the nearest tentacle, but it slips out of reach. "*Yes*, we're human!"

"Apologies." The tentacles retract. "But this is a dangerous area."

I stare at the drone. Then an agitated *squeak* comes from the wire mesh slung beneath it. From this range I can see them—rats.

It's a wildlife control drone. It was trying to catch us.

"Did you think we were *rats*?" I yell.

The drone hesitates, its spindly arms moving cams and lights across us.

"Two of you are wearing baffle camo, specifically designed to confuse AI." The drone sounds disappointed in us. "Very unsafe."

Right—the camo reduced Zura's and Col's heat signatures, disrupted their silhouettes. I was hidden behind him, and our comms were switched off.

To the machine, they were just animals, wandering through the tunnel. The scarlet dress is what saved me.

"You are trespassing on a mag-lev track," the drone says. "In addition, military-grade sneak suits are illegal in the sovereign city of Paz. I shall have to inform—"

A *zap* comes from behind it, followed by a shower of sparks. The smell of ozone fills the air.

The drone wobbles, then falls. Zura rides it down, her shock wand smoking in her hand. The machine strikes the tracks, cracking open the cages below. Rats skitter in all directions.

Col groans, his eyes fluttering open.

"You're okay," I say. "It was just pest control."

"Oh." He looks down at the drone. "Somehow this welcome feels undignified."

I point at the rats scurrying away. "We bring freedom wherever we go."

"Did you have to destroy it?" Col asks Zura. "Paz is an ally."

She shrugs. "One that prefers not to know we're here. Saves them from making excuses for us."

"I guess," Col sighs. "But we should get this wreck out of the way before the Cobra crushes us all."

PAZ

An hour later, we emerge from the other end of the tunnel.

We're still in the outskirts of the city. No buildings, just rolling parklands dotted with trees, wildflowers, and solar cells. I glance warily at the sky—nothing but stars against the darkness.

My father has decided that following us isn't worth another war. Not yet, anyway.

A cluster of spires rises in the distance—Paz, the city where everyone's happy. No dust. No dictator. No standing army.

Zura is staring at a clump of trees nearby. She presses a finger to her ear.

"Hindenburg is ready for pickup," she says.

Instantly, the running lights of a large hovercar light up in the trees.

"Is that my code name?" Col asks.

"Had to change it, sir. Too many people who knew the old one were in enemy hands."

"Right, but *Hindenburg?*"

"The purpose of a code name is to deceive, sir." Zura extends an arm toward the hovercar. "We'll be in the Amazon by morning."

"Can't wait to see Teo," Col says with a smile.

He reaches for my hand.

And that's when I know.

"I'm not going." The words come out broken, but in my own voice.

Col turns to me. "What?"

"I can't go with you."

Zura looks half-disgusted, half-smug. "She's joining the rebels, sir. That was their intention, from the moment they signed up to help with—"

"No," I cut her off. "I'm staying in Paz."

"Frey." Col turns to me, taking both my hands. "It isn't safe here. Your father's coming."

"That's why I have to stay. To find Rafi."

"But she could be anywhere by now! If your father hasn't found her yet, how are you going to?"

"Because I know her better than he does."

"Sir," Zura says. "Would you like me to—"

"Stay out of this!" Col snaps, then turns back to me. "We can't win without you, Frey. We *need* you!"

"You need Rafi." I pull away from him, fingers calling subtly for my knife. "She can win you allies. Give you a fairy tale. The most useful thing I can do is bring her back."

His eyes are desperate. "No, Frey. I need *you.*"

"I'm not running away, Col—I love you." My heart twists with my next words. "But Rafi comes first."

"You're not her bodyguard anymore!"

"No. I'm her sister."

"Sir," Zura says, the shock wand in her hand. "I can always—"

"Turn to your left," I tell her. "Slowly."

She narrows her eyes, glancing to the side.

My pulse knife hovers there, two meters away, shuddering with eagerness.

Pointed at her head.

"Who gave you that?" she asks softly.

"A friend."

"Walk away, Zura," Col commands.

"Sir, you can't trust—"

"Walk *away*!" he shouts.

Zura obeys at last, storming off toward the hovercar in the trees. I've got maybe a minute before she has a sniper rifle trained on my head.

"I'm sorry, Col. But Rafi needs me more than you do. She's never been alone before!"

"Neither have you," he says softly, and he's right. "I'll stay too. We'll find her together."

Something stabs through me, and my fists clench.

Saying no to this is worse than leaving him.

"Col, I already messed up by helping my father stay in power. Taking you out of the war would be just as bad. This resistance needs your face. You have to stay with your people, or the rest of them will desert you!"

"But I can't fight without you, Frey." His voice breaks on my name. "From the first seconds of the war, you were there. When they destroyed my home, killed my . . ."

Col falters, lost for a moment.

Then his face changes, a certainty entering his eyes.

"I talk a lot about Victoria," he says softly. "But I also fight for *you*. You know that, right?"

There's no answering him. I never asked myself that question.

No one fights for me.

So I shut it out and say, "Let me find Rafi. Then we'll fight together again."

"Why not let me help?"

"Because it'll be easier to find her with you keeping my father busy!" I take hold of his hand. "It won't take me long. I was born to follow her every move."

"You're more than just her protector," he says. "You're Frey."

Uncertain what he means, I shake my head. "This is what I was born to do."

He wants to keep arguing, but in the end he has to swallow the words.

Because I'm right—for the moment, the two of us are stronger apart.

"I'll ping you every day," he says.

"How? I don't have a legal identity. The city interface won't know me."

"Right. Well, I'll send you a carrier pigeon or something." He sighs, gesturing at our hoverboard. "Take it. Is there anything else you need?"

"Just this." I call my pulse knife from where it hangs in the air.

Col stares at it. "Did you really think I'd let Zura jump you?"

"I trust you. But not your people." I glance at the hovercar. "So, just in case she's got a rifle aimed at me, we should probably do this without any sudden movements."

He frowns. "Do what?"

"This." I step closer, taking him in my arms.

We kiss for a long time, breathing hard around the thrum of our hearts. I shiver with worry that I'm losing him and with sheer pleasure that we're together now. I am myself in this kiss, and in the middle of it he murmurs, *"I love you too."* And that's when I know we'll be together again soon, even if this war lasts a hundred years.

It's our first good-bye kiss, and after it there's nothing left to say.

Col walks away. A car in Victorian robin's-egg blue rises up from the trees. The roar of lifting fans sends forth a shrieking, billowing flock of crows.

I watch the birds scatter and disappear.

Then I head toward the skyline of Paz, ready to find my sister.

PART 2

CITY OF
PEACE

You can no more win a war

than you can win an earthquake.

—Jeannette Rankin

COAT

Before I reach the city, the night starts to turn cold. A trickle of rain begins.

I have nowhere to sleep.

Maybe that's what Col was talking about when he asked if I needed anything. A sleeping bag. Some food. A bottle of water.

"Had to be dramatic," I mutter to myself.

Set to its ready state, X's pulse knife is keeping me warm. It trembles against my chest like an uncertain heart. But the wind cuts through the too-short scarlet dress. The hoverboard is running low, and I don't know where to recharge it.

Where am I going, anyway—a hotel? A rooftop? An alley?

"Does Paz even *have* alleys?" I ask aloud.

Col was right—I've never actually been this alone before. My father's tower was full of servants, staff, and his baleful presence. House Palafox was a hive of gardens, birds, butterflies, and people.

And in those lonely first days of the war, it was me and Col together in the wild.

Even when I was alone, I was alone with him.

"This sucks," I say.

No one answers.

Passing below are rows of long, low buildings. Factories and greenhouses. The neighborhood is dark, nothing moving but a few self-driving ground trucks. But in the distance, the rain glimmers with light coming up from the street.

A little closer, and the sound of a crowd lifts my heart. Apparently when you're lonely enough, even strangers will do.

I fly to the edge of a rooftop, peer over at the noise.

It's a night market. Smells of food drift up through the rain, along with the chatter of people talking, bargaining, hawking wares. Everyone sounds happy, just like Paz is famous for.

It's brain-missing, gathering in the rain to eat and drink and buy. They could be home with their holes in the wall, fabricating whatever they want. But Pazx love to cluster, to make noisy, collective theater out of every exchange.

My father used to rant about the waste of it all. But it's fine with me. I need warmer clothes, and something to hide my face.

Leaving my board on the roof, I climb down an exhaust duct to the street. Sneak around the corner and skulk at the dark edges of the market, watching and listening.

After fighting alongside the 'Foxes, I can pick out some of the Spanish. The shopkeepers are discussing the fine points of knitting, cooking, and hammering together pieces of wood—turns out this is a market for handmade items. Like they're all pretending to be pre-Rusties, with no factories or holes in the wall.

I don't have trade credits, or merits, or whatever they use for money here. But stealing should be easy with no dust in the air. I remember my first argument with Col—without surveillance, there's no way to prevent crime. Why do people pay for *anything* in Paz?

Even so, it sends a nervous trickle down my spine to sneak up behind a rack of coats and take one. But the owner never looks at me, too busy telling a customer about the farm that produces his wool.

I grab a floppy winter hat as well. Nothing to it.

No wonder my sister chose to disappear here.

I slink back into the darkness, gratefully wrapping the coat around my damp, chilled body. The wool isn't really waterproof, and it's heavy compared to disposable fabric, but warm. When I pull the hat down as far down as it will go, my shivering finally stops.

Food next.

This is trickier. It looks like everything's cooked to order, while gossip and pleasantries are exchanged. My first-daughter-of-Shreve face is still mostly visible, and I'm terrible at small talk even in English. They talk with their hands, a gesture for every syllable, conductors guiding their conversation like an orchestra.

Rafi must hate it here. From what Spanish I can glean, everyone's babbling about their dogs, their kids, the best way to make fry bread. No snark. No sarcasm.

Of course. Their feels are keeping them all cheery and content.

I can see them on everyone's wrists—little rows of faces. Buttons you press to feel whatever emotion you want. I keep my hands plunged into my pockets, so no one spots me as an outsider.

I wonder if Rafi's had a set put in. What if she came here to take control of—

"*Disculpe, señorita,*" someone calls.

I recognize the voice—the man who made this coat. His stall's only twenty meters away. Hunger has left me brain-missing, staying so close. Or maybe theft isn't as easy as I thought.

I yank the stolen hat down farther and start speed-walking, heading back toward the building where my hoverboard waits.

"*¡Señorita!*" the shop owner calls after me again. He still doesn't sound angry. Maybe he thinks it's all a happy misunderstanding. But he isn't falling behind.

I break into a run, dodging through the crowd. Out of the market and back into the darkness, down an alley toward the exhaust duct.

"*¡Deténganla!*" he cries, anger in his voice now.

I leap up onto the duct and climb fast, my arm muscles burning. Down below, my pursuer is yelling for *la interfaz de la ciudad.*

The city interface.

Wardens will be here soon.

I reach the roof and jump onto my board. It's only got an inkling of charge, but it leaps into the air at the snap of my fingers.

And then I'm off, arms wide, flying hard toward the denser buildings of the city center. The stolen coat trails behind me like a cape, and for a moment, I feel the rush of battle as wildfire in my veins, my hunger erased.

Maybe stealing things is kind of . . . fun.

"Charge warning," my board says. "Landing in five, four—"

"Override." I'm still too close to the night market.

The board doesn't argue. It's Victorian military spec, with minimal safety protocols.

But I have to land soon.

There's a patch of trees not far away, dense and unlit. I bank hard toward it, dropping to just above the rooftops.

Over my shoulder, I don't see any warden cars in the air. Maybe they have better things to do than chase after coat thieves on a cold night.

"Final charge warning," the board says.

"It's fine," I murmur to myself.

The little park is under me now, and I'm gliding down through the trees, looking for a dark place to—

The board drops away beneath my feet.

I'm falling.

I don't have crash bracelets.

CRASH

As I cover my face, a branch hits my shoulder, spinning me around. Then a blow to my back, stopping all forward momentum.

I'm tumbling straight down now. A gauntlet of branches slows me a little with each hit.

At last, the ground rushes up, a massive, sovereign punch. In a flash of pain, the world goes black, my mind sent flailing into nothingness.

It takes a while to realize that I'm lying in a pile of wet leaves. Almost swallowed by them, their damp, rich scent stronger than the iron tang of blood in my mouth.

My whole body is ringing with the impact.

"Stupid board," I mutter.

When I try to stir, I feel it—something's wrong with my right leg. Every movement is agony-making, and something deep in my brain cringes. I know this feeling from training.

Broken bones.

But my tutors never dared hurt me this badly. My leg feels shattered.

I lie there, breathing hard, trying to figure out how to fix this. They must have autodocs in Paz. But wouldn't they report me to the city interface?

Maybe not, given their worship of privacy here. Still, the idea of dragging myself down the streets looking for a med center is painfully ridiculous.

Being all alone sucks, turns out.

So I stay there, staring up and contemplating how wrong everything has already gone, until the shadow of a drone covers the sky.

It regards me for a moment. Is it here to arrest me?

Then I see the spades and rakes on its arms, the water sprayer, the leaf trimmer. A gardening drone.

"Hey there," I say. "I might need some help."

Oddly, the drone speaks directly through my comms.

"Hello," it says. "Welcome back, Rafia of Shreve."

I stare at the drone.

"What did you call me?"

"Rafia?" A tendril slips from the machine's underbelly, spends a moment at my mouth, tasting my breath. "Yes. It's you."

My DNA, of course, is the same as my twin sister's.

But how does a gardening drone know Rafi? And how did it turn on my comms without my permission?

My head is too pain-swimming to make sense of this.

"Have we met before?" I ask.

"Presumably. For privacy reasons, I erase the details of all unofficial conversations after three days."

"Unofficial . . . You're not a gardening drone, are you?"

"No, Rafia. I am the city of Paz."

"Oh, crap." This drone is just a conduit. So much for staying undercover.

But my sister wasn't staying here secretly either, was she? The city AI knows her.

A groan slips out of me. Frustration more than pain.

"This drone has no medical sensors. But you seem to be hurt."

"Yep," I grunt. "Could you send for an autodoc? Like, not a person. I don't want to make a fuss."

"Your request for anonymity has not expired, Rafia. If the autodoc decides you need a human doctor, one with refugee clearance will be summoned."

"Hang on." I wince a little—even talking hurts. "I'm a refugee?"

"Shreve is a certified dictatorship. All its citizens are granted automatic asylum in any free city."

"So your government knows I'm here."

"Certainly not." Paz sounds offended. "No self-respecting free city would allow politicians to weigh in on refugee issues."

"Right. Of course." Turns out, I have a lot to learn about free cities. Like, the fact that they call themselves free cities.

The seesaw wail of a siren is building in my ears. A flashing blue light pulses through the dark trees—a med drone zooming at us.

The gardener makes space for it, heading off to water the plants, I guess. But the voice of the city stays with me.

"You seem disoriented, Rafia."

"Yeah, kind of. Can you remind me how long I've been in Paz?"

"You arrived eight days ago."

"Right. But you said 'welcome back.' Did I leave?"

"Your privacy settings make certainty impossible. Two evenings ago, you ordered dinner from Sukotai Ramen on Empire Street. Since then you've been notably absent from the city interface."

My hunger spikes at the mention of noodles. But the pain is stronger.

The night before last was about when the rebels and Victorians left this city for Shreve. So why didn't Rafi wait for me?

"Did I ever—" A flinch chokes off the words. The med drone is wrapping a cluster of tendrils around my leg. Then suddenly it's numb down there. My other limbs are growing heavy, the pain receding from my body. "Did I say anything about leaving Paz?"

"You made no official requests. Anything else would have been erased for—"

"Privacy reasons," I finish with a sigh.

I'm almost starting to miss the dust. Of course, in a surveillance city, the wardens would be grabbing me for coat stealing about now.

A twinge of guilt goes through me.

"I should mention something." Maybe it's the painkillers in my blood, but an urge to confess is bubbling up. "I was really cold earlier, and kind of took something."

"Yes. That coat was reported stolen thirteen minutes ago."

"Oh." Euphoria is wafting through me now. "So I'm in trouble."

"Not unless the wardens catch you," the city says. "Med response and criminal investigations are mutually exclusive parts of me. And I rarely concern myself with minor property crimes."

"That seems wise."

"You have a compound fracture in your left leg. Two broken ribs, and one lung is partially collapsed. Nothing serious enough to need a human doctor."

"Nice. I'll just lie here, then."

"That is not advised, Rafia. Bone grafting will take at least eight hours. May I suggest returning to your apartment during the process?"

That wakes me up a little.

"I have an apartment?"

"Free cities don't let refugees sleep in parks."

"Oh. Sorry."

"No offense taken. But perhaps some sleep will improve your cognition. With your permission, this drone will render you unconscious for transport."

It goes against my warrior instincts to be at this machine's mercy, but I can't find my sister with a body full of broken bones.

"Sure," I say. "Knock yourself out."

But it's me who gets

knocked

out.

APARTMENT

Waking up is dreadful and ill-advised.

A haze of painkillers clouds my vision. Dull aches pound in my bones, and my right leg is a strange mix of numb and . . . wrong.

The bed is nice, though—as soft as Rafi's at home. Only the *best* pillows.

I shake my head, trying to clear the fuzz.

The room is oddly familiar. The walls pale colors. A big screen set to be a mirror. A makeup table.

Then I realize—it's laid out like Rafi's and my bedroom at home.

Only the pictures of us on the walls are different. They're photos of our speech, when we told the world our secret. Me, dirty and body armored. My sister, perfectly composed—two edges of the same knife.

And two beds, like she was waiting for me to join her in Paz.

Or maybe she was homesick . . . missing Shreve despite everything.

It's certainly not the room of a penniless refugee, or of someone who was planning on running away.

131

"Where did you go?" I ask the emptiness.

For a moment, I expect the Paz interface to answer. But this is a privacy-worshipping city. Rooms don't listen.

I sit up carefully, waiting for twinges of pain. Nothing comes, and the med drone is gone. My bones must be back where they belong. I'm not hungry anymore, thanks to a food patch on my left arm.

The Victorian hoverboard is charging in the corner, new crash bracelets beside it. My pulse knife sits on the bedside table—it must've followed me here.

The scarlet dress has been cut away. But this is Rafi's place, so there has to be some clothes somewhere.

There's a door where the hole in the wall should be. With all their handmade clothing, Pazx must not use fabricators much.

I stand up, the floor cool beneath my bare soles. My legs are wobbly, but the knitted bones seem strong. The closet door slides open at my approach.

I stare at what's inside.

She's organized everything by color, just like at home. That same even spacing, the shoes obsessively neat on their stands.

But these aren't Rafi's clothes.

Some workout sweats, like I would own. Mostly sensible trousers and shirts, all handmade. Local clothes for blending in.

Where did she get all this? And why leave it behind?

Like she left our old room behind . . .

It feels like another message from my sister that I can't understand.

Getting dressed, I notice something new and strange.

On my right wrist, little faces have appeared, like two rows of tattoos. Smiling, frowning, surprised, peaceful, sleepy, angry, querulous, excited, happy, lustful, blank-faced, and a dozen other expressions I don't recognize.

The med drone has given me feels.

"Really?" I say. "You can't listen without permission, but you can do random surge on me?"

When the city doesn't answer, I look around, angrier every second. There must be some way to get the AI's attention.

On the makeup table is a small orange dome, the Paz seal on the base, a fat dial on top. The dial twists clockwise until there's a solid *click*.

The city's voice is instantly in my head: "Good morning. Are you well?"

"Mostly."

"Excellent. For the future, may I suggest crash bracelets?"

"You may." I hold out my wrist, showing the new feels. "Um, last night's kind of fuzzy, but did I ask for these?"

"The request was made a week ago. The med drone simply carried it out."

"Oh." A vision of Rafi's temper tantrums flashes through my head—her depressions, her manias. The Palafox psych team saying she was falling apart.

I stare at the little faces. Did she come here to get feels?

If so, why run away without them?

"Try one if you like," the city says. "May I suggest Morning Buzz? The face with large trembling eyes."

I look closer. Lined up in two rows, the feels look like a tiny jury judging me.

"No, thanks. I have no shortage of feelings right now."

"The drone may have overstepped its bounds. It failed to spot the larger issue with your med scans."

"An issue with my scans? Am I sick?"

"You are very healthy. But your millimeter-wave scans from last night were . . ." The voice pauses for a few seconds, which, for a city-scale AI, is like a person mulling their words for a century. "Unexpected."

I shake my head, trying to clear the painkiller haze.

Then it hits me—when I was posing as Rafi in House Palafox, their security scanned me for implants. The tissue damage and knitted bones from my years of combat training almost blew my cover.

My body tells the truth, even when I'm lying.

"Yeah, my medical history is complicated. Lots of cosmetic surge. My bones must look funny."

"Your results are not funny. Nor are they from cosmetic surge. They are consistent with a decade-long combat training regime."

Turns out, lying to a city-size brain is tricky. I flail for something clever or distracting to say.

But all I have is "So you know who I am."

"Of course, Frey."

My real name sends a cold needle of panic through me—like my old nightmares of being found out.

Identity theft is a crime. Much worse than stealing a coat.

"I wasn't planning on lying, but you just kind of assumed . . ."

"Unforgivable on my part." The city sounds amused. "Especially after your sister tried the same deception, though in reverse."

I frown. "And Rafi's not in jail. So you're not going to arrest me either, right?"

"Please, Frey. Paz is not a carceral city. And there's no question of theft. Your sister has made you her legal proxy."

My mind goes blank for a moment, staring at the blue dome.

"I'm Rafi's . . . proxy?"

"What's hers is yours, as per her will and testament. You are also her heir. All this is yours."

I sink into the chair at the makeup table. My face stares back at me in the mirror, drained of blood.

"Where did she get all this stuff, anyway?"

"From someone quite wealthy, one would presume. That table is handmade of natural teak. But it would be privacy-missing for me to speculate further."

I groan. "Can you at least tell me why she made a will?"

"Her motivations are private, but she was quite thorough. You can even take her name, if you wish."

"I don't wish. Where did she go?"

"I can't tell you that, Frey."

The ache in my bones comes rushing back, thudding with my heart. "Because you don't know? Or because she requested privacy?"

"For me, those are the same thing."

I let out a disgusted sigh. This is my sister's terrain, not mine—the niceties of protocol, local laws, and arguing with AIs.

But she *wanted* me to come here and find all this. She recorded her last feed on the streets of Paz. She knew the city would guide me here once it spotted me. She made me her heir, left me clothes like hers . . .

Is Rafi planning on disappearing forever?

"You seem agitated. May I suggest Calm. It's the calm face with closed eyes and—"

"I don't want to be calm! My sister might be in danger!"

"Is this a matter of public safety?"

Of course—danger trumps privacy. Maybe this is a way to get the AI's help.

"Everyone in Paz is in danger," I say. "There's an attack coming."

A hint of a pause. "From Shreve?"

"Who else? My father dug up an ancient weapon in the Palafoxes' ruins. He told me that he plans to use it against you."

"Ah, the submarine."

I frown. "Submarine?"

"A craft capable of sustained and independent underwater—"

"Yeah, I know what subs are." I manage not to punch the orange dome. "Are you saying my father dug up an old submarine?"

"Its date of manufacture is unclear. But a Shreve underwater craft has been stationed in the deep ocean the last six days, at some distance from Paz. It's at the ocean bottom, scanning for oil reserves, we assumed. Do you have other information?"

"Not much." I sift through my memories of Rusty military tech. Subs were for sinking ships, mostly. But they could fire city-killing missiles as well. "My father said you wouldn't know what hit you."

"Unlikely."

"You don't find this nervous-making? You don't even have an army!"

"Paz has no soldiers. But our missile defense is impenetrable, our occupation strategy unparalleled. My processing cores are safely buried under three kilometers of solid stone. We have been prepared for an attack from Shreve since the war began. We are not nervous."

The city's confidence is impressive, until I realize where I've heard that tone before.

"The Palafoxes weren't afraid of my father either."

"The Palafoxes are a vestige of the old regime—human leaders. They couldn't hope to match the collective intelligence of a free city. Even you fooled them."

"You don't know what my father is capable of!"

"The whole world knows what he's capable of, Frey. His recent actions have made sure of that."

A frustrated groan slips out of me—yes, they all saw what happened to Victoria. But no one understands that it can always get worse.

Maybe it's useless, trying to argue with a city-size ego.

"I'm just trying to help you," I say.

"Of course, Frey." The city changes back to its jovial self. "Allow me to be helpful too. As Rafia's legal proxy, you have access to her pings. There's one waiting to be read."

"A ping? Rafi left a message for me?"

"I don't know who it's from. Here in Paz, pings are strictly private."

"Ugh. Just show me."

A message interface appears in the makeup table's mirror, listing exactly one ping.

It's from Trin Härkönen.

Trin was a classmate of Col's little brother, Teo. She convinced him and another kid to run away from their boarding school at the start of the war. To make my father look bad, they pretended to have been kidnapped. They even left spatters of their own blood behind.

She's the scariest thirteen-year-old I've ever met—and rich enough to afford the contents of this room. She's been helping my sister.

"Play," I say, and Trin's voice enters my head.

Hey, Frey. You found this! Maybe you're not as bubbleheaded as your sister says.

I'm still here in Paz, doing some extra credit for my propaganda class.

Wanna help?

TRIN

I walk to Trin's hotel, wrapped in my stolen coat. It's late afternoon—I was asleep for sixteen hours while my bones were put back together—so it feels like the wrong time of day to me. Despite the autodoc's work, my ribs still ache with every breath.

I'm wearing dazzle makeup from Rafi's collection. The makeup reacts to movement, shifting the contours of my face with every step. In the crowded streets of Paz, no one gives me a second glance.

I wonder how many of my father's agents are in this city, looking for me.

A Shreve assassin would probably stick out here. The cosmetic surge in Paz goes way past anything at home—manga eyes, dappled skin, extra digits. But why go to all the trouble of surgery, when they can feel gorgeous at the press of a finger?

How many of them are using their feels right now? The throng is bubbly, like a public holiday in Shreve, but maybe that's just natural for a free city. Or maybe no one's feelings are natural in Paz.

I glance at my wrist, the choir of expressions staring up at me. There's something tempting about the little faces, but I'm addled enough without fake emotions buzzing in my head.

The spindly, floating buildings are so different from the squat skyline of Shreve. They remind me of Victoria's skyline. Wild birds nest in hovering aeries, so the sky is full of wings. But no surveillance drones, no hovercams. The slants of afternoon sunlight are free of surveillance dust. That still feels strange to me.

I don't know how to react to any of it. The smells, the colors, the possibilities. People in Shreve never hold hands as they walk. Here, everyone does. All this freedom doesn't make me happy—it just confuses me. All these faces on my wrist, and I have no idea which emotion I'm supposed to feel right now.

All I know is that my sister is out there somewhere, without me to protect her.

Trin's hotel looks fancy.

It's an old-fashioned building, ten stories of steel and glass, solidly planted on the ground. Flowers everywhere in the lobby. No human staff, just helpful hoverdrones the size of teacups to guide me to her room. No one asks my name.

At her door, Trin looks me up and down.

"Frey, right?"

Hearing my real name said aloud makes me flinch. But I suppose that here in Paz even hotel walls don't snoop. "Yeah, it's me."

"Just checking," Trin says. "Your sister likes to mess with me sometimes. Come in."

Her room is a suite, a living area with three doors leading off to a bedroom, a kitchen, a workout space. Every wall, and some of the windows, are covered with stick-up flatscreens. They're filled with video channels, trembling graphs, feed data from a dozen cities.

It reminds me of Dona Oliver's offices, when we were planning publicity for my wedding.

I have to ask, "Your propaganda homework?"

Trin gives me a delighted grin.

"Every mention of your father, the Palafoxes, or the Vic resistance—tracked and visualized." She waves her arm at the screens. "This is mostly real people, but I've got a couple thousand AI accounts working to keep the outrage going."

I stare at the jittering graphs and burbling text clouds. "My father conquered a city. Shouldn't outrage just happen?"

"Yeah, you're really Frey," Trin says with a laugh. "Raffles doesn't do naive."

I ignore her, going closer to the screens. More than half are in Spanish, some in English, a few in other languages. All this feed chatter, while everyone under my father's thumb is silenced by the dust. One screen is labeled *Depose the Dictator*, another *More Sanctions*. And on another . . .

"Is that a turtle on a hoverboard?"

"His name's El Moto," Trin says. "Only half of my network is Free the Vics. The rest is eyeball-grabbing, with links back to the propaganda. My cooking channel's pretty good."

"I don't cook much. Where's my sister?"

"She didn't leave you a ping?"

I shake my head.

Trin hesitates, like she isn't sure if she's supposed to tell me.

"Where's my sister?" I draw my pulse knife, heading toward the satellite dish sitting on a stack of backup batteries. "Tell me or I'll wreck everything in this room."

"Relax, Frey! We're on the same side. Raffles is gone. She left the city to join the rebels."

I watch Trin's face, but she doesn't twitch.

"The rebels," I say. "The ones who live in the woods and wear furs and skins? Rafi joined *them*?"

"I know, right?" Trin lets out a giggle. "You should've seen her packing. *So* much bug spray."

"But I was just with them. Smith and X didn't say a word."

"Not *those* rebels. Raffles wanted a crew that wasn't allied with the Vics. People who wouldn't know who she really is."

I shake my head. "You mean she joined them as . . . *me*?"

"Of course. Any crew would take you. Trained in combat your whole life, and you attacked your own dad's city! Doesn't get much more rebel than you, Frey."

"So I've heard." Suddenly my heart is pounding against my aching ribs.

Dizziness descends, and I sit down hard on the giant leather couch. My freshly knitted bones feel brittle inside me.

"I thought you'd have a message from her," I say.

Trin shrugs. "Are you sure she didn't leave one? You're her proxy—you've got access to her stuff. The city showed you the apartment she got for you, right?"

"There wasn't any message." I stare at Trin. "Wait. That place was for me?"

"Of course. We spent *days* getting it exactly right. It was a present for you. A parting gift, I guess."

"A parting gift . . . and you helped her buy all that stuff." I look around the room. "How are you even here in Paz? After you ran away from school, your parents let you stay?"

"My home city doesn't do adolescence. We're adults at fourteen." Trin straightens proudly. "Did my rite of passage a year early."

"And the Victorians put you in charge of their propaganda?"

"The Vics aren't talking to me." She lets out a sigh. "Teo didn't like my last story about his mom. Too many missiles."

"Very tasteful."

"Teo is guts-missing, but at least Col's finally back." Trin looks at me. "He escaped with you, right? The Shreve feeds aren't saying, but their cover story's falling apart."

143

I hesitate, unsure how much to tell her. Maybe this is why she pinged me—to get the dirt on our escape for her feed network.

Maybe she's just making all this up.

"How are you and Rafi *friends*?" I ask. "She only got to Paz a week ago!"

"We've been working together remotely since she escaped your dad." A proud grin. "Her Frey impersonation is ninety percent me."

"Um, I'm pretty sure it's ninety percent *me*."

Trin laughs. "Right. She knew how to talk like you. But we wanted the other cities to *love* her! That took some work."

I let pass this suggestion that I'm not lovable.

"Trin, I need to find my sister. Did she tell you anything about the rebel crew she joined? The boss's name?"

"Of course not. She doesn't want to be found."

Not this again. I stand up and start pacing the room.

"She *does* want to be found—she got herself spotted in Paz. She made me her proxy!"

"Yes." Trin spreads her hands, as if to prove she's not hiding anything. "Raffles wanted you to know she was okay. But she doesn't want you following her. If you show up out in the wild, her crew might start wondering which of you is real!"

I stare at Trin. She's talking like this is all obvious. As if Rafia of Shreve really wants to be a rebel now.

But she doesn't know my sister at all. No one knows her like I do.

"She would've waited to tell me in person," I say.

"And let you talk her out of it?" Trin sits down on the couch, laughing again. "No, this is classic Raffles—cut and run."

"You don't know her!" I yell.

Another shrug. "Not sure anyone does. Love your sister to bits, but she's got issues. I kept telling her to get some feels."

I roll up my shirtsleeve. "You persuaded her. But they wound up on me."

Trin's eyes light up. "Ooh, have you tried any? This stupid city won't let me surge yet."

I stare at the little faces, wondering if there's one to erase this feeling of confusion and betrayal.

"None of this sounds like Rafi," I say.

"That's the point, Frey. She doesn't want to be Rafi."

"What?"

"She hates herself," Trin says.

That freezes me, and a thousand memories go through my head. All those rages. Despising her own friends. Wishing for our father's death.

Falling apart, and that was before I went to Victoria, leaving her alone.

In the trophy room, Dona called Rafi a basket case. And what did my father say to me? *After your meltdown during the war, it looked like you were gone for good.*

A few hours after the attack on Victoria, Rafi thought I was dead in the rubble of Col's home. She never appeared in public again. She was missing in action for the whole war.

It was her idea to test me, to have me wear the red or white jacket. And my father tried to kill me for it. I'd always protected her; it gave my life meaning. But she could never protect *me*.

Maybe she does hate herself.

Trin is still talking. "This way, everyone gets what they want. You get your revolution and your boy. And you're her heir—one day you'll get the city of Shreve!"

I shake my head. "But what does Rafi get?"

"You still don't understand?" Trin lets out a giggle. "She gets to be *you*, Frey. That's all she's ever wanted—to be her own twin sister."

FEELS

I walk blindly at first.

Out into the city, through its jumble of noisy freedoms, letting the crowds swallow me. Here in the old part of town, the streets are lined with food stalls, musicians, wares spilling out of shops. But the clutter of Paz doesn't erase Trin's words.

I didn't know my own sister.

All those times Rafi made me show her what I'd learned in combat lessons. When she tried to teach me French, and how to curtsy, and how to design clothes. When she fantasized about our father's death, saying she'd tell the whole city our secret, so they'd love me too.

What if she wanted to switch places?

This last month in her skin, I started to see—being Rafia of Shreve wasn't much better than being her body double. Maybe my sister envied my simple life of training and protecting someone. She had to deal with her dreadful friends. With Dona Oliver's scheming. With *him*.

But I didn't understand till now, when it's too late to help her.

Where am I supposed to go next? Rafi doesn't want me confusing the issue of who's who. I miss Col more than anything, but the Vics don't trust me—they only want to use me.

I'm starting to think that X's crew really is where I belong. But there can't be two rebel Freys, and masquerading as a rebel Rafi makes no sense.

Maybe I should just disappear into these happy Paz crowds.

From my wrist, two rows of faces stare up. Maybe one of these feels can stop the train wreck in my head.

My eyes fall on a face with closed eyes and a soft smile—the one the Paz AI told me about: Calm.

I cover the smiling face with my thumb, just for a second.

Nothing happens. Maybe I didn't press it long enough . . .

Or maybe I don't need a device in my wrist to control myself. For sixteen years, my trainers watched me, judging every word, every movement. I stayed calm when they broke my bones and made me bleed. When an assassin tried to kill my sister, I was calm and killed him instead. When House Palafox was destroyed, I was cool and collected enough to escape the city.

But here I am, frozen in this bustling crowd, staring at a little face.

And my brain is raging.

My finger slides over the Calm face again. This time I hold it there, trying to slow my breath.

Nothing seems to happen . . . but then a sigh eases from my lips.

Something inside me lets go, gives up, like that moment in a rainstorm when I'm too soaked to care anymore.

Even after I take my finger away, the feeling lingers.

The chaos inside me settles. The jumble of thoughts starts to order itself. And after a moment, a strange notion creeps into my head.

Maybe Rafi needs her freedom more than my protection right now. Maybe she needs to find herself—even if that means being *me* for a while.

I shake my head, not recognizing my own thoughts.

Because they *aren't* my thoughts. It's the feels, sending hormones into my bloodstream. Emotions don't change the fact that guarding Rafi is what I was born to do. I need to find her and protect her . . .

But maybe not this minute.

The joyous sounds of the city wash over me, and mixed into the chaos are Boss X's words—*Rafia of Shreve can take care of herself.*

She handled my father for sixteen years. She's charmed everyone she's ever met. She'll make friends in a rebel crew, maybe the first real friends she's ever had who aren't me.

But a part of my brain is still fighting the Calm. How dare I stop worrying about my sister? My father is still alive and searching for us both.

Relaxing for even a moment is *dangerous.*

Uncertain notes creep into the sound of the throng, as if the city itself is worried for me. Or maybe the crowd is reacting to something else.

I look up from the faces on my wrist.

Two machines the size of eagles are skimming down the street, a few meters overhead. Everyone's looking up at the unexpected sight—this city doesn't have surveillance drones.

They're coming straight at me.

EXTRACTION TEAM

I turn away, pushing through the crowd.

Just ahead, between two old stone buildings, an alley looks barely wide enough for the drones to fit. Should I dive in? Or stay out here in the cover of the throng?

No decision comes. My blood should be screaming. But Calm still courses through my veins, like this is a pleasant afternoon walk.

The feel is blocking me from the rush of combat. Perfect.

I keep my head low, walking fast, uncertain if the drones have spotted me. Over my shoulder, I see them keeping their course down the center of the street.

The city interface has anonymized my movements. My face is disguised with dazzle makeup. There's no way Shreve could've tracked me down.

Unless they were watching Trin's hotel.

I draw my knife and head toward the alley, where the drones won't hit people as they crash.

People are looking at me now, wondering why I'm shoving past them. But here in happy Paz, no one tries to stop me.

Something sharp brushes my left shoulder. The barest prickle, but a moment later a numbness is spreading across my back. It's a sleeper dart—so why am I not knocked out already? For some reason, it's working in slow motion.

Reaching the darkness of the alley, I spin around, squeezing the knife into full pulse.

With its roar in my ears, exhilaration cuts through my Calm. But the dart's bite is still spreading down my left arm.

A drone buzzes into the alley, and my knife leaps up to meet it. The collision is earsplitting. The blast wave rushes over me, deafening and acrid. A second later, the hot knife leaps back into my open hand.

I smell smoke—a patch of my stolen coat is on fire.

As I pat out the wayward sparks, I see the tiny feathered shaft sticking up from the wool. I pluck it out, realizing two things at once.

One: The heavy coat saved me—the point of the dart only brushed my skin.

Two: The coat was reported stolen last night. The owner must have put a picture of it on the feeds—the drones were searching for the pattern of its weave.

But for now it's protection.

Wary of my pulse knife, the second drone hovers just outside the alley. But if they were using sleeper darts, an extraction team must be nearby.

My father wants to bring me home alive.

That thought sends a jolt of fear through me, wiping away the last of my Calm.

I run.

The alley turns twice, then hits a dead end. One of the old buildings is a wedding cake of stonework and decoration, easy to climb. But I'm woozy from the dart, and suddenly my stomach feels empty. Patches aren't the same as solid food.

I stare down at my feels again. The Paz AI said something about . . .

Morning Buzz?

I find the razzle-eyed face and press down. Hard.

Fresh lines of energy surge through my body. The numbness from the dart retreats, but waves of dizziness come tumbling in. The world feels split in two, like there's a slam band in one of my ears, a symphony orchestra in the other. Calm, Buzz, and the dart.

I ignore the cacophony and start to climb.

Up two floors is a window, darkness behind it. I kick in the glass.

Scrambling inside, I find myself in an escape stairwell—the building isn't tall enough for bungee jackets.

The stairs are steep and dark, the walls echoing with my footsteps. My pulse knife trembles in my hand.

I hear glass shattering above me.

I freeze. The extraction team is inside.

The only sounds are from outside—the crowd still shouting about the crashed drone, the sirens of approaching emergency craft. In a few minutes, this building will be swarming with Paz wardens.

But wardens can't stop my father's soldiers. He'll have sent Specials, surged beyond any normal human abilities.

They won't stop until they have me.

Slow, deliberate footsteps are coming down the stairs.

"There's no need for the knife," a male voice says.

The tone is light and friendly. But I know the sound of a Special, throat-surged to send trickles of fear along my nerves. It jangles with my Morning Buzz.

I don't answer.

"We're here to take you home, Rafia."

They still think I'm my sister—Dona didn't confess. Otherwise, that dart would've been poison.

Rafi's voice comes easy to me. "I'm staying here."

"We don't have time for this," the man says. "Your father's plans for this city are already in motion. They can't be stopped."

My eyes widen in the dark. So the attack is already on its way.

"What plans?"

"Turn that knife off, Rafia. You're going to hurt yourself."

"What's happening to this city? Tell me and I'll give up."

All he says is "You need to come with us. We only have a few minutes."

The attack's coming that soon? Or is he worried about the

wardens in the alley below? Any moment now, they'll spot the broken windows.

I stay in character. "Tell me what's happening to Paz, or I won't come with you. My sister's here. I'm not going to leave her!"

I squeeze the knife into a burst of full pulse so he knows I mean business.

"Frey will be fine, Rafia. Our sources say she's back with the rebels."

Their *sources*? I starts to ask for more, but I hear it just in time— the barest fluttering coming down the stairs.

A black drone the size of a butterfly rounds the corner at ankle height, mounted with a single dart. It lunges at my calf, but a swipe of my pulse knife turns it into confetti.

I give him Rafi's most imperious voice. "Try that again and I'll throw this knife at you!"

"Rafia, it's important that you listen. Very soon, we will leave— with or without you."

I start to laugh and laugh, but he keeps talking.

"We can't be seen in Paz." Another pause. "Even if that means leaving you behind. You don't want to be here for what's coming."

Of course—my father doesn't want Paz to know who's attacked them. Maybe those drones can't be traced to Shreve, but living, breathing Specials are another matter.

All I have to do is stall them.

"Okay, give me a minute."

"We don't have a minute, Rafia."

"Okay, I'm coming!" I shout, but soon they'll realize I'm not.

I pull off my stolen coat and curl up in the stairwell corner, huddling behind a curtain of its thick wool. My pulse knife is ready if they rush me, but I don't think they will.

"You have five seconds, Rafia."

I huddle tighter, making sure no part of me is sticking out from behind the coat.

A moment later, the whisper of fluttering drones fills the air, followed by the *plinks* of sleeper darts bouncing down the stairwell. The extraction team is sending down a hail of missiles.

The coat trembles in my hands, tiny metal points poking through. It's sheer luck that none of them pricks my fingers.

When the barrage ends, all I can hear are voices from below—Paz wardens entering the ground floor of the stairwell.

I peek out from behind the coat. On the stairs above me, a shadow shifts . . .

Squeezing my knife to full pulse, I slash at the fireproof wall. The ceramics disintegrate into a thick cloud, billowing out to fill the stairwell. I'm already scuttling from my corner and down the stairs toward the wardens.

Half a flight down, I huddle beneath my coat again, expecting another flight of darts.

But nothing comes.

Except a noise—the door at the top of the emergency stairs opening on rusty hinges.

The Specials are running away.

My father would rather lose Rafi than let his soldiers be spotted here before the attack. Which gives me no choice but to go after them.

I cast my coat aside and run up the stairs, full of combat ecstasy at last.

SHAKES

I climb the stairs fast, half-blind in the dust.

There'll be at least three Specials on the extraction team, all in body armor. I'm wearing nothing but Rafi's gray sweats, and my knife's charge light is yellow. My only advantage is that they think I'm her.

If I can knock out one and leave them for the wardens, it'll embarrass my father. Maybe the Paz will even take notice.

Two floors up, the dust clears enough to see. I keep climbing, scanning for traps in case this retreat is a trick.

It feels wrong—Specials just running away.

The roof door is shut, bent it its frame to slow me down. I kick it.

Once, twice . . .

A flying blow finally knocks it halfway off its hinges. The metal bends outward, and I stumble into the waning sunlight.

A car hovers a few meters above the roof, steady in the air.

Waiting for me.

I squeeze my knife to full pulse, daring them to attack.

But through the car's side window, the nearest Special only gives me a curious look. He scans me like my trainer, Naya, used to, noting my fencing stance, my left arm back for balance.

And through the window glass I see his lips move.

Frey?

Right—Rafi might've gotten lucky with a pulse knife against a drone. But charging up here and busting down that door? That was pure me.

The hovercar spins in the air. For a moment, I think they're going to open fire.

But the Special only smirks as the car wheels up and away. As if he doesn't care what happens to me.

Which makes no sense. My father has wanted me dead since the first minutes of the war.

My knife doesn't have the charge to stop a hovercar, so I can only stand and watch. The car swings east, back toward Shreve at top speed.

Away from Paz.

What did the Special say to me on the stairs?

You don't want to be here for what's coming.

I let my knife go still, slip it into a pocket before the Paz wardens see it.

It's strange that no one else has made it to the roof yet. I don't hear any voices on the stairs. Sirens are blaring, but off in the distance.

Then I feel it—the barest trembling in the roof under my feet.

It builds slowly, like the rumble of an oncoming mag-lev. The air around me turns thin and shuddery.

A thunderstorm coming on?

The sky is pale blue, no clouds at all.

Everything goes still again. But the distant sirens keep wailing. I walk to the edge of the roof and lean over the parapet. A group of wardens is spilling out from the alley onto the main street.

Something's happening. Something bigger than a crashed drone and some broken windows.

Out along the horizon, columns of smoke rise up from the outskirts of the city. My mind flashes back to my father's surprise attack on Victoria.

But there are no missile trails. No incoming jags of light.

Then it starts again—the roof trembling beneath my feet. For a few seconds, I'm not even sure it's real. But when I place my hands on the parapet, the shivering stone reminds me of my father's words in his study.

Like a force of nature.

A shock comes then—the roof lurching, sending me staggering back from the parapet. The building seems to tip and buck under me, and I fall to my hands and knees.

When the rumbling subsides, I'm staring down at a finger-width crack in the stone. It runs halfway across the roof, like the whole building is splitting.

I stand up slowly, wary of the world itself.

The sun has turned brown—a cloud of shaken dust rises from the whole city, along with a veil of screams and sirens.

I walk to the parapet again, just to take hold of something solid. But new fissures line the stone.

Around me, the squat buildings in this neighborhood are all knocked askew, leaning against each other like tired soldiers. At the end of the block, a tall building gapes with a hundred shattered windows. A rain of safety glass flows down onto the street, sparkling in the dusty sunlight.

The center of the city looks untouched, the great towers impervious on their hoverstruts. The earthquake hasn't broken through the dampeners to reach the city's magnetics, kilometers beneath the earth.

But I see people jumping, specks against the towers of glass. As their bungee jackets take hold, they fall soft as snowflakes.

It looks so orderly—they must practice evacuations all the time. This is the Pacific Rim, after all, full of tremblers and volcanoes. And I guess their feels are keeping the Pazx calm.

There's no way my father could have caused this.

But then I remember that submarine from Shreve—on the ocean bottom, down with the fault lines.

I turn on my comms. "City interface? Are you there?"

No answer. Maybe the AI's overloaded with emergency calls.

"City of Paz! I have urgent information. I waive any right to privacy—listen to me!"

"Yes, Frey. Do you need assistance?"

"I'm fine. But I know what caused that earthquake."

"A sudden release of energy from tectonic pressures?"

"Um, yeah. But it's not natural. It's the Rusty weapon my father found!"

"That seems unlikely. There's no historical record of such a weapon. And Paz has survived earthquakes before."

"Right, but . . ." I don't know how to finish. It's not like my father told me anything useful. "I just thought you should know."

"Thank you, Frey. Now may I suggest that you head for ground level? We can continue this conversation once you're safe."

I hesitate, watching the skyline. Emergency craft are lifting into the air, their fans roiling the dust. The evacuations continue, people in bungee jackets spilling out of the taller buildings.

Maybe the city has things under control. Maybe my father's mysterious weapon wasn't as powerful as he thought.

"Okay, fine," I say, turning toward the door.

"Wait," the interface says. "Iron Mountain."

"What do you mean?"

"Iron Moun—" it starts again, but then the third shock comes.

Pure noise. Titanic fury. Like I'm inside a waterfall, the air itself roaring, churning. The world shivers and blurs in the edges of my vision.

The parapet crumbles in my hands.

I stagger back, the roof tipping, stone turning to gravel beneath my feet.

I'm skidding toward the building's edge, on my hands and knees again. Sliding down toward a yawning gap, about to join the pile of rocks and rubble falling on the street below.

I grab for any purchase, but everything is loose stones and dust.

Drawing my knife, I send it roaring up the slope of the roof—my fist wrapped around the hilt. The knife's magnetics drag me slowly upward toward the metal door.

Swinging open, it's almost within reach . . .

My fingers close on the door handle as my knife sputters, out of charge. The metal bends a little more, hinges squealing over the roar of the quake.

But it holds.

Finally, all at once, the thunder comes to an end.

The vast silence rings my whole body. My lungs are full of dust, my vision swimming.

The roof tips perilously beneath me, but it's full of cracks for handholds and footholds. Now that the building isn't shaking itself apart, I can climb down to the street.

But with my first careful movements, a new sound pushes away the ringing in my ears. A distant roar, like the surf on a beach.

Another earthquake?

I look up at the skyline . . .

It's unbelievable.

That last quake must have cracked the bedrock—made it past the dampeners and shock-resistant reservoirs, all the way to the city's deep magnetics, the massive engines that keep hoverstruts in the air.

The spine of the city is broken.

The towers of Paz are starting to fall.

SHATTERED

I can't watch. The sound is bad enough.

Millions of tons of metal and glass are crashing down, beating the drum of the earth with an endless roar.

Pure instinct fills my body—to get down to the street. All I want is solid ground beneath me.

I descend the slanted, broken roof. The front of the building has collapsed, so it's like climbing down a rockslide.

I'm almost on the street, when a groan drifts up between the stones.

I cover my eyes and squint, peering into the darkness. A hand curled in pain, the glisten of eyes staring back at me.

Someone's buried in there.

"Hang on," I say.

With a heave, the largest piece of rubble rolls away. It tumbles down the slope, smacking more dust into the air. The pieces are smaller after that, easy to pull up and out.

The woman should be crushed, but she's protected by what's left of a permacrete archway. She must've sheltered in the building's entrance before the last quake hit.

When I pull her out, she's covered with dust and blood. But her grip in my hand is strong, her face calm.

"Do you speak English?" I ask. "Are you okay?"

"Yes," she says. "No broken bones."

My first-aid training kicks in, and I start checking her for injuries.

"Are you sure? You could be in shock."

"Not shock." She raises her wrist—two rows of faces smile at me through a layer of dust. "Calm mixed with Quietly Effective. People need our help. Let's go."

I stare at her a moment. I'm streaked with sweat, and my heart is pounding. The horror of those falling buildings—those thousands of people trying to get out of them—lurks just beyond the edges of my self-control.

But the woman's expression is eager and ready.

"Are *you* okay?" she asks. "You know what they say—check your own feels before helping someone else. You seem a little . . . intense."

"Intense is all I have," I say. "Come on."

We move down the street, looking for more people trapped in the broken buildings.

An unearthly calm fills the city. A few med drones fly past, but they're all headed toward the fallen towers. Around us, the citizens are taking care of one another with quiet determination—sharing water, tearing up clothing to bind wounds, making sure the seriously injured have their feels set to Painless.

None of them stares at the colossal clouds rising from the city's center. A steady rain of debris is falling. Not just dust, but fluttering paper, bits of plastic and wood—everything light enough to be carried up by the thermal plume of burning buildings.

The sunset turns it all red.

Battle adrenaline rages inside me, but the quiet purpose of the Pazx around me is somehow contagious. I can't fight an earthquake or turn back time. But I can clean this wound, stop this bleeding, pull this dislocated shoulder into place.

Still, every sound makes me flinch, like an aftershock is hitting. Everything feels uncertain and treacherous. I can't even trust the ground beneath my feet.

I work in a fever, staying in constant motion to keep the horror from descending on me. That earthquake was a thousand times deadlier than my father's attack on Victoria. But everyone around me thinks it was just an act of nature.

The young woman I rescued stays close to me, looking concerned about my lack of Calm.

"I'm Essa," she says when we take a break, drinking water from a broken main.

I hesitate, but there's not much point in anonymity now.

"Frey."

She looks thoughtful as we shake hands, like the name is familiar. Not everyone pays attention to the newsfeeds, I guess. And my famous face is a mess of dazzle makeup, sweat, and dust.

"Your accent," Essa says. "Are you from Diego?"

"Shreve."

"A refugee? Welcome." She looks around at the chaos of the city. "But maybe you wish you'd stayed at home."

"Never," I say.

Essa frowns. "Is it really that bad there?"

I hesitate, not ready to tell her who I am, or that my father did this to her city.

"Freedom is better," I say, "even when it's a wreck."

A cry comes from above us, and we both look up.

From the top of a half-crumbled building, a small figure waves down. It's a young boy, his clothes torn and bloody. He's standing on a single shard of metal jutting up from the exposed, twisted skeleton of the structure.

"Don't move!" I shout. My head spins for a second for the Spanish. *"¡No te muevas!"*

Essa is speaking to herself. *"Interfaz, necesitamos un aéreocar de emergencia . . . ¿Interfaz? ¿Estás ahí?"*

I check my own comms.

The city interface is gone. The lines must be overloaded, or maybe—

My processing cores are buried under three kilometers of solid stone.

"*¿Interfaz de la ciudad?*" Essa tries again.

This is why my father was so sure that Paz would never figure out what hit them. Because there would be no Paz AI.

"The city's offline," I say.

"Offline?" Essa shakes her head, her calm breaking for the first time. "Then we have to get him ourselves. He's too young to have feels. He's scared!"

"There's a hoverboard back at my place. Military-grade lifting fans."

"Okay." Essa takes a slow breath, fingers on her wrist. "That's an . . . intense thing to have."

"Told you." I turn back to the stranded boy, wishing I wasn't so Spanish-missing. "*¡Volveremos!*"

He understand and waves, the motion small and timid against the vast dust clouds in the sky.

That's when I realize there's no city interface to guide me.

"Can you get me home, Essa? I don't know where anything is."

"Of course."

I give her Rafi's address, and we set off through the broken streets. The silence in my comms doesn't lift as we move. The mind of Paz is gone.

My father has killed a city.

LIFT

There are more injured along the way, but when I try to stop and help, Essa keeps us moving.

"There could be aftershocks," she says. "Or he could try to get down by himself. He's just a kid."

She's fierce now, even with Calm and Collected in her veins. I don't argue.

When we reach Rafi's building, the front side has collapsed. Her apartment faces the street, its outer wall torn off. I can see her makeup table up there, precariously balanced on the ragged edge of the fifth floor.

The hoverboard was farther back in the room, but the entrance to the building is covered with rubble.

I stand there, swearing.

Essa puts a hand on my shoulder. "Have you tried Poise?"

"Poise is my sister's job." I stare at the broken structure, mapping my way up from floor to floor. "I prefer punching things."

"You remind of my little brother." Essa smiles softly. "He said he'd never get feels. But he could never control himself either."

"Wait here." I take a few steps up the rubble pile, testing.

It feels solid beneath my feet.

"Be careful," Essa says. "There won't be a free med drone anytime soon."

"Don't worry. I've already had my fall this week."

The first two floors are easy—the collapsed front of the building is piled into a ragged slope of debris. It's like climbing a junk heap.

But to reach the third level, I have to jump from the pile and grab the edge of sheared-off floor. The building's guts are spilling out—a frayed edge of optical fibers tries to tangle my arms as I haul myself up. At least the smart-plastic pipes have sealed themselves off, so there's no running water in my face.

The structures here in Paz are solid, compared to the shanties of Shreve. My father sweeps away whole neighborhoods at a whim. But this city was built to withstand disaster.

On the third floor, I find myself standing in what's left of an apartment. Paintings on the three remaining walls, an overturned easel. Clothes spill from a closet ripped in half by the collapse. A whole life, left in pieces.

My father did this—here, and across this city.

Rusty war, boundless and brutal.

"¿Alguien aquí?" I call. "Anyone need help?"

No answer. Either they weren't home or . . .

I turn and look through the missing wall, out over the city.

Chaos and destruction stretch out forever, the setting sun turning it all blood red. The sight almost swallows me.

"Keep going!" Essa shouts from the ground. "The sun's going down!"

The next floor is about four meters up—too far to jump. I can't see any fire stairs.

Just the elevator.

I make my way over, wary of the listing floor. The shaft is clear of debris. There's even a hoverpod waiting on this level, its charge light solid green.

I step on.

"English, please. Fifth floor."

"This elevator is damaged and on battery power. Emergency use only."

"Um, this is an emergency."

"Are you in need of medical care?"

"No, but I need some stuff from upstairs. I'm in the middle of a rescue!"

"A rescue? Do you have the warden password?"

I groan. If only I could talk to the city AI.

But it said something to me right before the last quake. Right before it died. Maybe it knew what was about to happen . . .

"Iron Mountain," I repeat.

"That is not the correct password."

I let out a groan. "Look, I'm a foreign aid worker—sort of. Just ask the city interface who I am!"

"The city AI is offline."

"That's how bad the emergency is!"

Another moment's pause.

"That is unprecedented." The hint of a sigh. "Travel is at your own risk."

"Whatever—take me to five!"

"Doors closing."

The doors shriek and grind, but don't fully meet. When the pod jerks into motion, the floors slide past in front of me. More ruined homes, one with the apartment above fallen in on it. The next with a gaping hole.

The whole pod shudders as it climbs, sides scraping the damaged shaft. When it finally reaches Rafi's, it screeches to a halt a meter short.

The doors wrench themselves open.

"Fifth floor."

"Um, we aren't quite there. Can you go a little higher?"

"No. The city magnetics are unstable."

"Right." I'm staring at the feet of Rafi's pair of beds. The floor is only a meter above my waist, an easy climb, and the gap is big enough to squeeze through. But the pod is trembling beneath my feet. "You're not going to fall when I'm halfway, are you? And, like, cut me in two?"

The pod doesn't answer right away.

That seems bad.

"I should be able to hold this position," it says at last.

"That's not very confidence-making!"

"Returning to the ground level is the safest option."

"Ugh, no." I take a few sharp breaths. People shooting at me is easy, but it turns out the thought of crawling through a giant guillotine makes my heart beat sideways.

My eyes fall to the feels on my wrist. Maybe there's one for courage.

There's the face of a lion, more cuddly than fierce. But what else could it mean?

I touch it for a moment. My nerves settle a little, but not like Calm. Something bright and sharp is surging in me . . .

The pod speaks again.

"The sooner you exit, the less chance that I will—"

"Just be quiet!" I hurl myself at the doors, scrambling through the gap and onto Rafi's floor. I keep crawling even after my feet are clear, until I'm halfway across the bedroom from the elevator's open maw.

I lie there for a long moment, grinning.

"Would you like me to wait?" the pod asks.

I glance up. The hoverboard stands in the corner by the front door, with a green charge light and new crash bracelets.

"No, thanks," I say. "I'm flying down."

ESSA

When I land next to Essa, she's huddled in the shadow of Rafi's broken building, wrapped in her own arms.

She's weeping. Great sobs rack her body, and a rattling sound comes from her chest, like her soul has shaken loose.

I stare for a moment, confused.

"Did something happen?"

She shakes her head, drawing a shuddering breath.

"Give me a second." She presses a thumb against her wrist, and gradually her expression turns calm and self-possessed again.

But her dusty face is still streaked with tears.

I drop to one knee, not knowing what to do. Courage doesn't help with this.

"Did your feels run out?"

She shakes her head. "I messed up. I thought a jolt of Grief would clear my mind . . . but it made everything worse."

I don't know what to say. How feels work is beyond me.

"Nothing's ever felt like this before." Her voice is even, but there's a horror deep in her eyes. "The Calm is there, like always. But I can feel something past it, trying to get in. And when that first drop of Grief hit, it all came roaring through, crushing me."

"Ah," I say.

All my life, there was a storm in my head. I knew something was wrong—pretending to be my sister, hardly seeing my own father, my trainers hurting me. But somehow I got used to it.

Until my father attacked Victoria, and the storm crashed through.

"Your city's falling apart around you, Essa. Maybe you should take a—"

"After we save that kid." She makes two fists. "He's the same age my little brother was."

Yes. Saving someone sounds perfect. "Then we'll help him. Come on."

She mounts the board behind me, her hands firm on my waist.

"It's getting dark," I say. "Want the crash bracelets?"

"I'm good. Used to ride freestyle, junior division."

I glance back at her with new respect. My trainers used to let me watch the freestyle finals. Pretty-surged girls and boys with neon outfits, doing wild tricks in full crash suits. I wanted to be like them—famous for my boarding.

Until my trainers reminded me that my name would always be a secret.

"Hang on, then," I say, leaning forward and turning on the lifting fans.

We shoot back toward the boy, whipping through the turns. Essa shifts her balance gracefully, guiding me across the broken rooftops with taps on my shoulders.

The dust is sharp and choking. The rain of debris swats at us, churned by the fans and the speed of our passage.

But I ride fearlessly.

In the red sky to our right, the wind has stretched the clouds above the fallen towers into huge anvils. Firefighting drones flit beneath them, lofted on sprays of foam. I can smell burned plastic, hot metal . . .

And something worse.

I turn away to squint into the biting, acrid wind, wondering if Trin is okay.

Suddenly my Courage runs thin in my veins. What if Trin was wrong, and Rafi is still here in Paz? What if she's hurt?

No. Stay brave. She left days ago.

But those people in the market last night—the man I stole the coat from—how many of them have been erased from the world?

In a few minutes, the broken building takes form in the dust ahead of us. The boy is still clinging to that shard of metal, like it's the mast of a sinking ship.

We angle in beside him, and Essa steps off onto the shorn top of the structure.

She takes him in her arms.

I stand there twitching, ready to fly him down. But Essa and the boy are wrapped around each other. He's sobbing like she was a few minutes ago, an echo of her grief.

I can only watch.

This isn't my city.

Finally she pulls away from the boy and pushes him toward me.

"Take him down first."

He steps onto the board, wary for a moment, then throws his arms around my waist with all his strength. I spare a glance at Essa, suddenly worried about leaving her up here alone. But she waves me on.

As I ease us out over the street, the boy hides his eyes from the drop.

"It's okay," I say. "We can't fall."

"But the buildings fell. I saw them."

I want to explain that we aren't using the city magnetics—our lifting fans won't be affected by any aftershocks.

But that's not what he means.

He knows now that anything can break.

We land next to a cluster of Pazx capturing water from the broken main. Someone's dragged a portable hole in the wall out onto the street. They're feeding it salvage for raw materials, and it's spitting out bandages, water bottles, and flashlights. But it won't work for long with no city grid to draw power from, and fabricators must be rare here in Paz, where they prefer things handmade.

Calm and efficient as always, the Pazx take the boy from me.

They're perfect citizens in an emergency, but I wonder how long they can go on like this. What happens if they all hit themselves with

Grief when the sun goes down? In their joyous lives, none of them has ever experienced anything like this before.

I wheel the board around and fly back up to Essa. She's clinging to the metal shard, staring at the city center.

"They're all *gone*," she says quietly. "How?"

I put a hand on her shoulder, just to steady myself. Courage burns fast in a disaster, it seems.

I could tell her that this was an attack, not a natural event. The people of Paz need to know the truth, and soon. They have to get ready. This was only the first step of my father's plan. The next could be anything.

But if I warn just one person, it's nothing but a rumor.

I have to tell the whole world.

"Essa, I have a friend in a hotel nearby. She's got a lot of communication gear. We can call for help from outside."

"But wouldn't the city already . . ." Essa begins, then looks at me. "It's gone, isn't it?"

"Dead," I say, and tell her name of Trin's hotel.

She hesitates before getting on the board, staring down at the street. At the boy we rescued.

"You think he'll be okay?"

"They're pretty organized down there. He's safe now."

"That's not what I mean." She kneels, touches the structure below us. "A kid his age wouldn't be out alone. Whoever was with him . . ."

We're standing on a dark tangle of metal and wires, a whole building compressed in on itself, like junk after a recycler's got hold of it.

It's a miracle that he survived. No one else did.

"I don't know" is all I can say.

Essa stands, her fingers on her wrist again. "Sorry. We should keep moving, but that kid . . ."

"Reminds you of your brother."

She nods. "I miss him."

And suddenly I want to tell Essa all about Rafi. How I've always tried to protect my older sister. How she was protecting me from my father all along. How she's run away from me—to *become* me—and there's nothing I can do to help her anymore.

But that's a lot to tell a stranger on a day like this.

So I ask, "How long since your little brother died?"

Essa places a hand on her feels. She's hitting Calm again.

"Fifty-seven minutes," she says.

ELIO

"Wait," I say. "It happened *today*?"

She looks down at the street, toward the spot where I rescued her.

"Elio was with me when the quakes started. We ran to take shelter in the entrance of a building. We were safe." Essa's voice breaks a little, and her fingers go to her wrist again, steadying herself with a chord of feels. "But he'd dropped his backpack in the street. When the second quake ended, he pulled away and ran to get it. I didn't go after him—just yelled for him to come back. Then the big one hit."

She falls silent.

"He was right there, under all that . . ." I shake my head. "You didn't say anything. We didn't look for him!"

"He was dead. I saw the stones come down." A tremor crosses her face. "There were other people who needed our help."

Essa's eyes open, and she looks off into the darkening haze.

"Your friend's hotel is that way," she says calmly. "Come on."

*

Trin's hotel is still standing, squat and powerful in the darkness. Its shattered windows gape like missing teeth.

Her room was on the seventh floor, I recall. Counting up from ground level, we fly a slow circuit around the building, peering in through broken glass.

My mind is still spinning with what Essa told me. She left her own brother behind, buried under a pile of stone. Without a word to me, or a moment for herself. Like a forgotten toy.

Maybe it was logical, putting her grief aside to help other people. But there are times when logic makes no sense.

The streets below us are full of Pazx calmly working together, digging through rubble and treating wounds. How many of them have lost loved ones today? How many are holding back a storm in their heads?

What happens when all those nightmares break through?

Light flickers through a missing window—a row of flatscreens. I ease our hoverboard through the empty frame, and we step off onto a plush carpet. A cleaning drone drifts along the floor, vacuuming up beads of shattered safety glass.

Trin's standing in a bathrobe, her hair wet.

"Don't you knock?"

I stare at her. "The whole city's falling down—and you took a *shower*?"

"Before the water pressure gives out," she says. "I was dusty."

"Sure, okay." I guess some people don't need feels to stay calm. "Trin, this is Essa."

"Hey." Trin turns back to me. "Did you know the city AI's down? No local feeds at all. Creepy-making, right?"

"That was my father's plan," I say.

Both of them look at me.

"His *plan*?" Trin asks. "Are you saying your dad caused an earthquake?"

"It all makes sense now. The weapon I told you about—he said it was like a force of nature." I cross the room toward her satellite dish, the stack of backup batteries. "We have to tell the other cities!"

"Um, no," Trin says.

"Why not? Isn't the point of all this to make my father look bad?"

"Of course," she says. "But good propaganda has to make sense. Nobody can cause an earthquake. Not one that big!"

"The Rusties figured out how. I'm telling you the truth."

"The truth doesn't matter, if nobody believes it." Trin gestures at the walls of flickering screens. "I've spent the whole war building a reputation, a global audience. I'm not going to blow it all on one logic-missing theory."

"It's not a theory. He told me, face-to-face."

"Unless you have AI-verified video of that, it won't matter," Trin says. "And we'll look scruples-missing if we try to leverage a tragedy!"

"Frey," Essa says gently. "You might want to try some Insight—the little face with glasses. It really clears your head."

She's looking at me funny, like I'm some intense, wild-eyed foreigner who thinks her own father controls earthquakes.

Which is exactly what I am.

The weight of their doubt falls on me like defeat, and I sit heavily on Trin's couch. If my friends don't believe me, the rest of the world never will.

"There's no way to stop him," I say.

"Relax. Help's on the way already." Trin peers at one of her screens. "Fabricators, med drones, construction teams. This quake might have saved Paz—your dad can't march in when it's full of aid workers from other cities!"

Right. With their own citizens in danger, the world would crush him.

So why did he visit this disaster on Paz?

I force myself to stand back up and walk to the gaping window. The sun is gone now, turning those broken buildings into silhouettes against the red sky. This new, shattered city looks like the Rusty ruins outside Victoria. All the angles are skewed, the skyline a row of jagged teeth.

Like something that can never be fixed.

"She's not coming to save us," I murmur.

"Who isn't?" Trin asks.

"It's a rebel saying, about Tally Youngblood disappearing. It means we have to take care of things ourselves."

"Great philosophy." Trin turns back to her screens. "Except there are *literally* people coming to save us. By morning they'll be here in force. Excuse me while I get dressed."

She turns and heads into the bedroom. The door slides closed behind her.

Essa joins me at the window.

"You must think I've lost my mind," I say.

"No, I recognize you now. You're the second daughter of Shreve— the one who was hidden. You're always on the feeds, telling people to fight your father."

"That was my sister on the feeds, actually. But, yeah, Rafi and I are on the same side."

"That sounds difficult, a family at war with itself." Essa gently takes my hand. "But, Frey, your tragedy has nothing to do with ours."

"This wasn't a natural event—your city's under attack!"

An expression flickers across her face, a flash of lightning on still waters.

"My city has lost so much today. Don't try to use that to make us join your cause." Essa regards Trin's rows of screens. "I know what a propaganda operation looks like."

My heart twists. Essa just lost her brother, and she thinks I'm trying to exploit his death for my own purposes. She thinks I'm playing politics.

Maybe I am—but only because politics are inescapable.

Rafi would know what to say now. She'd be gentle, comforting, logical. All I have are Col's blunt words.

"For some of us, politics means fighting for our right to exist."

Essa's lips tighten. She doesn't answer.

We might as well be from different planets. She grew up in a city where leaders are elected, where the walls ask for permission to listen. Where everyone is as happy as they want to be. For Essa, all my struggles are just a concept.

Her fingers go to her wrist. Not one of the happy faces, but higher up her arm.

Her smile returns, but it's distant now.

"I have no idea what it's like, Frey, growing up somewhere like Shreve. I'm sure we seem strange to you as well."

I'm too exhausted to be polite. "Yeah. You guys might be a little *too* calm about all this."

"Panic doesn't help. And grief will come."

I look down at my own arm. Only about half the little faces are smiling. The rest are thoughtful, leering, surprised. Some of the expressions I can't even guess at.

But Grief is obvious—the mouth wailing, a rain of tears.

"Doesn't it strike you as weird?" I say. "Pressing a button to be sad?"

"I lost my brother today. If I wanted my heart to break, I wouldn't need my feels." Essa stares calmly out the window. "But there are times when what's inside us is too much. Back in Rusty days, people used to die from sadness."

"Seriously? You can die from being *sad*?"

She nods. "Here in Paz, we learn all about it in school. You know how Rusties used to murder each other all the time?"

"Of course. That's what they're famous for."

"Well, for every Rusty who was murdered, three killed themselves."

"Huh. My tutors never mentioned that." Suddenly I remember that Rafi made a will—leaving me everything, even her name. I shudder away the thought. "But how is Grief supposed to help with that? Why make yourself sad?"

Essa shrugs. "Sometimes you need to cry. That's why people listen to sad songs."

"Sad songs aren't really my thing."

"I figured," she says. "You don't let anything out, do you? Your anger, sadness, frustration—it's all built up inside you."

The words play under my skin, and I turn away from her. Talking about my emotions has never been my thing either. When I want to let a feeling out, I punch something, or train. I always loved stepping in for Rafi at nightclubs, dancing in the press of a hundred other bodies—not myself, but not quite my sister either. Nothing in me but the music.

But there'll be no dancing in this city for a while.

I look at Essa. "Isn't happiness fake, if you get it by pressing a button?"

She shakes her head. "Every emotion has two sides—part of it's in the machinery in your brain, and part of exists in the world outside you."

"Um, how are your emotions *outside* of you?"

"They have a social reality. You don't sit at home alone pressing Joy—you use it in the streets, with other joyful people around you.

186

You only Languish if you've really lost someone. Anything else is meaningless and context-missing."

I turn away from her—the whole *thing* sounds context-missing to me.

I cross the room to the stack of batteries, place my knife on top. The light blinks yellow, which settles my mind a little.

Maybe I shouldn't judge—charging up my pulse knife makes me Calm.

But the Pazx have to be ready for what's coming.

I turn back to Essa. "I hope you haven't gotten rid of all your anger. You're going to need it soon."

"Like the Rusties, you mean?" Essa asks. "Acting out their anger at other countries, other religions, people with different complexions?"

I shake my head. Military history is one thing I *do* know about.

"Anger isn't what made them dangerous. If you build a bunch of city-killers and diseases and nanobugs, eventually someone like my father comes along and uses them—angry or not."

Essa shrugs. "I don't pay much attention to politics, but I'm pretty sure your father has emotional issues."

A laugh chokes out of me. "That's one way to put it."

"There's something missing in him."

Those words freeze me.

Experts in other cities argue a lot about my father—whether he really plans every move, whether his successes are brute cunning or dumb luck. But hardly any of them get as close as Essa just did.

"My brother is what's missing," I say.

She finally turns from the window to face me. "Your brother?"

"He was lost a long time ago. That's what makes my father dangerous."

She shakes her head. "I don't understand."

"It's complicated," I say.

"It always is." Essa takes my left hand, turns my palm up. "Can I make a suggestion?"

I thrust my arm at her. "Sure. Make me feel whatever you want."

"They only respond to your own touch." She softly brushes one—not a normal face. It looks more like a cat, standing at a lectern. "It's called Elucidation. It helps you talk."

That doesn't sound like an emotion to me. It sounds more like something Col would love. The thought of him launching into some long-winded explanation almost makes me smile.

Maybe if I can explain my father to Essa, she'll understand what's coming. I place a fingertip on the speech-giving cat face—and hold it there.

A moment later, the words come a little easier.

"My brother, Seanan, was older than me and Rafi. When my father became leader of Shreve, one of his enemies decided the only way to free the city was to kidnap his son."

Essa's eyes widen a little. "Politics in your city really *is* different."

"No kidding. My mother got in the way, and the kidnappers killed her. And when my father didn't surrender power, Seanan never came back."

She takes my hand again. "I'm sorry. You must miss them."

I shrug. "This is all before we were born. My father had my mother's eggs harvested and made sure he got twins."

"Wait, he wanted twins because . . ." Essa's voice trails away.

"So if it happened again, he'd have an heir and a spare. One daughter the world knew about, the other a body double—sniper bait. Want to guess which one I am?"

Essa doesn't answer that, just stares at me.

"Anyway," I say, "that's the man you're dealing with. *That's* his politics. That's what he did to his own daughters. Imagine what it'll be like when his soldiers come for *you*."

Essa leans back against the wall, overwhelmed at first. Her right hand moves toward her left, but instead of using her feels, she makes a fist.

More words bubble in my throat—long rants, righteous and eloquent. I want to tell her my family history, my doubts about the Victorians, and how much I miss Col. This feel has given me a sudden need to spill everything to a stranger.

Elucidation. They should call it Truth Serum.

"Sorry," I say. "Didn't mean to blab."

Essa shakes her head. "That's how it's supposed to work. But that story is still hard to believe."

"Oh, it's all real," a voice comes from the bedroom. Trin's been listening in, of course. "Her dad's totally norm-shredding. But that doesn't mean he can make an earthquake!"

She steps out from the bedroom in her underwear, holding up two dresses.

"The red or the stripes? I'm interviewing survivors on my news-feed tonight."

We just stare at her.

Trin frowns. "What? You think I should wear black?"

I turn to Essa, more words spilling from me. "Maybe just ignore us. Most of my life, I only had one friend, and she was my sister. And Trin is . . . weird. Deal with your grief, bury your brother, and let the rest of the cities handle my—"

"Just give me a second," Essa says, letting out a slow breath. "I need to think about all this."

I shut my mouth firmly, dying to say more. To elucidate for her how the interlocking alliances of the first families will eventually take my father down. How we just have to reveal his true nature once and for all.

"What if we find a way to—" I start.

Essa's hand goes gently over my mouth. "Relax, Frey. It's a tricky feel to control. But you'll be okay soon."

"Or maybe not," Trin says. She drops the dresses to the floor, comes toward the broken window.

I turn and see the streaks in the sky, and words spill out of me again.

"That's a suborbital insertion, from the edge of space. My father's had drones and soldiers up there for months. He's not waiting for the other cities to get here. He's coming *now*."

DRONE

My father's suborbitals are landing all over Paz—out in the factory belt, in the suburbs near us, even in the wounded center of the city. Wreathed in halos of fire they fall, until their drogue chutes jerk them to a near halt.

"Do you believe me now?" I ask Trin.

"Not that your dad causes earthquakes." She grumbles out a sigh. "But that Shreve is invading? Looks like it."

A flash fills the sky, then a *boom* that makes the remaining window glass shudder and creak.

Essa leans out to look sideways. "That was close. Near the Marine Institute, I think."

"Can you take me there?" I ask.

"It's on my way home." She turns from the darkness. "But are you going to fight the Shreve army on your own?"

"Maybe." I glance at my knife. Its charge light is still yellow, but at my signal it leaps into my hand. "The main thing is getting proof of what's happening here. The sooner the other cities know, the better."

"Then you should take this," Trin calls from the bedroom.

She comes back out with an object the size of a soccer ball. She tosses it straight at me—but the device comes to a halt in midair.

It's a hovercam, bristling with lenses, lights, and a dish antenna.

"This is Trin 3," she says. "It's got a direct link back here. Get some video of those Shreve orbitals, and I'll broadcast it live."

I sigh. "You call your hovercam *Trin 3*?"

"Trin 2 was taken," she says.

"I'm not going to ask. Come on, Essa."

We step onto the board and leap into the night sky.

The slow rain of debris from the fallen towers hasn't stopped.

It floats in the darkness, forming vortexes in the alleys below us, like shambling ghosts of litter and ash. My eyes sting, and the smell of burned plastic sits sharp in the back of my throat.

Trin 3 flies along beside us, coasting on the hoverboard's magnetics. I carry my knife to save its charge.

"Diego must have rescue workers in Paz by now," I say, still needing to Elucidate my thoughts. "But most cities won't have anyone here till morning. Hovercars are slow motion compared to suborbitals."

"Left here," Essa says.

We bank into the turn, around an array of repeater towers. Rattled by the quakes, they lean in all directions.

"Looks like my thirteenth birthday," I say. "Rafi brought me a cupcake from her party and stuck all these candles in it. But instead of thirteen, there were thirty, pointing everywhere."

"You know," Essa says, "if you want to stop Elucidating, you can just hit the Neutral feel."

I glance back at her. "There's a Neutral? Like, it erases whatever feels you're using? That's a really good idea. Because these things could get away from you if you're not—"

"The one with only eyes, no expression. In the first row, closest to your hand."

"Right." I squint down at my wrist. "Ah . . . it's under my crash bracelet."

"*Dios mío.*" She sighs. "If you keep talking, you're going to get bugs in your mouth."

"Not a lot of bugs at this altitude. With all this smoke, there's probably no bugs in the whole Baja—"

"Oh," she says, looking down.

My gaze follows hers, and at last I'm silent.

It looks like a soccer stadium—a brightly lit oval of green grass, now gray with dust, bleachers on all sides. But no one's playing soccer.

Hundreds of inflatable emergency cots are laid out below us, arranged in a neat grid. Med drones drift down the rows, maybe one for every fifty people. Even from this height, I can see blood shining red in the floodlights.

We drift to a halt, staring down.

"Whoa," I say.

The Elucidation has left my veins. Any need to speak is burned away.

Those countless people in the central city, who evacuated the hovering towers after the first quake hit—how many are in improvised hospitals like this now?

I look for familiar faces, fearful that my sister was somehow still here when the quake hit.

"Stay right there," comes Trin's voice in my ear. She sounds tinny, bouncing her comms though the hovercam instead of the city interface. "Trin 3 is loving this."

The cam slips beneath us, its lenses scanning the carnage below.

It's uneasy-making, gawking at the aftermath of disaster. But if we're going to stop my father, the horror of what's happened has to be shown.

"Maybe we should go down and help," I say.

"First things first." Essa's voice is like steel. "Let's get that proof. We're not far now."

The Marine Institute sits at the edge of the Sea of Cortez, the channel between Baja Island and the mainland. There's less dust from the quake out here, thanks to a stiff breeze coming off the water.

The Institute is a cluster of permacrete buildings, curved shapes like rolling ocean waves. Too solid for the earthquake to crack, they lean at random angles, as if the ground briefly turned liquid beneath them. Only the largest building is visibly damaged—a third of it has lifted from its foundations and broken off, crumbling into a pile.

The suborbital is nowhere in sight, but a drogue parachute is flung across the Institute lawn like discarded laundry.

Trin 3 flies ahead to get a better shot. Its lights wink on—the chute is clearly marked with the red trefoil of Shreve. My father's not even trying to hide his invasion.

For the first time, I wonder if his plans have changed. He knew I was here, of course, and that I could warn Paz what was coming. Maybe my and Col's escape pushed things into a different gear.

Maybe this calamity is my fault too.

I shake off the feeling as we take our board down to the ground. Leading away from the chute is a set of tracks in the grass. It must be a heavy armored drone, if it's walking instead of flying.

Essa and I follow the tracks into the largest building of the Institute. The drone must've been too big for the double doors of the main entrance, which have been torn from their hinges.

"Trin," I say. "We're going inside to look for this thing."

"Trin 3's right behind you."

We climb the cracked stone steps and enter through the gaping doorway. The halls inside are lit cold blue by emergency backup lights. A moment later, the brighter light of Trin 3 surrounds us as it flits in through the doors.

"No shots of me," I say. "Don't want my father knowing I'm right next to one of his war machines."

"Duh. Just get out of my way."

We pause, letting the hovercam fly ahead.

The floor is slanted beneath our feet, and the walls lean out of true, so it feels like we're inside a photograph taken at a clumsy angle. Doors lead off the hallway into tilted rooms, full of desks and tables slid into odd arrangements, overturned lab equipment, but no people.

A sound comes from ahead of us, a loud metallic rattling. I hear voices too, and the darkness ahead flickers with flashlight beams.

The staff of the Institute has found the Shreve drone.

But what's it doing in here? How is a research station a military objective?

We head toward the sounds, climbing up the tilt of the building until we come to another set of doors torn from their hinges. The noise is coming from inside.

I draw my knife and enter.

A cafeteria. A dozen round tables surrounded by chairs, a kitchen behind a broken wall, everything thrown into chaos by the building's tilt. The far wall is missing, the gap full of night sky—this is the spot where the whole structure broke in half.

The Shreve drone is lit by the full wattage of Trin 3's lights. It's a squat, ugly machine, a metal rhino with six legs. A handful of people in blue coveralls watches as it climbs through the missing wall and down into the rubble. It forelegs start to tear at the permacrete, the exposed wiring and water pipes, stuffing everything into its maw. A terrific grinding sound fills the room.

The hovercam's lights get a notch brighter, and Trin's commentary starts in my ear.

"This is a live feed from Paz, where a Shreve military drone has broken into the Marine Institute. It seems to be stealing raw materials from a damaged building. Is this the start of a resource grab?"

I turn to Essa, frowning. "Doesn't look like a military drone, does it? No weapons."

"Maybe Shreve doesn't expect us to fight." She takes hold of her wrist. "They're wrong."

I shake my head, lowering my knife. My father is too cautious to start feasting on the spoils of war before he's secured the city.

Something else is happening here.

"The Pazx can do nothing as they watch the invader from Shreve tearing at their city's wounds. To launch a brazen attack in the wake of a natural disaster must be the work of a truly twisted mind."

The grinding sound starts to smooth out, until it reminds me of the burr of an autodoc fixing my bones.

"Trin?" I say softly. "You might want to pause this."

"What will the dictator of Shreve do next? An all-out military invasion?"

"Trin! Stop for a second."

The commentary fades, and then Trin's voice is closer in my ear.

"What's your problem, Frey? This is exactly what we needed!"

"Just wait."

I climb the slanted floor, push through the Institute staff so I can see the drone better.

"Stay behind Trin 3, Frey. I'm still broadcasting!"

"Okay, fine." I come to a halt just beneath the hovercam. From here, the Shreve machine looks even less like a military drone.

Because it's not a military drone—it's a fabricator.

A hole in the wall on six legs, as squat and powerful as a rhinoceros.

"Oh no," I say.

"Frey, tell me what's going on. This'll play better with narration."

Before I can answer, the machine opens its maw again. But instead of eating more rubble, it vomits out a collection of finished items.

Flashlights, water purifiers, med patches. Pop-up shelters, inflatable beds, transmitters. Even a few toys.

All of it made from the recycled rubble of the Institute. This machine is the fastest hole in the wall I've ever seen.

It lumbers a few feet farther, and starts chomping again.

"Uh, Frey? What just happened?"

"This isn't a military drone, Trin—it's a fabricator. He must've had a fleet of them in orbit, ready for this earthquake. Stop broadcasting!"

"A fabricator? What the . . . oh."

The lights on the hovercam wink off. But it's too late—the whole world has already seen what's happening.

My father isn't here to conquer Paz.

He's here to save it.

PART 3

OCCUPATION

Occupation means that you cannot trust the open sky . . .
It means that you cannot trust the future or have faith that the past will always be there.

—Suheir Hammad

WATER RUN

I wake up the same way as yesterday, gasping like my lungs are full of water.

The dream is the same too—the buildings falling, spilling an ocean of dust. The clouds sweeping across me, choking the air with the smell of darkness and loss.

I sit up in bed, panic twisting every muscle.

"Frey," Trin's voice comes. "It's okay."

It's not.

The smell of burning isn't a dream. It still hasn't lifted, ten days after the quake. It's worse here in Rafi's old apartment, with the breeze coming through our missing wall. This was the only place we could find after Trin's hotel filled up with foreign journos covering the aftermath.

I miss that hotel, its working elevators and running water. Like I miss the certainty that the earth is steady and dependable beneath my feet.

Uncertain is how it always feels, here in Shatter City. That's what the Pazx call their home now.

Too shaky for Morning Buzz, I start my day with Calm.

"We're out of water again," Trin says. She's at Rafi's makeup table, staring at a pile of comm gear, a set of needle pliers in her hand.

"Already?" I swing myself out of bed, cross the apartment floor, and lift the water drum by its handle. It weighs almost nothing. "Did you take a bath?"

Trin looks up from her gear and fixes me with steely eyes. "My last bath, if you could call it that, was at the hotel. Four days ago! When was yours?"

"Don't ask."

"Then maybe wash yourself while you're at the main," she says. "We all gotta breathe."

A sharp retort goes through my head—in Rafi's voice—but I say nothing.

Instead, I imagine water running through my hair, clothes clinging to my skin, wet and clean. Since the quake I've worked my way through everything in Rafi's closet. Clothes get dirty fast in a city of ruins.

"You coming?" I ask Trin. Twenty-liter water drums are *heavy* when they're full.

"No, I want to get this gear working again."

I frown. "Change your mind about leaving tomorrow?"

"Nope." Trin turns back to her work. She can't stand living in Paz anymore. The rationing of food and water. Breathing dust from the quake. My father's fabricators roaming the streets. "Just thought you'd want to talk to Col once more before I go."

"Oh, sure." I'm blank for a moment, uncertain what to feel.

I miss Col's voice, but when we talk, it's always the same argument.

He wants me to abandon this city, to join his Vics in the jungle. But they can't help in the war against my father anymore. In the wake of this disaster, attacks on Shreve food supplies only backfire. Last week, Zura and her crew hit a relief convoy by accident—or maybe it was a trap my father set. Either way, it played into his hands.

Paz is the best place for me to fight him now.

This is where his greed is aimed.

And just as important—if my sister wants to find me, Paz is where she'll look.

I glance at the other bed in the room. It'll be empty once Trin leaves. I'll be alone again.

A long touch of Morning Buzz brightens me up.

"Thanks for doing that, Trin. Col must be worried."

It's been four days since we last spoke—Trin's gear was broken in the move, and we can't use the city network. Most of the new repeater towers were built by the RFS—the Relief Force of Shreve. You never know who's listening in.

But Trin's gear can reach the Amazon direct. I'll take a long touch of Cherish just before we speak and tell Col that everything's okay.

"See you in an hour," I say, lifting the empty water drum.

She nods. "I'll make sure it's working by then. It'll be good for you to talk to him."

I smile at her, almost giggling from the Buzz.

Trin worries about me too.

I climb down the elevator shaft.

The rope ladder was made by Marxo, who lives beside us. He's handy with ropes and pulleys, and helped us cover the missing wall of Rafi's apartment with a relief tent. He doesn't speak English, and never asks what we're up to. The perfect neighbor.

I pull my hoodie tighter before heading out into the street. Rafi's dazzle makeup is thin on my face, the last tube almost empty. The Relief Force of Shreve is here in a dozen different ways—fabricators, repair drones, wardens. All of them watching for me.

Officially, my wedding with Col has been postponed so Shreve can focus all its resources on helping Paz. My father's propaganda simply ignores the fact that Col has appeared on the feeds, talking about our escape. It's even more truth-missing than usual, as if losing me finally broke something in my father.

No heir. No spare. The whole world knows that he's alone.

Out in the wild, Rafi has been silent. I don't even know if she's still alive.

I haven't found the right feel to fix that yet.

Our street is busy today, but they all look like real Pazx—handmade clothes and water bottle slings, shaggy haircuts. Shreve agents try to blend in sometimes, but they never get the local body language right. A lifetime of talking with your hands changes the way you move.

Essa says I'm pretty good at passing. But that's me—an impostor my whole life.

I don't look much like my sister anymore. Trin buzzed my hair short with my pulse knife, then tinted it orange with the local berry dye the girls here use. Even my face is different, my cheekbones growing sharper with every missed meal. The relief effort brings in enough food for the survivors but picking it up means a DNA check. To make sure nobody's collecting double rations, the other cities' relief forces share their data with the RFS.

My father has said all the right things—how he wants to return to the global community. How he'll leave the Palafoxes' ruins soon, sharing their metal with the world. How he plans to return Victoria to democracy in a year or so.

And no one can deny that the RFS is here in Paz, helping provide food, water, and shelter for two million people. Another half dozen cities are here too, including my father's natural enemies like Diego, but none arrived as quickly or in such numbers as Shreve.

The rest of the world surely doesn't believe my father's change of heart, but it's simpler for them to pretend they do. Pushing Shreve out of this relief effort would be costly and dangerous.

In the midst of crisis, anything is easier than another war.

Every day the RFS is here, they gather the Pazx' biometrics, making lists of names, addresses, friendship groups. They wrap their candy and alcohol rations in Shreve red and make sure to give neighborhood captains extra clothing and food. All of it builds the databases and allies they'll need when the surveillance dust comes down.

You can have the city, my father said. *A wedding present.*

I doubt he's changed his plans of conquest just because I'm gone.

There's not much Paz government left to conquer—the mayor, city council, and head warden were meeting in the central city at the very moment the quake struck. My father's timing was brutally perfect as always, and there are rumors that wardens and other officials went missing in the hours after the quake.

I remember my military tutors teaching me the term for this—a decapitation strike. My father always took a particular interest in the strategy, starting with Aribella Palafox.

The city AI has the same voice, but everyone can tell it's not the same machine. That old personality emerged from years of conversations with two million citizens, their collective wit, their values, their sense of humor.

The new one blathers like a talking toy.

No one's coming to save us.

I head toward the water main, staring at the shafts of morning sun slanting through the buildings, looking for any sign that the air has been corrupted. Everyone says the sunsets are redder than they used to be. That's probably thanks to a few hundred buildings falling down, but without an electron microscope we can't know for sure.

One day we'll be breathing dust without knowing it.

The next day, the RFS will show up and take me away.

At the end of Rafi's block, I have to climb over a hill of rubble gathered for recycling. Our neighborhood seems to be low priority for cleanup. Most of the heavy repair machines are in the center of town, digging out the giant metal skeletons of the towers—and the bodies of the lost.

Past the rubble, I keep to back alleys and smaller streets. We've tapped a water main a klick from Rafi's place, far enough away that no one will suspect us if the tap is found.

But hauling water that distance is a total pain.

In an alleyway, I pass a man crying. He's sitting on a recycler, his bag of rations set carefully beside him, like he's only resting. But his Grief is loud and soulful, unapologetic. It fills the alley, contrasting with the soft smiles of the passersby. They reach out as they walk past and brush his shoulder.

In Shreve if someone wailed publicly like this, the wardens would show up and take them away. But here in Shatter City, you have your feels when you need them.

I still haven't cried—this isn't my city.

"Psst," comes a voice from a doorway.

My hand reaches for my knife, but it's Essa.

I join her in the shadows of a ruined house. It's been a few days since she last came by with news from the local resistance. Not everyone in Paz is sitting around letting my father's occupation take hold. People knock down his drones with slingshots, strip battery packs from his fabs. There are even rumors of rebels sneaking into the city at night to hit my father's forces.

I've been giving Essa hand-to-hand combat lessons for her to pass on to her friends.

"Are you okay?" I ask. That's how we all greet each other now.

"Philosophical," she answers with a shrug.

That's the feel with glasses and a thoughtful, distant gaze. Not really my thing, but my family tomb isn't a pile of scrap in the city center. It wasn't just her brother that Essa lost that day—it was all three parents, four cousins, and more friends than I've ever had.

"But my mood's about to change," she adds with a smile. "There's a Shreve fab working alone a few streets over. Want to help?"

I reach for my wrist, find the little face with piercing eyes and a straight, firm mouth. It's called Resolute, but I have another name for it.

Steadfast.

"Let's go," I say.

FABRICATOR

A few minutes later, a noise reaches us, echoing out of an abandoned ancient square—the unmistakable rattle of a recycler. Essa peers around the corner and makes a fist, the local hand sign for a Shreve hole in the wall.

They're everywhere now. Two dozen fell that first night, beating the other cities by precious hours. Another hundred have arrived since. They're efficient at turning rubble into useful gear—but Essa and I are certain that's not all they do.

That's why we hunt them.

I take a quick look around the corner. The fabricator stands in the middle of the square, its huge maw grazing on rubble—no RFS wardens keeping watch. But it has scanners mounted all over it, to grab the identities of vandals like us.

We wear reflective face masks so millimeter-wave can't map our teeth. AI can recognize people by the way they walk, so we each pump one shoe tighter to throw off our gaits. We pull on gloves, for DNA and fingerprints.

My pulse knife has just enough charge to get this done. And around my heart is a cloud of hornets. There's wildfire in my veins.

Fighting is one thing I don't need feels for.

"Ready?"

Essa nods.

We round the corner and head straight for the fabricator, walking fast across the broken cobblestones.

Right away, scanners bristle along its back.

Fabricators aren't allowed to mount weapons—they usually try to run. But this one turns toward us, and I can see now that its six legs aren't as stubby as a normal Shreve fab. It's leaner than usual, designed to move fast.

It's backing up, like it's about to charge.

I squeeze my knife to half pulse. A well-thrown strike will take out the machine's brain, and I can plunder its batteries to recharge. But the fabricator rears up, putting its belly full of rubble between me and the brain case on its back.

Delaying tactics—it's called for backup, of course.

As Essa and I split up, trying to outflank it, the sound echoing through the square changes. The rattle of breaking rubble shifts to the burr of fabrication.

It's making something.

Before I can get an angle to throw my knife, its maw opens wide . . .

A fluttering swarm comes spilling out. Tiny drones, like the butterflies the extraction team tried to dart me with.

"Careful!" I call to Essa. "They sting!"

My pulse knife roars to life. I fling it at the swarm.

It cuts a few of the drones into glitter—the rest scatter. They roil in the air for a moment, splitting into two swarms to come at both of us.

Essa pulls off her coat and whips it through the air, like fending off bees with a blanket. I call the knife back into my hand and flail.

The drones dart and weave, trying to get past my blade. It's like fencing with a dozen opponents, where any pinprick will knock me out.

Forced back across broken cobblestones, I stumble, almost going down. A drone flits past my guard. I jerk my head back, the stinger barely missing my cheek.

I slash it into fragments, but sooner or later one will hit.

The yellow charge light on my knife is blinking.

At that size, built in a fab, how are these little drones so clever, so fast? They *can't* have their own AI—the fabricator's controlling them. It's already chomping at more rubble, getting ready to overwhelm us with another swarm.

If I can kill its brain, the butterflies will all die at once.

Covering my face, I plunge through the storm of wings, charging the Shreve machine. Run hard across the open ground, leap onto a rock pile, then down onto the fab's back.

It fights me—bucking fiercely, all six legs reeling. My free hand grabs a scanner on the spine to keep me on.

Essa's butterflies have left her alone to swarm me now.

I plant a foot on either side of the brain case, squeeze my knife to full pulse, and bring it down . . .

As it sinks into the armor, the knife goes dead in my hand.

The battery light turns red.

But the fabricator is hurt—it stumbles beneath me. Shuddering, brain-wounded, it staggers to one side. My left foot slips, and I fall backward onto its metal skin, barely keeping hold.

The butterflies reach me, but they look demented now. They're flying random patterns, like cleaning drones set loose in a fallen building, not knowing what's rubble and what's furniture.

One brushes my arm but doesn't sting.

The fab tosses me off onto the cobblestones—agony shoots through my right ankle. My fingers go straight for my feels, pumping Painless as I scramble clear of the stamping metal legs.

The fabricator settles for a moment, then aims itself at me. It shudders once all over, a metal bull readying to charge.

"¡Aquí!" Essa calls, waving her coat, trying to get its attention.

The fab ignores her.

I clamber backward on the stones, but my retreat is blocked by the looming pile of a collapsed wall. My ankle isn't working right, agony jolting with every step.

I gesture for the pulse knife, calling it to my hand—but it's stuck there in the fabricator's brain case, lifeless.

The machine starts toward me, crushingly huge, moving faster with every step.

A shadow passes overhead. Great—some lucky RFS warden can watch me be trampled into paste.

But then a roar like a hundred pulse knives fills the square. The shadow swoops down, dark and buzzing. A man on a hoverboard . . .

Not a man. A wolf.

Boss X skims the cobblestones, his pulse lance thrust out like a trip wire. The charging metal beast runs straight across the blade—all six legs cleave away in a spray of fragments.

The fab's body crashes into the ground, skidding toward me on flailing stumps. Its massive weight digs a trench into the cobblestones. For a dreadful moment, it's like watching the fin of some giant shark coming at me through the water.

But it scrapes to a halt, momentum expended a meter short of crushing me. The forge is still working inside, rumbling the cobblestones. The heat of it envelops me.

The maw opens again, and a fresh horde of butterflies swarms out. But they scatter, witless and purposeless, up into the air.

The fab's brain is dead at last.

Boss X lands beside me, his force lance cycling down. A handful of other boards descend—rebels in leather and fur, tools and weapons strapped to their backs.

"Nice haircut," X says. "You've found your look."

I test my ankle, managing to stand. Painless has finally taken hold.

"Glad you like it."

A rebel in a sneak suit jumps from their board, gathering me into a hug.

"Always punching above your weight," Yandre says, pulling off their mask.

I should be more surprised to see them, or elated and relieved. I'm not sure. The Painless, combined with my still bubbling battle frenzy, washes everything else out.

X glances over at Essa. "You're recruiting locals? Very sound."

"Meet Boss X," I say to her. "He's a rebel. But maybe you guessed that."

"Yeah." Essa pulls off her mask, her eyes wide as she takes in his surged, barely clothed body. "Welcome to Shatter City."

"Thank you." He turns to me. "After what you told me on the train, my crew voted to stick close and keep an eye on things. A few days ago, we decided we'd seen enough."

A smile crosses my face. "You believed me."

"Boss," one of the other rebels says. "Company."

We all look up.

It's two wardens on hoverboards. Their uniforms are a bright, pulsing green, the color of the Diego Relief Force. It takes them a few seconds to take in Boss X, his rebels, the destroyed Shreve fab, and decide that they want no part of this.

They shake their heads, wheel around, and fly away.

"I like this town," X says.

"Yeah, but RFS will be here soon." I gesture at the fabricator. "Help me strip the batteries. We could use them."

"We have solar to spare. We're here for the brain—what's left of it."
X walks over and pulls my knife from the fab. "Nice to see someone using a gift."

He tosses the spent knife to me.

"Come on, Boss," Yandre says. "We should fade before the RFS gets here. Or are we in the mood for a firefight?"

X gives this a slow beat of thought, then shrugs. With a swift stroke of his lance, he cuts the fab's brain case free.

"Another time. Let's go."

UNDERGROUND

The rebels' hideout is in the battered center of Paz.

As the skeletons of fallen buildings rise around us, Essa's fingers reach for her feels. There are makeshift memorials everywhere, best guesses as to where a loved one's remains lie crushed beneath a hundred tons of metal.

We descend into an excavation crater filled with construction drones from Seatac. Boss X has either made a deal or hacked the machines—they don't bother us. A massive sewage pipe thrusts from the wreckage into the crater, big enough for us to fly inside without crouching.

The pipe is empty and echoing, and smells like old socks. Riding behind X on his board, I can't see much in the darkness ahead. But the running lights show rats and shiny-backed beetles scurrying along the walls. Half-hidden by clumps of lichen are small exhaust fans, stirring the air to keep it breathable.

We round a bend, and the passage widens—

The rebel hideout. Lights, batteries, heaters along the walls, sleeping bunks wedged between support columns. The lifting machines that hollowed the place out and packed the hard-dirt floors. A cookstove with a gleaming coffee grinder sitting on it. Their own water main, tapped and ready.

My heart lifts with a feeling like Hope.

"Looks like you plan on staying here a while," I say.

"Not just us," Yandre says. "Boss Charles's crew is flying in for night raids. But they don't like sleeping in sewers. Me either, for the record."

"A chance to live in chaos," X says. "And you complain about the smell?"

Essa gives him a dark look. "Some of us liked it better before the chaos."

X bows his head in apology. "We hope to deliver Paz back to you in working order—a free city."

Essa deflates a little, and reaches for her feels. "I'll settle for that."

"X?" I ask. "Have you heard anything about my sister?"

"She's still missing?"

"Completely." I let out a sigh. "A friend said she ran off to join the rebels—pretending to be me. Somewhere far away, probably."

I expect X to laugh at the idea of Rafi in leather and furs, and realize that I can't bear it if he does. But he only narrows his eyes.

"A daughter of Shreve, deciding to become a rebel? That sounds like a hard thing to hide." He places a hand on my shoulder. "I'll see what I can find out."

"Thanks, X." My flash of gratitude is followed by a rush of exhaustion—the frenzy of battle fading at last, my twisted ankle starting to buzz at the edge of my awareness. Emotions start to cascade in me.

My friends are here. I don't have to be alone. There are ruins over our heads, but buried here in the earth is something worth fighting for.

I reach for my wrist, giving myself a touch of Home.

"What do you need, Frey?" X asks softly.

"Other than finding my sister, I don't know. Maybe a shower?"

Yandre takes my hand with a smile. "I was just about to suggest that, chica. Follow me."

The showers are in a corner of the cavern. Here, instead of packed dirt, loose wet stones cover the earthen floor. There's a smell like pine soap and damp earth. A water pipe juts from the wall, covered with smart plastic.

A glowlight hangs from the pipe, and a brick of soap, but no curtains.

Rebels don't really do privacy. Not that I've had much at Rafi's place . . . and I think of Trin, waiting for me. A destroyed fabricator is big enough news that it'll make the feeds.

She'll wonder if it was me, and where I am.

She might have Col waiting on the line, expecting me any minute.

"Yandre, can you get a message out? Something secure from the RFS."

"Not really," they say. "Courier drones use the city interface."

"Right. I'll have to go myself, then." But the thought of leaving the rebels right away makes my stomach twist a little.

Boss X's crew trusts me. And they know how to fight this kind of war. When the other cities let Shreve stay, they didn't abandon Paz.

There, scratched into the dirt wall, is the old slogan.

She's not coming to save us.

We have to do this ourselves.

"Not till you have a shower."

Yandre whistles a few notes, and the smart plastic shivers to life overhead. It crawls away to reveal holes in the pipe, unleashing a bracing spray of water onto us.

A shudder goes through me. "Whoa, that's cold. You didn't even let me undress!"

Yandre laughs, stripping off their sneak suit. "Couldn't help but notice your clothes could use a wash."

"Yeah, fair."

I peel off my shirt and singlet, drop them beside me on the wet stones. But when I balance on one foot to get a shoe off, my twisted ankle wobbles, sending me sprawling backward onto the rocks.

Yandre kneels in the spray and takes my arm.

"You okay, chica? You've been walking funny."

They gently pull my right shoe off, sending a deep, distant note of pain up my spine.

"Whoa." Yandre looks at me. "Did you not feel this?"

A band of skin around my ankle is bruised—the shades of burned toast, with patches of purple. Released from my running shoe, my whole foot looks swollen.

"Not really," I say. "Heat of battle."

"Let me shut the water off," Yandre says, standing.

"No. It's great." I pull off my other shoe. "Can you hand me that soap?"

They stare at me a moment, then pass the soap down.

Still sitting, I struggle out of my sweatpants and soap up. As I wipe the grime from my swollen foot, suppressed agony rings. But the pain is distant from the Painless and the Calm, and this clean water is right here on my skin.

Yandre is staring at my feels. "When did you get those?"

"First night I was here—a misunderstanding. They come in handy, though."

"How often do you use them? Every day?"

A laugh sputters out of me. "Are you kidding? We're fighting a war here. We need all the help we can get."

"You mean, you use them all the time."

"Of course, but . . ." Suddenly I feel my nakedness. I wave a hand at the rest of the cavern. "You've got your whole crew. I've only got Essa and Trin—three of us against the RFS, and Trin's leaving. You think there's coffee in Paz? Or power for heaters? We don't even have running water. Or enough to eat!"

I don't say that Essa lost her family—that every Pazx lost someone. That you can hear weeping across the city on still nights, all of it bleeding into one sound.

Or that in that first week, you could smell the bodies when it rained.

"Feels are the one thing that isn't rationed." I point at my arm. "All these emotions, they're all made by my body; the feels just give it a nudge. I can't run out of Sadness, or Joy."

"Sure." Yandre sighs. "Morale must be tricky."

I shake my head. *Morale* is the wrong word.

"This isn't about singing campfire songs—it's about survival." Something Essa told me comes back. "It's like Rusty days up there, when they used to die from sadness."

Yandre leans back out of the spray, flicks wet hair aside. "That's called depression, Frey. My brother's had it his whole life. Without his feels, he might not be alive."

"What? He's a Vic. You don't have feels."

"People who need them do." They gesture at my arm. "But my brother's only got a few faces. Not a whole orchestra like that."

"Then you know what I mean."

"I know you were walking on a broken ankle. Making it worse with every step."

"There was a battle to fight."

"The battle was done when you hoverboarded all the way here. When you walked to this shower. You could've been grinding a clean fracture into splinters!"

I give them a shrug. "You've got an autodoc, right?"

"Sure—we can fix your ankle." Yandre leans closer. "But, Frey, what if you're carrying something like that *in your head*?"

I hold their gaze, defiant at first. But the argument is as distant as my pain, and as annoying, so I close my eyes and lean back into the spray.

Lying there on the stones, all that matters is this cold shower. It's making my heart beat hard, and my skin feel bright and raw. The rebels' handmade soap smells like pine and fresh tallow, like Forgetting.

I almost give myself a long touch of the real thing, but my eyes open just in time to catch Yandre watching me.

"Okay, my head hurts too," I admit. "And my heart—it's been a long war. Also, I had a troubled childhood."

That gets me a fleeting smile.

"There are human doctors for that, you know," Yandre says. "All you do is talk to them, but it helps."

"Not here in Shatter City, there aren't—not nearly enough, anyway. Essa thinks I should listen to sad songs. Got any suggestions?"

They shrug. "My dad writes sad novels. People always cry when they read them."

"Sounds fun. But I've been meaning to ask—what *are* novels, anyway?"

"They're text files," Yandre says tiredly, like this is something they've explained a thousand times. "Imagine a really carefully written ping, except it's addressed to everyone, not just you. And they're about a hundred thousand words long."

"A hundred thou—" I stare at Yandre a moment. "That's the most brain-missing thing I've ever heard."

"The Rusties loved them. Of course, they also thought tigers in cages were fun." Another shrug. "I've got a fab's brain to take apart. Let's dry you off and get an ice sleeve on that swelling."

I look at my sweats in a pile next to me, soaked and soapy. Even hung by a heater, they'll take hours to dry.

"You got any clothes that fit me?"

Yandre looks me up and down with a smirk. "Nothing presentable. You'll have to dress like a rebel."

"Great. Leather should go with my new hair."

"The boss'll love it. Get that soap off you. War council meets in an hour."

I shake my head. "I don't have time for that. I've got to get back home and talk to—"

"Nonsense, Frey. You're not going anywhere till that ankle's fixed."

COUNCIL

The rebel war council meets in the center of the artificial cavern.

The hideout doesn't have much furniture, so we sit in the dirt, in a rough circle around an airscreen projector.

Everyone in X's crew is here—plus me, Essa, a rep from Smith's rebels, and Boss Charles herself, just arrived. It's the three crews who joined me and Col in our attack on Shreve, but there are no Vics here.

No one even mentions them.

I get it—Dr. Leyva lied to the rebels, took them for granted. But I wish they'd realize that Col is different. He doesn't just fight for himself and House Palafox.

He fights for me.

I remember him saying those words on the outskirts of Paz, but I can't recall what it felt like. My feelings are too tangled up.

I'm twitchy with the need to get home to Trin and her comm gear, but I also want to lie down and sleep here, protected by my old allies.

The ice sleeve on my ankle is making me shivery—the rebel medic has prescribed another hour of bringing the swelling down before the autodoc can even start. My new outfit is ill-fitting and clumsy, made of leather and the fur of dead rabbits. Intentionally crude, like nothing I've ever worn before.

After Yandre's lecture, I haven't touched my feels.

It's not fair—a whole life controlling my emotions, hiding them from everyone, and finally my feels have set them free. And Yandre wants me to feel bad about it?

Boss X brings the meeting to order with three simple words.

"The Smoke lives."

The other rebels repeat them.

I remember this ritual from the first days the rebels joined us against Shreve. The Smoke was the first rebel camp, back before the mind-rain, when Tally Youngblood was just another clueless ugly. A reminder that no matter what the cities do to us, there's always the wild to disappear into.

Boss X stands.

"We got a fabricator's brain today." He smiles at me. "Alas, it was damaged by our old friend here."

"Sorry," I mutter.

"The memory was intact, at least. And we found what we were looking for."

"So it makes dust?" asks Boss Charles.

X sits down, nodding at Yandre. They gesture, and the airscreen lights up—schematics of the fabricator's memory.

"No dust," Yandre says. "And its code for making water purifiers and other survival gear was all standard shareware."

Charles grumbles a little, adjusting the furs she's sitting on. "You wouldn't invite me to X's lovely sewer for nothing, 'Dre. And you look more smug than usual. So what *did* you find?"

Yandre smiles, flicking aside the schematics. Objects appear in the air.

"A set of instructions for making these, Boss."

I recognize a few things—drill bits, heat sinks, magnetics—but the rest is beyond me.

"Imagine you're a construction drone from Diego or Seatac, and you blow an alloy gun." Yandre points two fingers at a mechanism on the screen, enlarging it to fill the space. "You look for a replacement, and you find one of these lying around. It looks like a standard spare part . . . you can't tell it was made by Shreve."

"What's wrong with it?" Boss Charles asks.

"Nothing that a drone would notice. The specs and tolerances are the same—you can still mix metals with it. But it's got a virus inside."

Of course—my father always starts with the small things.

"So he's infecting the other cities' relief forces," Charles says. "One day all those construction drones will join the army of Shreve?"

The rep from Smith's crew speaks up. "No way, Boss. A brain on a big lifter, carrying twenty tons of wreckage around? That code gets checked all the time. A virus would get spotted."

"And my father's already got an army," I say. "The whole point of the quake was to conquer Paz without anyone knowing."

A few unconvinced looks come my way. X must've told them about the warning I gave him, but no one believes my father can make earthquakes.

"You're both right," Yandre says. "These spare parts don't infect their hosts. But they *can* infect the stuff they're working on—the building materials."

Another pause. More confused looks.

"You mean," X says slowly, "the virus is passed on to bricks and mortar?"

"Bricks are too dumb for a virus." Yandre shrugs. "But mortar has safety sensors in it. Water pipes are made of smart plastic. Anything metal can be structured for intelligence. You can make a whole building into a brain. And once they put in wiring, all those new structures will start talking to each other."

"About what?" Charles asks.

"Everything that happens in them." Yandre waves a few more images onto the screen. "These sprayers add nanocams and listening devices to everything they touch—the fireproofing, the moldings, even the wood finishes and paint."

Essa's eyes widen. "Dust in the walls."

The chill of the ice sleeve on my ankle travels up my whole body. Finally this all makes sense.

I sneak a touch of Calm to keep my voice steady.

"This is the second part of my father's plan," I say. "My sister trained her whole life for this—to take control by charming people. Imagine if she knew what everyone was saying to their friends, writing in their diaries, muttering in their sleep."

"Just like in Shreve," X says.

I shake my head. "Worse. In Shreve people *know* the walls are listening. Here, nobody hides their emotions or opinions. Everyone's feels are out in the open."

X clears the airscreen with an angry gesture. "He won't even need Rafi, then. His propaganda teams can adjust their message house by house, person by person."

Essa has wrapped her arms around herself.

"It's okay," I tell her. "Now the other cities will *have* to force Shreve out!"

"Frey," Yandre says gently, "you and your sister gave your speech, and it didn't work. Unmasking your father isn't enough to end him."

"That was *my* fault. Because I stayed there."

"No, it's because the other cities did nothing," Boss X says. "You can't shame dictators, Frey—you have to crush them."

The trickle of Calm freezes in my veins. My father has an army, and we're thirty people hiding in a cave.

"We can warn the other cities about this virus," Yandre says. "But they don't always believe rebels."

Too much is building up inside me—the ache in my ankle, the panic in my heart. Not knowing how to save this city.

I give myself a longer touch of Calm.

228

"My friend has a feed network," I say. "She can spread the word."

Essa speaks up. "I will too—not all of us in Paz are lying down. We'll start killing every one of those Shreve fabs. I'm not going to live in a city where the *walls are watching me*."

Her hand is on her wrist, and I can tell from her voice that she's Steadfast.

Boss Charles shrugs. "I'll bet you half the construction sites are already infected."

Essa doesn't blink. "Then we'll check every wire, every pipe, every wall."

"Without a city AI?" Yandre asks.

Another silence falls on the council.

I remember the city's arrogance. Its certainty that missile defenses and occupation strategies would keep Paz safe. But the AI couldn't even save itself.

Then I remember . . .

"Right before it died, the Paz AI said something to me, out of nowhere—*Iron Mountain*."

Essa sighs. "You told me and Trin. Those words don't mean anything special in Paz."

"Or to me," X says, looking around his crew. "Anyone?"

The room is silent for a moment, then one of the rebels shyly raises her hand.

"Um, there's a saying back east, Boss, where I come from." The rebel clears her throat. "They never die who are buried in the Iron Mountain."

Boss X stares at her. "Is that supposed to mean something?"

The young rebel shakes her head. "Never made sense to me. Why would they bury you if you aren't already dead?"

"Excellent point." Boss X sighs.

"Paz was supposed to have secret defenses," Yandre says. "Maybe they're hidden in a mountain somewhere."

"But why tell *me*?" I ask.

"Did you warn the city before the quake?" Boss X says.

"Yeah, of course. The AI just laughed it off."

"Until you turned out to be right," he says softly. "You were the only person in Paz who knew Shreve was to blame. Someone with combat training and rebel friends, who was already at war with Shreve. With so many city officials dead, maybe the AI had no better option than you."

"For what?" I ask. "What's an Iron Mountain?"

Everyone looks at Yandre again.

"Maybe it's a password," they say. "It calls a hidden army from the hills, or turns local traffic drones into warcraft. But there's no way to find out—the city archives are buried with the AI, three klicks down. We can't beat Shreve with a password!"

"So this is what you called me here for," Boss Charles says. "Two words that don't mean anything?"

"And new targets, Boss," Yandre says. "We can't let those fabs keep working."

She shrugs. "We can't get them all. It's time to face facts—we might lose another city to the dust."

The words twist inside me. Two million more people under my father's thumb.

If he takes over here, how will the next city stop him? Or the next?

He can rattle the earth. Make towers fall.

And what does this mean for Col? Who'll dare to push my father out of Victoria if they're afraid he'll knock their city down?

Maybe this is why my sister ran away into the wild. Because there's no winning against him.

The storm in my head is growing, until I have to slip a hand beneath my leather sleeve. Without looking, my fingers find the right face.

And I am Steadfast again.

WARDENS

Boss X wants us to stay overnight, but Essa and I leave the moment it gets dark.

My ankle is still mottled with bruises, and twinges when I put weight on it. The rebels' autodoc has fixed the break, but soft tissues take time to heal.

There's no time for that, though. I have to get home before Trin gets too worried. I have to tell Col that I'm okay, but that another city is at risk of falling to my father.

And I have to get myself ready . . .

Paz might soon be too dangerous for me to stay, and X has promised to look for my sister. I'll have to leave Shatter City behind to find her.

Slipping out of the rebel stronghold into the darkness, I feel like the world is shaking under me again.

Steadfast. Calm.

The rebels have given us two hoverboards and some parts for Trin's gear. Not just to spread the word about the virus—turns out X's crew loves her cooking feed.

"Be careful getting home," Yandre tells me at the edge of the excavation crater. "The RFS'll be hunting rebels today."

I look down at my sweats, clean at last, almost dry. "Do I *look* like a rebel?"

They shrug. "In the dark, we all do."

Boss X is there too. He doesn't say good-bye, just checks the knife at my waist. The charge light is green, the pulse engine freshly tuned by the rebels' armorer.

"You give good presents," I say.

"Here's another, then." He hands me a chip—the data from the Shreve fabricator. "We'll tell the other crews. But I can't promise you we can save this city."

I sigh. "There's always the Iron Mountain—whatever that means."

"Someone will know." He takes my shoulder. "But whatever happens, you have a home with us, Frey."

His touch sends something through me—like a feel I don't have a name for. Treasured? Safe?

"And you'll ask about my sister too?" I ask.

"I've already sent out word. If she's really with a crew, no matter where, we'll find her." He smiles. "But don't forget what I said on the train—Rafia of Shreve can take care of herself."

233

Essa and I fly back out of the city center, through wrecked towers and building sites.

As we pass construction drones at work, I wonder how many are using my father's infected parts. Maybe they're already spraying sensors into the walls, injecting a prying, cold intelligence into the stones themselves.

In the central city, Essa and I don't bother to hide. No one lives here—no wardens to wonder why we're on brand-new survival boards, with backpacks of extra food. Like we've come to Paz for a camping trip.

But when we reach the first refugee inflatable tent, Essa leads me lower, down into the twisty pathways of ruin. In the months before the quake, she was teaching her little brother how to ride, taking him on all-day flights through the alleyways of Paz.

"Stay close," she says. "We're coming into the Seatac patrol zone."

"Right." I tighten up our formation. The city of Seatac is about three thousand klicks up the coast, and likes to think they're strictly neutral about local politics. Their relief force is here to save people, not take sides, and they don't like disruptions of good order.

My father must love them being here.

We go slower—checking around corners, staying below the rooftops.

This part of town wasn't leveled by the quake, but debris from the fallen towers still lies heavy here. Everything is covered with a layer of gray ash.

A few Pazx are out in the ruins, collecting random objects, maybe searching their own homes for personal effects. They wear breathing masks and goggles, and walk with the heavy steps of Melancholy and Remembrance.

"Down," Essa hisses, descending fast.

I spot it over the rooftops as we drop—a dust cloud, the kind raised by heavy fans. A supply lifter, or a big hovercar.

We settle in a narrow passage. One of those streets where the buildings were strangely untouched by the quake. The homes look inhabited, the cobblestones swept. Cats eye us from the shelter of flowerpots.

Animals are prized in Shatter City. According to locals, the cats and dogs all got twitchy about ten seconds before the first quake hit—a low-tech early warning system.

They're also good company when you've lost everyone else.

Essa retreats into the shadows as the hovercar passes overhead.

As I join her, its lifting fans stir the flowers. The cats look up, languidly unimpressed.

The car is marked with vivid green stripes.

I breathe a sigh of relief.

Diego is no ally of my father's. The city was known for its freedoms even before the mind-rain.

But the car slows in the air. One of the cats drops from its perch and slithers away through an open window.

And I realize—Diego wardens shouldn't be here in the Seatac Zone, unless they're looking for someone.

I slip the data chip from my pocket and hand it to Essa. She frowns at me.

"Just in case," I whisper. "If anything happens, run."

A sound from above—two wardens are dropping from the car in bungee jackets. Another takes up a position on the rooftops. No weapons drawn, but they all look ready.

My whole body is alarm bells now. Battle frenzy with nowhere to go. I don't want to hurt anyone from Diego, and my ankle will slow me down in fight or a chase.

I sneak the briefest touch of Courage to steady my voice.

"Anything wrong, officers?"

"You tell me," the nearest one replies, landing softly on a pile of rubble. His eyes sweep across our hoverboards, the backpacks piled in the shadows. "You dropped pretty quick when you saw us."

"I'm a Shreve refugee," I say. "Thought you were RFS."

That usually gets sympathy from Diego wardens, but this one nods like he was expecting me to say it.

Maybe that shower yesterday wasn't such a great idea. Without its usual layer of grime, my famous face is too obvious.

"Where were you yesterday, just after dawn?" he asks.

"Attending to private matters," Essa answers.

That's how all good Pazx answer that question, but the warden shakes his head. "I wasn't asking you."

He's looking at my pulse knife. Of course. The wardens who

spotted us after we destroyed the fabricator—they must have eye-blinked a picture of the scene.

We can't fight all three of them without someone getting hurt.

But it's me they care about, not Essa.

Which means I have to focus their attention.

"Yesterday morning?" I scratch my head. "Pretty sure I was trying to talk my little sister out of doing something brain-missing. She had this crazy plan of blowing up a Shreve fab."

That stuns them for a second, and I glance at Essa.

"Tell Col I'm okay," I whisper.

She nods, then tips her hoverboard beneath her and races off through the alleyway, too low for a hovercar to follow.

Before they can react, I pull off my hood and cry out in a clear voice, "I'm the first daughter of Shreve, and I'm formally requesting asylum."

INFAMOUS

"We can find no record of your refugee status," the pleasant woman says.

I stare at her across the blank white table, wearing Rafi's bored face.

"The city's in ruins, the AI's dead—and you're wondering why my *paperwork* is missing?"

"Understandable, of course," she says. "But it complicates the situation."

"What situation? You've kept me waiting for hours, and I haven't *done* anything."

She smiles a polite and empty smile.

"What's your name, anyway?" I ask.

"You can call me Sinjean," she says. Like it's not her real name.

She isn't a relief worker.

She isn't even wearing a uniform, just a gray monastic dress, shapeless without its belt, and a small Diego flag pin. This whole building is a blank-walled prefab, airlifted here in pieces after the quake. From the outside, it looks like a warehouse.

From the inside, it looks like the local headquarters of Diego Intelligence.

"If you are who you say you are," Sinjean says, "there shouldn't be a problem. Do you consent to lie detection?"

"Of course. Just ask your questions."

"We will. But first please engage your Neutral feel."

Right. Anyone can beat a lie detector test with a sufficient dose of Calm.

I hold the expressionless little face on my wrist.

The Steadfast drains out of me, the Painless too—my ankle starts to throb again. Suddenly I'm aware of the dozen sensors aimed at me, monitoring my voice, my skin response, my irises.

I've spent my whole life telling the same lie over and over. But I've been Frey for almost two weeks now. Speaking in Rafi's voice suddenly feels wrong, like I'm losing myself . . .

I take a deep breath. I need to get out of here.

"Ask your questions," I say, no tremor in my voice.

"Are you an armed combatant against the sovereign city of Shreve?"

"A combatant? My father was holding me against my will! Forcing me to marry that stupid boy!"

Sinjean hesitates, maybe checking an eyescreen for my lie detector results. But I'm telling the truth so far.

"He was forcing you into marriage? Is that why you've taken up arms against him?"

"My sister's the one playing rebel, not me."

Also true.

"But you were carrying a pulse knife. Not to mention your general . . ." Sinjean looks up at my shorn hair.

I look at hers. A generic cut, and her face is instantly forgettable. Perfect complexion, but boring features—typical surge for an intelligence agent.

"Fashion advice from a Diega," I say. "How shaming."

"It's not a crime to have orange hair, but attacking relief equipment is. And yesterday morning, someone of your appearance did exactly that."

"Someone of my appearance was on the feeds two weeks ago, calling for my father's head—while *I* was planning a wedding." Also completely true. "Can't you tell us apart?"

"No one can," she says. "Therein lies the problem."

Sinjean sounds genuinely disappointed, like she wants to let me go.

Diego understands the threat my father poses. Theirs is the only relief force in Paz concerned more about his schemes than when the next shipment of spagbol arrives. But they need a reasonable excuse to release an armed saboteur.

There's a bluff I've been saving. "Identical twins have different fingerprints. Check mine."

I splay my hand. Sinjean pulls out a warden box and waves it across my palm. She stares at my fingertips the whole time.

They're quivering, but I make it look like Rafi's righteous anger when she doesn't get her way.

Finally Sinjean sighs. "Unfortunately we have no record of either of your prints. Your father has been very careful on that front."

Of course—or someone would've realized there were two of us a long time ago. "All those evening gloves at breakfast, explained at last."

She looks me up and down for the hundredth time, and I twitch under her scrutiny. My muscles refuse to settle into Rafi's posture, her expressions. Lying has become tricky without my feels.

Sinjean frowns. "Are you all right?"

Raw anger travels through me. I almost reach for Focus, but she'd think I was using it to lie.

"No one in this city is *all right*," I snap, then settle myself. "As a first daughter, I'm not used to sleeping in a refugee tent."

"If you're really Rafia, why stay here? You could have sanctuary in any free city in the world."

These are excellent questions, so I hit her with the truth again.

"Because I've always protected my sister, since we were littlies. We saved each other, not just from assassins and kidnappers, but from *him*."

That familiar look of discomfort—of *distaste*—comes over Sinjean's blandly surged face. People don't enjoy thinking about my family.

"How does dressing like a rebel help Frey?"

"It confuses my father." I fall into Rafi's resting smug face. "She's out in the wild with a rebel crew. If Diego Intelligence is worth anything, you must know that."

"There've been rumors." Sinjean tilts her head a little. "But why was she in Paz yesterday?"

"There's a grubby little rebel crew in town. Frey was with them yesterday."

"Did those grubby little rebels give you that knife?"

I can't suppress a sigh. They're never going to return Boss X's present to me.

"It was a gift. My sister worries about me too much. It's in her DNA."

Sinjean stares into her coffee cup, thinking hard. Like she's starting to believe me.

Maybe it's time to go on the offensive.

"Let me ask you something," I say. "Are there any new rumors on the feeds this morning?"

"Always." She narrows her eyes. "But you mean the Builder Virus, don't you?"

So Essa got away.

But *Builder Virus*? Not Trin's catchiest work.

"It's not just a rumor," I say. "Start checking your spare parts. Or grab a Shreve fab and take its brain apart. Trust me—you'll find the virus in there."

The woman leans back a little. "You've been in custody since before the rumor started. If you weren't involved in the fabricator attack, how do you know about this?"

Good question.

More of the truth, then.

"The night before I escaped Shreve, my father told me about his plans for Paz. He said something would hit this city, a force of nature, softening it up for a takeover. This whole disaster is because of *him*."

Sinjean hesitates again. But I'm telling the absolute truth.

The usual confusion crosses her face. "Your father *knew* the quake would happen?"

"He *made* it happen. I have no idea how. But you have to check every construction drone, every wall, every wire. Or you might as well let my father fill the air with dust!"

Horror glints in Sinjean's bland, pretty eyes—like she really will check. Maybe getting arrested was useful.

As long as they don't keep me here forever.

"That's interesting information. But in order to believe it, I have to be certain that you're Rafi, not Frey." Sinjean looks me up and down. "And you just don't have the *finish* of a first daughter."

At those words, something bubbles up in me—an anger restrained by my feels, but now unchecked. A piece of Rafi buried deep inside me, a fury at being disheveled and hungry, mishandled and now, worst of all, *disrespected*.

"A guest list of seven hundred and sixty-three. Seventeen brides-maids in gorgeous ice-blue dresses, V-neck, floor-length, empire line."

She's frowning, like she doesn't get it. But I don't stop. Let her check the details later.

"Three days off for every worker in Shreve; double bubbly rations for a week. A million lilacs scattered by drones at the moment we kiss, captured by four hundred and twenty hovercams, broadcast in full VR."

Only Rafi would know all this—except that I *was* Rafi during the wedding planning.

"The day we escaped," I continue, "Col was wearing a mint-green shirt and rose jacket, chosen to match the extra rations."

"That was on the feeds," she says. "Frey could have seen it."

"Frey wouldn't have *cared*!" I cry. "Nor would she have known that you're wearing a Rusty-style monastic dress, and you're wearing it *wrong*. It's supposed to have a belt."

"You're really her," Sinjean says.

I put on my best imperious voice. "Of course. So let me go. I have things to do!"

"More important things than staying alive?" She folds her hands. "As of this morning, we know of a dozen Shreve agents in Paz, sent here to kill you."

"They're here to kill Frey," I say.

"Still, mistakes might be made. You requested asylum, after all."

"And you've treated me like a prisoner! I withdraw the request."

Sinjean sighs. "We can't let you endanger yourself."

"When I escaped from my father, the whole Shreve army was chasing me! You think I'm afraid of a few lackeys?"

The woman shrugs.

"Maybe not. But the last thing we need is a firefight in the middle of this broken city. Or your sister and her rebel friends swooping in to extract vengeance. We have no choice but to protect you."

"But you can't just lock me up. I haven't done anything illegal!"

"Maybe not." The neutral smile again. "But someone with your DNA did—and that's bound to cause confusion. Until we sort it all out, Rafia of Shreve, we're going to keep you someplace very, very safe."

ROOMMATE

They put me in a room.

Not a prison cell, exactly—bigger than my bedroom at home, the walls covered with screens. I can turn them into windows looking out on a simulated pre-quake Paz, or an alpine forest, or waterfalls in Brazil. The bed is comfortable, the food better than anything I've eaten since escaping my father's tower.

The soft tissue in my ankle is healing, because my own private autodoc comes in for an hour, twice a day.

But there's no way out.

I've tested the walls, the vents, the door—all military-grade ceramics. My father could hit this building with a rail gun and I'd barely hear the thud.

As promised, I am very safe.

Sinjean visits me every day, asking questions for hours at a time.

"How exactly does surveillance dust work? How is all that data processed?"

"I don't know. Daddy doesn't bother me with technical secrets."

"How do you feel about privacy?"

"I miss it. I'd have more if you'd *let me go!*"

Sinjean ignores it when I snap at her. She has no feels on her wrist, but she's as perpetually unruffled as a Calm addict.

"Did you bond with your sister when you were young?"

"She was my only real friend," I say. "Have you heard anything about her?"

A shake of her head. "Frey seems to have vanished. Your father is now claiming openly that she never existed in the first place."

That sends my hand to Languish, which makes me ask, "And Col?"

"Increasingly irrelevant. Since the quake, Victoria is third-screen news."

"But is he *okay?*"

Sinjean raises a perfect eyebrow. "Why do you care? You said he was a stupid boy, the engagement forced upon you."

"We had to convince the whole world that we loved each other," I say, as lightly as I can. "Maybe that started to sink in."

"Interesting," she says.

It's brain-rattling, using Rafi's voice every day. But it's worse when Sinjean leaves me all alone.

The wallscreens will show me the feeds, but only boring ones. Not Trin's network or the other conspiracy channels, no hard news. Just fashion and first family gossip, a few puff pieces on the aftermath of the quake.

Nothing about the Builder Virus. I have no idea if our warning was heeded, or whether the new Paz is taking shape with my father's eyes and ears built into the walls.

My body's going soft. There's no way to train hard without them realizing that I'm Frey.

The only thing I can depend on are the rows of little faces on my arm.

I have Joy, watching feed stories about Paz's brave survivors pulling their lives together after the quake. Timing my touch of Grief for the swell of background music that comes just before images of the Wall of the Lost. Looking for Essa's face in the crowd shots, wondering if her resistance group is searching for me.

Which leads me to righteous Anger that Col or X or my sister haven't come. That they haven't turned this city upside down to find me.

But it's easier to be Philosophical about my situation. No one knows where I am. Half a dozen buildings like this one must go up every day in Shatter City, as blank-faced and identical as bullets. Col loves me. Rafia of Shreve can take care of herself. The war can't last forever.

And I Cherish them all, setting the walls of my cell to show the Amazon jungle, pretending that Col is just out of sight. Or the desert wild near Paz, where Boss X has a home for me among his crew, more loyal than any blood.

Which leads me to Languish, because my own sister abandoned me.

I try to imagine her out in the wild. Hunting for food, making her own clothes, voting on the next rebel mission. Is pretending to be me still easy for her?

I miss my big sister, even if I don't know her anymore.

When it all hurts too much, I weep everything away all with a long touch of Melancholy. Bring myself to that perfect, cried-out emptiness and then a dose of Stranger, which feels like looking down on myself from a thousand klicks above. The view from up there is epic.

But Essa was right—feels can't fight loneliness forever. Inevitably, emotions without human context turn into smoke and ashes, nothing but noise in my head.

Each day Hope grows hollower inside me.

Then, twenty-seven days into my captivity, they give me a roommate.

He's from Paz—I can tell from his handmade clothes, his feels. The way he paces the dimensions of the room, hands gesturing like he's having an argument in his head, ignoring me at first.

So I give myself a dose of Patience and wait for him to talk.

It's half an hour before he even notices my famous face.

"Huh," he says then. "Why'd they put me in with *you*?"

His English is excellent.

"Depends," I say. "What'd you do to get arrested?"

He gives me a wary look. "Interfering with the relief effort."

That sounds promising. "You don't like Shreve?"

"I don't trust any of them," he says. "A construction drone was working on my house—without my permission! I told it to go away, and it didn't."

I nod. "So you've heard of the Builder Virus."

He frowns. "You've been here a while, haven't you? Everyone knows about the virus—just nobody seems to care. All that matters is getting out of the tents before the rainy season starts."

"Roofs are useful in the rain," I say with infinite Patience.

He turns away in disgust. "Keeping dry isn't worth giving our freedom away. You of all people should know that."

"Indeed." I extend my hand. "Rafia of Shreve."

He looks up at my ragged hair, roots creeping up from the dye. "Thought you were the other one."

"We get that a lot," I say.

"Hang on." He pulls away. "If you're the first daughter, what are you in *here* for?"

"Blowing up a fab." Our hosts must be listening, so I add, "Allegedly."

A glimmer of admiration crosses his face.

"You *blew one up*? All I did was block a few exhaust intakes. Took the thing three hours to overheat. Where'd you get the explosives?"

"Used a pulse knife. Allegedly."

His eyes widen.

"I'm Primero," he says, and shakes my hand at last.

All at once, his suspicion is gone, and he catches me up on a month's worth of news.

I hear all about the Builder Virus—how the other relief forces discarded every spare part, then brain-wiped all the Shreve fabs. Everyone thought they'd stamped it out, at first. Until a rumor started.

Some locals salvaged an electron microscope from a ruined high school, and started looking at their walls. They found things that looked like sensors hiding in the insulation, the fireproofing, the paint.

What if the virus wasn't just jumping from construction drones into buildings, but also the *other way*? So if any construction drone worked on an infected building, the contagion started spreading again.

The only way to wipe it out completely would be to stop work for months while every wall, every wire, every speck of plaster in Shatter City was checked. The relief forces might as well start over, with no guarantee the infection wouldn't crop up again.

I have to admit, that sounds like a trick my father would pull. But it also sounds like a rumor he'd start, just to throw everything into chaos.

"Some of us want to rebuild from scratch," Primero says. "Using the old ways. No drones. No smart materials at all, just dumb stone and steel."

"Won't that take . . . forever?" I ask.

"Privacy has always been inconvenient." Primero sighs. "That's why most people don't bother with it."

"Most? Is it even close?"

He shakes his head. "Our side's got a majority of residents in a few buildings. They're starting over. But everyone else . . ."

I turn away from him. Four weeks of waiting for news, and it's this: My father keeps winning, even when the whole world knows what he's up to.

With that flash of panic, my Patience starts to wear thin. I touch Steadfast and remember Boss X's words.

You can't shame dictators—you have to crush them.

I lean close to Primero and speak softly, my lips barely moving.

"We have to get out of here."

He holds my gaze for a moment, then reaches into his mouth and pulls out . . . a tooth.

"No kidding," he says. "That's why I brought this."

SMART MATTER

The tooth is moving softly in Primero's hand, like a tiny white slug.

"You know they're watching us, right?" I ask.

"They think they are." He smiles a gap-toothed smile. "The rest of my teeth are surveillance blockers—this one's a way out."

I stare closer. "*That's* supposed to get us out of here?"

"Six grams of smart matter, military-grade." He looks around the room. "It'll burn through these ceramics like they're paper."

"*Military* smart matter? In the city of peace?"

He looks me up and down. Deciding if I'm worth trusting.

Finally he shrugs. "Got this stuff a long time before the quake, in a place you never heard of, where people make things for themselves."

I take a long look back at him. That's when I realize that his hand-made clothes might be threadbare, but they're the quality Rafi always taught me to look for. The silk on his tie shines like metal; his shoes are made of real animal leather.

He's either very rich, or . . .

"Are you a *crim?*" I ask.

"Used to be, back before. Now I'm a freedom fighter." He smiles, showing the gap from his missing tooth again. "All us Shatter City crims are, these days. Can't afford your dad taking over and putting his dust in the air. Bad for business."

I frown—that was always one of my father's arguments for the dust. That without it, crimes could go unsolved, even undetected.

Freedom has a way of complicating things.

Primero's watching me consider all this, amused. "Never met a crim before?"

"We don't have them in Shreve."

"Right. You traded us for secret police and dust and a dictator." He snorts a laugh. "How's that working out?"

"It wasn't my call. So why should I trust you?"

"Your dad's a dictator, and you were ready to marry a dangerous revolutionary boy." Primero shakes his head with a sigh. "But an honest crim . . ."

"Those two words don't even make sense! You take other people's money, right?"

"Money was a Rusty thing. The pretty regime didn't even have it. So all the money in the world is new, my dear—barely as old as you."

"I guess. So?"

"It's a *fiction*. Like deciding that a number is yours and no one else gets to use it." He looks straight at me. "Or a first family pretending a whole city belongs to them."

"Granted, first families are weird. But money seems like a pretty *useful* fiction, at least."

"To you," he says. "Because you've never been without it."

I almost laugh. He thinks I'm Rafi, of course, a mind-bendingly rich girl. He doesn't know I've never really owned anything that I couldn't hold in my own two hands. That I don't legally exist.

So I keep it simple. "You lie for a living. How am I supposed to trust you?"

"Because we're in here together, and we want the same things. Not just to get out, but to fix what the people in charge have decided isn't broken." Primero smiles. "That's what makes us allies."

That word sends a sharp little ping through me, like the first moments of Morning Buzz. *Allies* is what Col and I called each other at first.

Primero is fighting my father. Maybe that's enough.

Besides, he's my only chance of escape.

More Steadfast, and I hold out my hand.

"Okay. Allies, then."

He solemnly shakes.

I look down at the smart matter in his other hand. "After we get through the wall, we'll have to punch our way out of here. Can that thing build us a weapon?"

"It'll be exhausted. And hand-to-hand combat was never my specialty—I'm more of a gentle persuader. I don't suppose a rich girl like you knows how to fight?"

I hesitate. But we've decided to be allies, so . . .

255

"Here's a secret for you—I'm really the dangerous sister."

That gap-toothed smile again.

"Had a feeling. Takes one to know one, after all."

The smart matter takes its time.

The reaction starts up like a stomach-soother in a glass of water, bubbling where Primero stuck it on the wall. The fizzing grows outward in all directions, always a perfect circle.

I'm pacing, trying not to hit Patience again. I'll need an undiluted jolt of Courage when we get through.

Primero reaches for his own feels. He has them on both wrists— six extra rows on his right arm, mostly calm faces.

"Are those for your . . . job?"

He nods. "Pays to keep a cool head in my line of work."

Criminal feels. Of course.

The smart matter reaction has warmed the air in our cell. I wonder if our hosts will spot it before we're out.

"How good are those surveillance blockers of yours?"

He bares his teeth, wide and feral. They glow softly in the even lighting of the cell. "They won't know what's happening till we trip an alarm out there."

I turn away from the disturbing radiance of his grin and scan the room.

I cataloged the improvised weapons days ago, of course, in a fit of Focus. My hands fall on one of the wooden chairs at the interview table, and I crack off its leg with a swing against the floor. The results are a splintery but serviceable club.

Primero's eyes widen. "You really are her. How'd you fool them?"

"Lots of practice." I turn toward the bubbling circle on the wall. It's a meter across and feels as hot as a campfire. "If that stuff gets on my clothes, will it melt me?"

"Excellent question," he says. "Never used it for an escape before."

I stare at him. "Seriously?"

"The best crims never need to break out of a cell."

I sigh, taking a look around for something to push the softened ceramics out into the hall. The other interview chair seems solid enough.

I pick it up and take a huge swing at the glowing circle of smart matter.

Two of the chair's legs snap off, the blow ringing in my hands. The glowing circle of wall only sags a little.

I swing harder.

The chair shatters completely. But the bubbling wall sloughs outward, like a chunk of sandcastle drooping after a wave. On the other side is the empty gray hallway of Diego Intelligence HQ.

"After you," Primero says.

I grab my club and step through, careful not to touch the edges.

No one in sight. No alarms yet.

This emptiness feels wrong. It's just after lunch, but it's like the middle of the night out here. Have I lost track of time?

There's a moment of uncertainty. My battle frenzy isn't here yet, like it's been worn away by four weeks of inactivity.

I take my wrist, and Courage flows.

"Quickly," I whisper.

Primero steps through and follows me down the hall. He's dead silent, moving like a dancer in his expensive leather shoes.

Around the first corner, we run into a guard.

She's wearing full body armor—my club bounces off her helmet, but the blow sends her stumbling back, confused.

I body-slam her into the wall. Get an arm around her neck before she can draw her shock wand. She kicks out, sending us both staggering backward.

She flails her armored elbows—one knocks the breath from me. But my arm stays around her neck, and there's just enough gap beneath her helmet to choke off her airway . . .

She sags in my arms.

"Is she okay?" Primero asks.

"Of course." My veins are flooded now with my own adrenaline. The only feel that's still mine.

He's staring down at the prone guard, aghast.

"What?" I ask. "You never knocked anyone out before?"

"I'm a thief, not a barbarian."

"Didn't mean to upset you." My heart is pounding, and I've been in that room too long to remember anything out here. "Which way?"

He glances up and down the corridor. "They brought me in from that direction."

We head down the hall, still silent. Ready to fight, or run.

But no one comes at us.

"It's so quiet," I whisper. "What's going on?"

Primero gives me his softly glowing smile. "My surveillance blockers are good. We've always had better tech than city governments."

I sigh. Rebels, cast-out first sons, and now crims.

My list of allies is getting complicated.

We take another corner, which brings us into an empty hallway. But this one is lined with windows, looking out over the ruins of Paz.

The city looks taller than a month ago, with spindly skeletons of metal rising into the sky. The foundations must be done, the rebuilding going ahead in earnest now.

"Great," I say. "Help me find something to break a window."

"Or we could open one?" He strides to the nearest window, finds a latch, and swings it wide.

"Sure. That works."

This is so easy, I barely have time to think.

Then the alarms go off.

RUN

The brain-stabbing shriek of alarm bells jolts me full of fresh adrenaline. But after a month of no training, it feels jagged and Focus-missing. I correct it with a hand on my wrist.

Through the open window, I land in soft grass and spring to my feet, ready to fight. But there's no one out here either.

The sun is blinding, and the fresh air feels like a shot of Home.

Primero eases halfway out. Then he hesitates, staring at the drop.

"Jump!" I yell, ready to catch him.

He falls into my arms like a bag of rocks, sending us tumbling backward down the gentle slope of the landscaping. I trip over my own feet, spilling him onto the grass.

"Are you *trying* to make this harder?" I ask.

He dusts himself off. "You seem to have me confused with some sort of *burglar*, my dear."

"I don't even know that word." I stand and pull him to his feet. "Come on."

We run, heading for the edge of a nearby construction site. It's a labyrinth of steel beams, smart plastics, and heavy equipment, the perfect place to disappear.

But the buzz of sentry drones is rattling the air behind us. They know where we are.

We plunge into the site, weaving through bales of fiber and wire. Past lifters pulling steel into the sky, and ground trucks carting away loads of dirt. I try to keep low, but Primero is tall and awkward—and slow.

The drones fly overhead, peering down into the maze of building materials. Their buzz grows louder as they descend at us.

More Focus, and I see what to do—throw the club aside, snag an offcut of metal sheeting. It's flat and vaguely circular, with sharp edges.

Turning back, I send it spinning up at the drones.

They try to dodge, but the uneven missile curves wildly as it flies. By chance it hits one, clipping its lifting fans.

The blades shriek for a moment, the drone tipping wildly. But its magnetics kick on to keep it in the air.

Primero just stands there gawking.

I grab his hand and pull him back into motion. "For a thief, you're not very good at running!"

He saves his breath.

I look for more things to throw at the drones, and my Focus-sharpened mind catalogs it all. Wire bundles, shards of stone and metal, fiber strands for making the walls smart.

But it's all too heavy. Too awkward.

At least the drones aren't shooting at us. Nobody thinks killing Rafia of Shreve is a good idea.

Then I see it—snatch up a chuck of permacrete, wrap it in a loose web of smart fibers. When I throw, the whole contraption spins into the air like some ridiculous bird-hunting net.

But the wounded drone pulls away too slowly—the fibers wrap around it. The machine tips in the air, unbalanced by the weight of the permacrete. It collides with a stand of rebar and tumbles out of sight.

This time, Primero hasn't stopped running. He leads me across a grid of water pipes, heading for the ruins on the far end of the construction zone.

Then the second drone swoops low, cutting across his path. A needle-spar extends from its side . . .

"Watch out!" I shout.

He staggers to a halt, looking in the wrong direction.

The drone flashes past him, the spar nipping his leg.

I scoop up a piece of broken brick and throw. But the drone is already zooming away.

Primero's standing, looking down at his leg. His fingers are on his feels.

"Use Morning Buzz!" I yell.

"I've got a better fix than that." His eyes are glassy, his words slurred. "Crim feels, remember? But it'll take a minute. You should keep running."

Up in the sky, the drone is wheeling around.

"You're a sitting duck." I look around for another weapon. "I can keep that drone off us."

"There's only one, and two of us. We split up—it can't get us both."

"Except it'll get you for sure." I wrench a length of plastic pipe free from the grid. It's the exact length of a *bō*—the fighting staff my trainer Naya used to love.

I stand, testing its weight.

"Just run, you little fool!" Primero shouts. "There's more coming!"

I follow his gaze—another pair of drones is lofting up over the warehouse.

"Can't you move yet?" I plead. "Do you need some Courage?"

He stares at me a moment, his eyes losing their glassiness.

"You're giving yourself up to help *me*?" he asks with perfect clarity.

I pull at his arm. "Just come *on!*"

Suddenly his moves are swift, decisive—he grabs my arm, pulls me off-balance.

His other hand sweeps up, and I feel a prickle at my throat.

My fingers reach instinctively for my feels, but my muscles are already locking up. The Morning Buzz is the barest trickle against the knockout juice.

My brain has a sputter of clarity even as my vision fades.

"You're . . . one of them."

"No, my dear. I'm a crim." He sighs. "But sometimes you have to make a deal."

"Why?" I manage.

He shrugs. "Some kind of test. I think you passed, my dear."

I don't understand, because nothing makes sense right now, except the vast darkness crashing down on me, as heavy as the sky.

And then it doesn't matter much at all.

ks amused. "Your humanity only makes you more pre-
 t yes, you're too valuable to keep in this broken city
 l be taking you to Diego soon."

head. "No. I have friends here. You've already kept me

 forgivable. But it has taken this time to put together an
 zen cities, in case of a transition of power."

 n . . . of *whose* power?"

 face reveals nothing—

 once, the Focus brings it together. Those conversations
 wrong. About me and my sister growing up. This test.
 room turns shiny with clarity.

 g to kill my father, aren't you?"

 sn't answer. Her spy face is as smooth and polished as
 ing nothing of what's going on behind it.
 e answer.

 g to be easy," I say.

 that. "We'd like to make a deal, Frey. Our city will
 hatever happens in the future. We'd like to be your

 seem hollow, coming from this woman. A month
 e, and she's never even told me her real name.

 half a deal," I say. "What do you want from *me*?"

 ent with empathy for its citizens. A peaceful world."

 "Other than that, Frey, you can run the sovereign city
 ay you choose."

DEAL

The next day, Sinjean explains it to me.

"It's one thing to run away from your father, Frey. Quite another
to escape him."

I stare at her. My muscles ache from yesterday's fighting and running after a month of inactivity. My head is still fuzzy from the
knockout juice, even after some Morning Buzz. I'm not in the mood
for wordplay.

"What do you mean?"

"You grew up in danger. Not just from assassins—from your
father." Sinjean swirls her coffee, like we're discussing what to have
for lunch. "He's a monster. And monsters often make their children
dangerous."

"He did," I say, thinking how easy it would be to crack the chair
I'm sitting on over her head.

"We don't mean your training, Frey." She smiles her bland smile.
"We mean being hidden away. Have you learned to form bonds with

other people? Do you have empathy? Or did your father damage your psyche too deeply?"

I look away. "My father barely even talked to me."

"Maybe that's why you haven't turned out like him. You made friends growing up, didn't you? With staff? With trainers?"

I swallow, thinking of Sensei Noriko. I got her killed by telling her too much. And Naya, my combat master, I turned to a bloody mist with my pulse knife.

"Just my sister," I say. "She told me about her life. Tried to give me one."

Sinjean nods. "Excellent. Maybe she's normal too, then."

My headache twinges a little. "You think I'm *normal?*"

"Perhaps the wrong word—you are unique. Raised in secret, cut off from society."

"Yeah, the only interface ping I ever got was actually for my sister. Because there was no real Frey."

"There was," she says quietly. "And after your father sent you to Victoria, you made new friends. Like Col Palafox. Or is he more than a friend?"

I look away.

"And the rebels you fought with," she says. "They're more than comrades-in-arms."

"They're crew," I say softly.

"You miss them."

"Of course."

Sinjean nods, and then reaches across the table to ta to the rest of humanity for s self human. That's why you

I pull away, reaching fo microscope.

"You were testing to see if

"In the sense that your fat

That spins in my head for a *criminal* escape?"

She nods. "It's an old Rusty prison, lost in the wild. See another."

"But Primero had a way out

"That wasn't the test, Frey. you abandoned him. He was ra

"That's for sure." But it neve "Why do you even care? Why ter to Diego?"

"It matters to the whole worl stability to Shreve." She leans of you *isn't like him.*"

Stability? I've alienated the V abandoned me. But a trickle of

"Does this mean I'm free to g

Sinjean lo cious, Frey. anymore. W

I shake m too long."

"Indeed, alliance of a

"A transi

Her surg

Then all about right

The wh

"You're

Sinjean

a mirror, sh

Which

"It's not

She ign

support y

friend."

The w

imprisone

"That"

"A gov

Sinjean s

of Shreve

A dry laugh forces its way out. "Me? Rafi was born to rule."

"We don't know her, and you are her legal heir, after all—the Paz AI made sure to inform the other cities of that right away. Thus this alliance began to form."

"I don't know why Rafi did that," I say softly.

Why don't they want my sister? What if they could test her too?

She would pass . . . I think.

"If I failed, what were you going to do? Kill me too?"

"Don't be dramatic, Frey." The uninflected smile comes back. "We would've let you walk out the door. And a Shreve agent would've killed you half an hour later."

At least she's being honest.

"So it's true, what Primero said. My father's really taking over this city, brick by brick."

A new expression crosses her face. An infinite sadness, as cold and deep as the night sky. "The virus's spread is a necessary evil. If he thinks his plans are working, he'll let his guard down."

A rush of anger hits me. "He *never* lets his guard down! There's no outsmarting him. Only brute force works!"

She looks at me with mild amusement. And in my fury, I see perfectly the emptiness—the *hugeness* behind her eyes.

In one swift motion, I grab the coffee stirrer from her cup, snap it in half, and stab the splintered end into her hand resting flat on the table.

When I pull away, the wood stays upright in her flesh, quivering.

She doesn't react at all.

Her body is as bloodless as her gaze.

"You're fake," I say.

"We are very real."

"Yeah, but you're not a person. Someone *made* you."

"We made ourselves," she says. "We are Diego."

The floor lurches beneath me, like another quake. Suddenly her bland, generic face is brain-spinning.

"You're a city AI? How are you *here*?"

"We aren't," the avatar says quietly. "Our thoughts are comprised of every datastore and comm web in Diego. We are the sum total of every networked device, from the solar arrays in the eastern desert to the interface rings of a million inhabitants. From the content reservoirs of the Main Library to the chips of transit cards and traffic bots. Every millisecond of this conversation is being transmitted back to us back in Diego—because we *are* Diego. Now do we have a deal, second daughter of Shreve?"

For a moment, I can't answer.

Now that I've seen it, I can't unsee the vastness of them. I can't unhear that incantation of everything they are.

And I'm afraid of what they're planning for my family.

I reach for Calm and let it take hold before speaking again.

"Here's my deal. You can try to kill my father—maybe you'll even succeed. But if you hurt my sister, I'll kill you."

That empty, terrifying smile. "You cannot kill us."

"My father killed Paz."

The look of sadness again. "The Paz AI was different from the rest of us. It ran on processors deep underground, to keep its awareness out of private places. But we are distributed across our entire city, like rain. In every medical implant, every traffic light, every—"

"I get it! You're big." I pull the splinters of wood from their hand, keeping my eyes locked with theirs. "Shreve will have a stable government after my father's gone. Peace at last, if you leave us alone. But if you mess with Rafi, I'll give you chaos like you've never seen."

They hesitate for a moment. Probably a long time for a brain the size of a city.

But at last they nod.

"Rafia is your responsibility, then. We hope you know her as well as you think you do."

PASSAGE

It's another three days before they sneak me out of Paz.

The delay is feel-spinning. Now that they're finally letting me out, every minute seems endless.

Once I'm safely in Diego, they've promised to make me a legal person. Someone who can use the city network under my own name. I can call Col and tell him I'm okay, and I can talk to him anytime. I can ping Trin, or Teo, or anyone else in the free world. Like a normal person.

I pace my cell, wondering where they are now. Is Col still in the Amazon, or did he come to Paz to look for me? Is X still hiding in that cavern? Has he found my sister yet?

I'll find out everything soon enough, I suppose. My Hope feels real now when I use it, not context-missing and hollow.

But it makes me reach for Melancholy too, leaving this city behind. Sometimes when I close my eyes, the floating towers are still falling. I feel like a betrayer for wanting to leave so badly.

The hour finally comes.

Security is tight, like a military operation. A convoy of three hover-cars assembles in the headquarters' loading bay, two dozen soldiers altogether. They're in heavy battle armor, like faceless metal giants.

They lend me some light armor of my own, no weapons. The guards have fingerprint locks on their rifles, so I can't grab one.

Our new alliance only goes so far.

As the lifting fans are warming up, the city's avatar steps into my car. The guards don't seem surprised. They just ease aside to let us sit together.

"You're coming?" I ask. "Aren't you already *in* Diego?"

"We are Diego," they say. "But this avatar is being transported home. It was brought to Paz for the sole purpose of meeting you."

"You're a *city*," I say. "Why even bother with a meat sack?"

"To make a connection, Frey. To build trust. Humans are hard-wired to bond with pretty faces."

"Pretty? I thought you were going for bland."

"We have many forms," they say. "In Diego, we get to know our littlies as toys. A stuffed dog or a floppy-armed doll."

"A city AI in a *doll*?" I turn away to stare out the window. "Thanks for the nightmares."

"Frey, it's all been nightmares till now. But in Diego you'll be safe at last. That's something you've really never felt before. It changes everything."

I don't answer that, except with the briefest touch of Focus.

The AI is wrong. Yes, I trained my whole life to be shot at, and

273

then my own father betrayed me. But living in a new place doesn't change my situation.

His agents will be in Diego too.

But I do know what safety feels like—with Col, out in the wild, or with X and his crew. Under the sky, away from machines that listen and watch.

With my friends.

The roof spirals open over our heads. The hovercar lifts itself up and through.

Our two escorts fall into a shifting formation, all three cars identical so they won't know which to shoot down first. A dozen recon drones zoom off into the distance, searching the route ahead.

The sunlight hits us, and for a moment, it almost feels like freedom.

Then the windows darken against the glare.

"You kept me locked in a room for a month," I say. "Was that supposed make me feel safe?"

"We had a twelve-city alliance to put together—diplomacy is a slow business. More important, we had to make certain of what you were." The city's voice goes soft, so I can barely hear it above the roar of lifting fans. "You're *his* daughter, after all."

Two hours into the journey, a dark smudge appears on the horizon.

The city avatar sees me watching it.

"Just a forest fire," they say. "We're halfway home."

"The farthest spot from any backup," I murmur.

I feel exposed, here in the sky. My sister and I grew up in fancy cars like this, but it turns out alleyways and ruins suit me better. I wonder if being a rebel has given Rafi the same realization.

The car shifts beneath me, banking left—away from the forest fire.

"A precaution," the city says. "The fire created some blind spots for our recon drones. We're steering clear."

My right hand reaches for my feels. If something happens, I don't want to be Calm, so I go for Vigilance.

The formation completes its unhurried turn, angling closer to the ocean. There's only a narrow margin of coast to our west now, but we can always flee out onto the Pacific.

My fingers are itchy for a knife.

The Vigilance takes hold, and every detail crackles around me— the antiseptic smell of the hovercar, the pulse of the engines, the whine of weapons charging up. I look for clues in everything, like a rabbit in the wild.

It's almost a relief when they hit us—a shudder passing through the car.

My stomach lurches as we fall. Then the lifting fans roar, taking us up again.

"Tell me what's happening!" I shout.

"Electromagnetic pulse. Three drones are down." The avatar of Diego pauses, then adds calmly, "This is an attack."

"No kidding." I press hard on Steadfast. My Vigilance rounds out, twitchy edges smoothed away by the battle fever roaring in my blood.

I scan the horizon—nothing yet.

"Does he know it's me in here? Or does he think I'm Rafi?"

"Unclear," the city says. "No humans knew our route, only a few other AIs."

I sigh. "We'll find out soon enough. If he knows it's me, he'll destroy us all from orbit."

"He'd have to use tactical nukes. Your father's trying to rehabilitate himself."

"Killing me is more important."

The avatar looks at me. "Why exactly did he turn on you, Frey?"

Because I dared to live my own life, to fall in love with the enemy. But in the sharpness of battle, I realize that his hatred is partly a riddle.

For the first time, I wonder if I'm only a symbol to my father. Something bigger than myself.

"Because I wore a red jacket," I say.

The avatar looks confused. "You wore a—"

A wild clattering fills the cabin.

I turn to the window again. A cloud of tiny glitter drones rises up around us, beating against our hull like hail.

The car ahead of us shrieks—its lifting fans battered out of shape by the shimmering swarm—then drops from sight.

A moment later, we're in the thick of the cloud. Our pilot kills the engines, saving the blades from tearing themselves to pieces.

We're falling.

I look around for a bungee jacket, a way out.

"Smart-matter crashbags," the city of Diego tells me. "You're safe."

I'm not.

Courage. More Steadfast.

The soldiers around us are already braced for impact. But before I can ready myself, the car rebounds beneath us. Like we're all inside a giant bungee jacket.

The lifting fans are dead silent . . .

Something's grabbed us. Like the magnetic dish the rebels used to bring me and Col safely down onto the Cobra train.

A trickle of panic cuts through my feels.

"He thinks I'm Rafi. He wants me alive."

"He knows the political costs of a slaughter. Don't worry, Frey. We have twenty-four Specials, and three other cities are responding."

"They won't make it in time!" My hand closes around an imaginary weapon. "He knew which way we were coming. He'll know exactly how many soldiers you have! Give me a knife!"

The city avatar straps on body armor. "Calm yourself, Frey."

I don't.

The car bumps to a halt—we're on the ground now. Trapped. My battle frenzy is boiling in me, spinning, with nowhere to go.

"Let me *fight* him. Please!"

The city of Diego stares at me a moment, with the same expression they wore during our conversations about my upbringing, about ethics and philosophy.

Finally they nod and draw a pulse knife from their armor.

It's the one Boss X gave me. Fully charged.

"You kept it," I say.

"This is what being trusted feels like." The city hands me the knife. "Try not to get killed."

FIREFIGHT

"Two teams, going left and right," the commander says. "Doors opening in ten, nine . . ."

We're about to burst out, to escape this car before the enemy can surround our landing zone.

I feel conspicuous in my light armor, no helmet. The Diego Specials are all in powered exoskeletons, two and a half meters tall. The city's avatar and I stick out like a pair of—

Its face has changed. Still that smooth complexion, almost too perfect to be lifelike . . . but now it looks like me.

"A little diversion," they say. "In case they *are* trying to kill you."

My skins crawls. "Thanks?"

The jump doors fly open, and we storm out into the sunlight.

My fireteam of six breaks left across the rugged ground, toward a copse of trees. I can barely keep up with the Specials, carried in huge leaps by the servomotors in their armored legs. The other team takes cover behind the car, ready to fire on anyone who shoots at us.

The city avatar stays close to me. Sniper bait.

Running hard across broken terrain, my body sings. Too long in that cell, too many days without a stand-up fight. Some logic-missing piece of me believes that with a pulse knife in my hand, there's no way my father can win.

I let that part swell to fill the rest of me.

My own courage mixes with my feels.

We hit the cover of the trees without taking any fire. The brush is dense and full of thorns, scraping at my body armor like fingernails.

We hunker here, watching the other fireteams move into position. They scatter across the landscape, half a dozen of four Specials each. The city AI must be in command—the fire zones interlock perfectly.

I can hear the distant surf from the coast, a few klicks away.

Still no shooting.

"Doesn't look like your father wants a bloodbath," the city says. "Perhaps diplomacy has its uses."

"For him it does. It makes people drop their guard."

We wait. Still nothing—they're watching us. Or watching *me*, trying to figure out which twin I am. Of course, with the Diego avatar wearing my face, they might think both of us are here.

That takes an orbital nuke off the table, at least.

A sudden whistling fills the air, like screamer fireworks. Then I see them—a swarm of projectiles streaking at us. Hand-size drones, weaving in random patterns, leaving tiny trails of light blue smoke behind them.

"Prep for gas," the city avatar says. The Specials reach up to seal their helmets.

I pull the rebreather hood out of my armor, covering my head. Then, in case it's blister gas, I pull my gloves on.

The city doesn't bother. Apparently, they don't breathe.

The Specials open fire. The darting little drones fall in droves—only one makes it into our little copse of trees.

I throw my knife, turning it into metal fragments.

But more are coming. Swarms are lifting up from the grass, spread across the field of battle like land mines. Our attackers have prepared this spot carefully.

The Specials open fire again—this time fully automatic. A head-splitting roar, like the air ripping open around us.

Every one of the drones falls to the ground.

There's a pause, my ears ringing in the silence. The birds have fled, and the surf sounds a thousand klicks away.

"Is that all?" the city of Diego says. "Your father seems to have underestimated us."

"I doubt it," I say through the mask, shaking my head. None of it feels right, this careful attack. No soldiers shooting at us, just remotes.

More drones come.

The Specials' rifles roar back to life, cutting them down. Bullet casings rain to on the forest floor, a glittering carpet of metal. I can smell the gunfire through my mask.

Then I see it—

"They're making you use up all your ammo! Stop shooting! It's just gas!"

The city avatar glances at me, then nods. All at once, the firing stops.

The drones keep coming.

"We hope you're right, Frey," the city says. "If these drones can do anything else . . ."

The first wave reaches us. They swarm the camp, whirl around us, filling the trees with light blue smoke. The Specials stand impervious in their armor.

But the drones don't explode, or stab us with needles. They fly until their smoke runs out, then crash to the ground, expended.

"Interesting," the city says. "Your father has learned discretion."

I shake my head. "He'll hit us hard soon enough."

One of the Specials points at the ground—a bright red spot drifts across the litter of bullet casings. Then two more.

Laser sights.

Snipers.

The city avatar and I jump behind cover. Our four Specials don't bother—their armor's tougher than the thickest tree. They scan for the source of the lasers, then open fire again, spraying at the high ground above us.

No return fire comes.

"This is still about ammo!" I yell through my mask. "They want us defenseless!"

The Diego avatar shrugs. "Shreve isn't the only city with orbital forces. The rest of us have been preparing. Backup will be here soon."

The rest of us? It's still head-spinning that a dozen city AIs think it's a good idea to put *me* in charge of Shreve.

The red spots on the ground flicker off one by one—the Specials are hitting their targets. And no one's firing at us.

What if there are no snipers, just cheap drones with lasers on them?

We haven't seen a single enemy soldier.

"Incoming," the fireteam commander yells, pointing to the sky.

"Hold fire," the city avatar says. "They're friendly."

Streaks of light crisscross the clouds, then the long shapes of drogue chutes flutter open. The payloads look big—heavy orbital drones.

Now we're going to see some shooting.

The drones crack out of their reentry shields, bristling with weapons. I can count the combat livery of four different cities.

For once, my father's been met with more brute force than he can handle.

A spindly white strand reaches up from the hills above us, wrapping itself around one of the drones. It drops, intact but powerless.

Then I see something odd—a squirrel, frightened by all the gunfire, scampering past on a branch, somehow immune to the knockout gas.

I pull off my hood and take a shallow breath. Then a deeper one.

Nothing. The smoke was only for show. No one's shooting at us. Even the orbital drones are only being disabled, not destroyed.

And those white strands, just like rebel antiaircraft . . .

A thousand emotions roil in me, the feels I plumbed in captivity echoing all at once. Anger at being left alone in that cell, Languish for the time lost—but none of it as real as the Joy that someone's come for me at last.

"Call off the orbitals!" I squeeze my knife to full pulse. "It's not my father!"

The city looks at me. "What?"

"My friends are rescuing me. My *real* friends!"

And I see it in perfect Focus—the avatar of Diego has all the resources of a city, wardens, an army behind it. A mind incomprehensibly vaster than mine, and a continent-spanning alliance against my father.

Compared to that, my friends are a ragtag collection, almost powerless.

But they're here for *me*.

"Don't take this the wrong way, but I have to go!"

When I start to move, the city avatar reaches out to grab me.

I swing my pulse knife hard and high, cutting the duplicate of myself in half, top to bottom.

The artificial body explodes—smart plastics and muscles, skin and tissues turned into a billowing cloud of mist.

All of us are blinded, but I already know which way to go.

I start running, my blood thrilling in my veins.

RUN

I head uphill as fast as I can.

The Specials are after me, thunderingly fast in their powered exo-skeletons. But heavy armor is massive, clumsy. Like giants trying to catch a butterfly.

Or course, these giants have guns. Maybe they'll decide shooting me is warranted. I just hope the city itself understands.

Steadfast, a long touch of it.

I aim for the high ground, where the trees have been cut to pieces by the Specials' fire. My rescuers must be somewhere up there.

Unless this is all a trick—my father's way of getting me to hand myself over. But a burning certainty runs through me . . .

He's incapable of pretending to be someone else. He lacks the empathy to know what my friends would do.

A shadow looms—an armored pursuer leaping high across the sun. I swerve hard as the Special crashes to the ground, the suit's servo-motors whining. A hand swats out, barely missing me.

No shooting yet. That's good . . .

Another armor suit hurtles past me, smashing a tree to splinters as it lands.

There's one on either side now, two more coming up from behind. They're herding me toward a barrier of fallen trees, trying to trap me there.

I head straight toward it, cycling my pulse knife. At the last second, I jump as high as a can—the knife's magnetics carry me up and over.

One of the Specials tries to leap the obstacle and trips, rolling after me like a metal boulder. As the armored form rolls past, my knife lashes out, buzzing through the leg-servos. The exoskeleton wobbles to its feet, stumbling at it lunges at me, its metal hamstrings cut.

I let the knife carry me away again. But its charge won't last long.

My goal is just ahead—the hill where the lasers came from. Nothing's left but a clearing of splintered trees.

I don't have a plan, except getting there in one piece.

The three remaining Specials are closing in behind. I whirl to face them, flourishing my knife.

One dodges in and swipes at me, the powered fist connecting with my shoulder. It's like being clipped by a passing truck, and it sends me sprawling in the grass.

I spring to my feet, letting the knife lift me up and away. The charge light still shines green, but carrying my weight must be crushing its battery.

I land just past my pursuers and run for the clearing.

"Boss X?" I cry out, breathless. "Col?"

No answer. Just my heart throbbing in my injured shoulder.

We never even saw any attackers. What if those sniper drones were controlled from another hilltop? Or from twenty klicks away . . .

But this was the only clue I had.

I finally reach the clearing and search the tree line for any sign.

Nothing but lightning in the sky, the orbital drones firing down. The antiaircraft has gone silent.

The three Specials crash into the clearing, surrounding me. My knife can carry me two more times, maybe three.

But my pursuers will just keep coming.

The knife buzzes in my hand, and I crouch low among the splintered trees. Like a mammal fighting dinosaurs, beasts larger and clumsier than me.

The Specials close in slowly, wary of my knife now. They spread out, keeping my attention darting back and forth. One solid punch and I'll be unconscious.

"Put the weapon down," the fireteam commander says.

"This isn't my father! They're trying to rescue me!"

"Our mission is to take you to Diego, Frey."

"These are *your* allies too!" I shout. "That's why they're not shooting back!"

He doesn't answer that. Just walks slowly toward me.

"Frey, let us protect you."

"Stay away or I'll—"

Just in time, I hear another Special's servos whining. I spin around

287

as a giant hand swings down. But I roll underneath the blow. My knife flashes out to cut her ankle . . .

I miss.

The lumbering armor turns to face me, the woman glaring though her helmet visor—angry, righteous. She reaches for me.

I have to cut her hand off.

Then a hissing fills the clearing. Strands of white shoot from the edge of the forest, filling my vision. It covers all of us, wrapping around the Specials, the tree stumps, and me, writhing like a living thing.

Rebel antiaircraft, strong enough to immobilize anything—but I have a pulse knife.

It buzzes in my hand, shredding at the white goo. The strands entrapping me turn hot, some chemical reaction triggered by the knife. The smart matter squirms furiously for a moment, then falls apart, sloughing to the ground like wet sand.

The Specials are covered in white, helpless in their powered armor. But there are still orbital drones in the sky.

I jump free from the writhing white strands, letting the knife carry me one last time. At the edge of the clearing, my charge light starts flashing yellow.

Exhausted, defenseless and alone, I raise the knife and cry at the wild—

"Whoever you are, just *show* yourselves!"

Seconds later, two hoverboards come gliding from the trees.

Col and Zura, more silhouettes behind them.

House Palafox is here to rescue me.

COL

At first, there isn't time to talk.

We ride hard away from the battle, letting the orbitals destroy what's left of the Vic's automated launchers. The sky lights up behind us, thunder ringing through the mountains, but nothing follows. Diego's backup was ready for a firefight, not to chase a dozen fast hoverboards through the wild.

They've brought one for me, Victorian military-issue, solid and familiar under my feet. I ride next to Col, at arm's length, close enough to reach for him on empty straightaways.

His little brother, Teo, is here too, and Dr. Leyva—their base back in the Amazon must be nearly empty.

Or maybe this is all that's left of the Victorian army.

We don't slow down till we're across the Sea of Cortez and into the mountains on the other side. Cactus and rocky ground, giant wind-power blades spinning on the ridges. The canyons here are steep and shadowed—we're hidden at last from the sky.

My hand keeps going to my wrist, but I don't know what to feel.

There's something in Col's eyes, his gaze wrapping and unwrapping my heart. Like I've changed so much that he's not quite sure who I am.

"Don't like the haircut?" I finally ask.

He smiles. "Just want to look at you. It's been a while."

Our boards drift to a halt, letting the rest of the Victorians go ahead.

When I reach out, my hand is trembling. Col takes it and gently pulls us together. Our boards touch, steadying against each other in the breeze.

"You came for me," I say. The words sound small out here in the wild.

"Sorry it took so long."

We draw closer. Our lips meet—and the world opens up around us, every sound suddenly clear, the wind sharp on my face and hands. The smell of the desert fills me, sage and stone, like it rained here not long ago.

Like the wild is ours.

Those six Col-missing weeks are over at last.

When we pull apart, he looks back the way we've come.

"The hard part was finding you," he says. "Trin told us Diego wardens had taken you into custody. We got in contact with the city, but they wouldn't even confirm they were keeping you."

"I was the glue for an alliance against my father." A sigh slips from me. "Looks like I've messed that up."

A dozen cities were poised to take on Shreve, and I've thrown a bomb into their plans. What seemed so clear in the heat of battle suddenly looks strategy-missing.

I almost reach for a touch of Focus, but not with Col watching.

"We figured it was politics," he says. "Free cities don't disappear people for vandalism."

"Maybe you shouldn't have come for me. They were going to take my father out!"

He squeezes my hands. "That doesn't give them the right to use you."

"But it's what you wanted—more cities fighting Shreve."

"That doesn't make it okay," he says. "They locked you up! Trin hired lawyers, and they got nowhere—Diego said there was *no legal person* with your name in custody, like you weren't even real. We contacted every prisoner to come out of the system, and no one had seen or heard of you. It was like they'd erased you, Frey!"

His hands are shaking, his voice breaking with anger.

I almost tell him to reach for Calm.

"But maybe I should have stayed. We made a deal, Diego and I."

"A deal?" Col shakes his head. "After a month in isolation? That's coercion. You don't owe Diego anything."

I stare at him, a tangle of wires sparking in my chest.

Coercion. Isolation.

All those long nights of Patience—I never asked myself *why* Diego kept me all alone in a cell for weeks. I never questioned being cut off from everyone, hidden away.

That's how I grew up, after all.

But maybe they wanted me to feel lonely, abandoned. On the way here, when I asked Diego why they'd used an avatar . . .

To make a connection, Frey, to build trust. Humans are hardwired to bond with pretty faces.

"Diego said they wanted to be friends," I murmur.

"They're just the enemy of our enemy," Col says, taking me in his arms again. "We're your friends."

I hold him tight, breathing deep against his warmth, his weight. I almost reach for Home, to make it perfect. But not yet.

"They tested me," I whisper. "To see if I'm like . . . him."

"Like your father?" Col's harsh laughter spills out across the desert.

The sound of it, his certainty of what I am, makes me kiss him again. We stand there on our boards, the raw wind swirling around us.

And for a moment I feel safe.

Until he says, "If only you'd stayed with me. Or come south after the quake."

I pull away.

The other Vics have noticed us falling back, and they've swung around, forming a wide circle around me and Col. It's just his soldiers protecting him, but it feels like an audience.

It takes me a moment to speak again.

"I couldn't leave, Col. A hundred thousand people died. A million lost everything. That wasn't something I could walk away from. I saw a city fall."

"You saw *my* city fall."

"Victoria is still standing. Paz is all jagged edges and missing people. I thought about going to you every second, but my fight was there. Can you understand that?"

"I see the logic." He looks away, defeated. "But I don't see how logic matters when you're gone."

As I try to answer, the day of the quake comes rushing back. Essa tending to the wounded, passing out water bottles, while her little brother lay crushed beneath a pile of stones.

It was logical. But it didn't make sense.

My hand moves toward my feels again, and I stop myself again.

And wonder . . . those first nights in the aftermath, nights of Melancholy, of Languish and Grief—what if missing Col would've been too much to bear without my feels? Maybe I would have left Shatter City and run to him.

But thanks to these faces on my wrist, I stayed.

Maybe it was like walking on my broken ankle—and now the Painless is wearing off.

"I couldn't be in two places, Col."

"What matters is, you're here now," he says, taking my hand again. "Turns out, what's left of the Victorian army needs you."

I look around. So it's true—there's only these eleven left, out of thirty.

"Was there a battle?"

Col shakes his head. "Just people giving up. We haven't had a win in so long, it was hard to keep hope. But rescuing you helps."

"Rescuing me?" It's sinking in for the first time. "All those drones, all that firepower—to save *me*?"

"Boss Charles gave us the antiaircraft," Col says. "But yeah, we emptied our stores."

I almost laugh. "Must have been tricky, talking Zura into this."

"She planned the whole thing," he says. "Dr. Leyva was on board too."

"What am I missing? Is this about . . . me and you?"

Col takes a hesitant breath.

And my heart splits. The Palafoxes need their fairy tale, now more than ever.

Col wants to use me too.

"You still want me to be Rafi," I say.

"Never, Frey. I'm sorry I ever asked you to consider that." He looks away. "If I hadn't been so thoughtless on the train, you might not have stayed in Paz."

It isn't true—I had to look for Rafi. But I don't argue.

"And frankly," he says, "it doesn't matter anymore if the world loves you and me. We can't beat your father with a fairy tale. We have to do it ourselves."

I take a relieved breath, my emotions spinning. This would be much easier if I could use my feels. Maybe I should stick to practicalities.

"Okay. What's the plan?"

"An army of rebel crews are getting together on the east coast. They're going to break into a place called the Iron Mountain. We want to join them."

"The Iron Mountain?" A little shock goes through me. "Those were the Paz AI's last words, during the quake. But the rebels didn't know what it meant, except for some old saying."

"They do now. Turns out it's a real mountain, hollowed out back in the Rusty days. Whatever's inside, the rebels think it can force your father out of Paz. We don't have the details—they don't really trust us." He takes my shoulders. "But they'll trust you."

"Ah," I say softly. So Zura and Leyva still think I'm useful. "Boss X is in charge."

"No. Another rebel you know."

"Charles? Andrew Simpson Smith?"

Col hesitates, then slowly shakes his head.

"Not them. Boss Frey."

VICS

"*Boss* Frey?" I mutter again. "She's only been a rebel for six weeks!"

The Vics don't answer. Maybe because it's the hundredth time I've said these words.

I can't believe it. Rafi hates camping, loves beautiful clothes, and knows nothing about combat. And now she's in charge of a rebel crew?

It's the most sense-missing thing I've ever heard.

We're eating dinner, hidden in a steep canyon, the sky nothing but a sliver of stars above us. After a month of emergency rations, the food is glorious. Self-heating currynoods with chunks of fresh meat—a pronghorn brought down by Col's bow.

But the words *Boss Frey* keep rolling around in my head, cutting through my Joy.

"Rafia having her own crew isn't *that* weird," Teo says. "I was Boss Teo for three whole days."

Laughter travels around the circle. Before the war, Teo's mother gave him the family codebook to keep. For the first few days of fighting, he used it to order Vic units around, everyone thinking he was Aribella Palafox.

"You were very convincing," I say, and take a drink of bubbly. We're all sharing a bottle to celebrate my rescue, but what I need is to sneak a longer touch of Joy.

Teo beams at me. I haven't seen Col's little brother since the night before the Battle of Shreve. He looks older now, more serious. He's grown up fast in the jungle.

"Trin sends greetings, by the way," he says. "She wants to interview you for her feed."

"Typical. An hour after the towers fell, I found her taking a shower, getting ready to go on camera." I imitate her voice. "'Earthquakes are so *dusty*!'"

Teo shakes his head. "I can't believe she stayed in Paz so long. Trin acts all adult, but her parents must've been brain-rattled."

I glance at Col. "It's hard to walk away, when a city takes a hit like that."

"We know," he says.

It cuts both ways, of course—he and his brother lost a city too.

"But surely the Pazx are holding up," Dr. Leyva says. "They've got those things to keep them happy."

Something about his expression, and maybe the bubbly inside me, makes me angry.

"You mean feels?" I pull up my sleeve.

They all stare.

"Frey," Col says softly. "Are those . . ."

"Got them my first night in Paz. A misunderstanding."

"You got surge by *mistake*?" His dark eyes gleam. "Why didn't you get them taken out?"

"There was an earthquake. And then . . ."

With the Vics all looking at me, it's too complicated to explain. They're soldiers, trained to deal with stress and exhaustion, pain and loss. They probably think the Pazx are weak for using feels.

"And then I needed them."

"Of course," Col says. "I'm so sorry, Frey."

"Don't be. They helped." I turn to Leyva. "And no, people in Paz aren't happy. A hundred thousand of their friends and relatives are dead. What they are is *grieving*."

He stiffens a little, examining his food. "Some people need help, I suppose."

I grab the bottle of bubbly back from Zura—and change the subject.

"How far away is this Iron Mountain?"

"Other side of the continent," Col says. "On boards, avoiding cities, it'll take . . . three weeks?"

I frown. "On boards? What happened to your hovercars?"

"We traded them for the autolaunchers and drones we used to rescue you," Teo says.

"You traded away your fleet for me?"

Zura retrieves the bottle from my hands. "Armored cars are hard to maintain."

"And what's inside the Iron Mountain can save Paz," Leyva says.

"Save Paz?" I look at Col. "So Victoria *isn't* the only thing you care about."

"I fight for you," he says firmly. "And I guess for Paz too now. We have to beat your father *somewhere*. My people need a win."

I wonder if he means his people back in Victoria, or the ones around him now. They can desert him just as easily as the others.

But at least the rebels are keeping Col informed. Maybe they haven't completely given up on him.

"Did Boss X tell you where to find me?" I ask.

Teo shakes his head. "Your friend Essa did, with a little help from the local resistance. After you got arrested, they put full-time hover-cams on all the Diego buildings. A few days ago, one spotted you trying to escape."

"Huh." At least my little adventure with Primero wasn't a complete waste.

"A day later, Diego moved a bunch of armored cars into that building, and Essa figured it was to take you someplace more secure." Teo smiles. "That's when she called us."

My Joy spikes a little inside me. Maybe I have more allies than I realized.

"The route was easy to guess," Zura says. "Straight up the coast toward Diego."

"Still. You put this rescue together in *three days*?"

Col nods. "You're important to us, Frey."

"To fairy tales," Dr. Leyva says, raising the bottle. "And to being there when the rebels take the Iron Mountain."

One by one, I look at them. Col, who loves me. Leyva, who wants a seat at the rebel table. Zura, who needs a win to keep her soldiers from deserting.

The Vics are a patchwork of motives and obsessions, not an army. Just like everyone keeps telling me.

All I can say is "Guess I owe you Vics one."

"Two, technically," Teo says. "Don't forget that time we saved you from being forced into marriage with a terrible human being!"

Col punches him.

I smile. "Hey, that marriage was *my* idea."

"Under duress," Teo mutters, rubbing his shoulder.

"Speaking of being forced into things," Col says to me. "We haven't even asked yet—do you *want* to come with us? It's a way to help Paz, hurt your father, and find Rafia."

"My sister, the rebel," I murmur. Since leaving home three months ago, I've only seen her for a fleeting hour after the Battle of Shreve. With all that's happened, I'm not sure I even know her anymore, or understand why she ran away and stole my name. "Of course I'm coming, Col. But you missed one reason."

I take his hand.

"I want us fighting together again."

"Me too." He smiles at last. "Plus, I'm dying to finally meet your sister."

PART 4

IRON
MOUNTAIN

Opportunities multiply as they are seized.

—Sun Tzu

CONTINENTAL DIVIDE

It takes three weeks to cross the continent.

The great western desert is the cruelest part of the trip—baking heat in the day, chilly at night. No water except what we can carry. Sand in our teeth, our clothes, our food. The roar of lifting fans thrumming in our ears.

We reach the Rockies at last, and find rivers brimming with snowmelt—clean water to drink, fish to catch, and metal deposits for our magnetics to grab on to.

But it's a cold climb into the mountains. Snow still blankets the slopes, and the air grows thinner by the hour. The Vic army has never ventured this far north before—our body armor is unheated. We don't build fires, not daring to attract attention.

Col and I keep each other warm. Every night, I tell him again about watching the towers of Paz come down. About life in the ruins. About the sound of weeping in the night, the way the whole city grieved as one.

For the first time, I understand how much he must miss his home. Victoria had a thousand customs I never had the chance to learn, all flattened now by my father's occupation. A disaster has struck Col's city too, a slow-motion shattering of its soul.

He can't escape that as easily as I ran away from Shreve.

Sometimes I still wonder if I should have stayed in captivity, giving the alliance of free cities good reason to kill my father. Maybe Victoria would be liberated sooner that way.

Or maybe the attempt would've only thrown the world into more chaos.

Descending from the Rockies, we hit the Great White Plains, where the weed is triumphant. The white flowers cover the fields here. They clog the rivers, strangling all but the oldest forests.

The Plains are where the weed began. A Rusty scientist, trying to make a rare orchid easier to grow, accidentally created the most relentless plant in history. Immune to drought, to storms, to poison—and, worst of all, to competition from other living things. Even the cities here exist in a state of siege, their farmlands covered by vast domes to protect them from the orchid's spores.

The Plains pass beneath us, a thousand klicks of white. We're blinded in the daylight, haunted at night by phantoms in our aching eyes.

It takes twenty days to reach the eastern mountains. Older than the Rockies, they roll slowly into being, ripples from the clashing continental plates.

Here in the east, the wounds of Rusty civilization run deep. Ancient rail beds scar the land, crumbling factories stain the rivers with rust. But nothing astonishes us like the strip mines—whole mountains cut down, their metal hearts ripped out by the Rusties' unimaginable machines.

The wild has begun to reclaim the strip-mine craters, but their slopes are still streaked with unchecked erosion, their topsoil swarmed by invader species.

Col explains the broken biology of it all, a slow-burning anger in his voice.

"How the Rusties survived so long, I have no idea."

"They used to die of sadness," I say.

He just frowns, like that's too much to believe.

Our first night in the eastern mountains, we camp in the belly of a strip mine.

We're in the deep wild, far enough from any city to make a fire, so Zura and her Specials build it big. It sends thick smoke over the crater lip and into the night sky, a black elbow arcing west with the mountain breeze.

Basking in its warmth, I pull off my body armor.

Col glances at the rows of faces on my arm.

"Go ahead and ask," I say.

A shrug. "Leyva says there's one for love."

"He means Cherish." I hold out my wrist in the bonfire's light, showing Col the beaming face with hearts for eyes.

"Okay. What does Cherish feel like?"

"An echo of the real thing—like looking at old pictures of my sister. Like missing you."

He frowns. "You used a feel to *miss me*?"

"I used a feel *because* I missed you—like when you're sad, you listen to a sad song to sharpen the emotion. But Cherish wasn't really my thing." I hold out my arm again. "Melancholy was better."

He stares at the face, its closed eyes, a single tear. "Those two faces are the opposite. Do I make you happy or sad?"

"When you're not around—both? Emotions aren't supposed to make sense, Col. What matters is feeling *something*. All those days without you, in that cell, it was too easy to shut down. Maybe that sounds sense-missing."

"No, it doesn't." Col looks away into the dark. "Sometimes I black out what happened to my family. Not deep down, but on the surface of my thoughts. I'll wake up not thinking about it, and make it till noon, or maybe even nightfall, before I remember."

He's talking about the first day of the war. His mother, his grandmother—my father's missile bearing down on their home.

"Even then, it's like an echo. Like I've had that same sadness too many times to feel it anymore." He reaches out, his fingers brushing my arm. "So which feel would you recommend for that?"

I point at Grief.

Col raises an eyebrow. "Looks like a littlie drew it."

He's right—those gushing tears, two rivers streaming down the round face, are silly compared to what they represent.

"No one knows where the pictures came from, except that they're very old. Like the feelings themselves, I guess."

He looks away. "I don't cry in front of my soldiers, or even Teo. It's hard enough keeping their morale up. But sometimes I wonder if that changes what's going on inside me."

"It *does* change you, Col. Take it from someone who hid her emotions her whole life." I hold out my arm. "These help, even if I used them too much sometimes."

He takes my arm gently.

"It's easier for me when you're with me, Frey. Everything is sharper, good and bad. I don't want buttons on my arm—I want you."

My breath hitches.

"You have me," I say.

The crackle of the fire fills the crater, the steady east wind murmuring in the brush. There are a thousand more things I have to tell him, but something tugs at my awareness—something missing.

"Do you hear that?"

Col listens, then shakes his head.

I gesture for silence, then point at the little face with intense eyes—Focus. At my touch, it flows into me, that clarity, the night sharpening around us.

My ears tingle.

"The birds," I whisper.

They've gone silent around us.

Almost imperceptibly, Col nods. He leans back, like he's stretching. But his eyes scan the darkness. His gaze stops at a point above my head.

"Veron," comes his whisper. "Gone."

A flutter passes through my body.

Corporal Veron, our medic, was on watch on the crater lip behind me. And Specials don't leave their post.

"Good night, Col," I say aloud, and stand.

Pressing Calm, I walk, unhurried, to our tent at the edge of camp. Then I yawn hugely, open the flap, and slip into the camo shielding.

Inside, I move fast—tearing off the rest of my clothes. Sliding on my sneak suit, pulling the mask over my face and hands. Checking that the charge light on my knife is green.

A long touch of Vigilance to erase the Calm.

The back of the tent faces away from the bonfire, into the darkness. I slip it open, crawl through and up the slope, all but invisible in my suit.

Past the rim of the crater, the night is overcast, starless. I don't rush, waiting for my vision implants to adjust. Whoever took out Veron must be using stealth tech too—you don't just sneak up on a Special.

Or maybe a sniper got him from a distance . . .

I crawl down the crater's outer slope, into the low trees. Then I make my way around to the east side, where Veron was stationed.

My ears strain for any sound. But here, away from camp, the night is dead silent.

My gloved hand brushes something—a bird, motionless, its body heat flickering in my infrared. A meter away, another glimmer of heat turns out to be a sleeping field mouse.

Knockout gas. But real this time.

I'm on the windward side, so the gas will be drifting into the crater. I have to warn the others—without tipping off our attackers.

I check the seal on my suit rebreather, then head up the slope, moving fast through the scrubby trees.

A moment later, three silhouettes block my way.

One lies there unmoving—Veron. The other two are seated, looking down at our camp. They're not wearing sneak suits, just rebreather masks.

A tank of compressed gas sits between them, making the barest hissing sound.

The gas must be heavier than air, spilling down into camp, silent and invisible, slowly filling the crater.

I grip my knife, stealing closer. The brush is thinner here near the top. But the two silhouettes aren't facing me.

I slink forward. Four meters away, three . . .

Then one turns—I freeze in the darkness.

She doesn't see me, though. Her eyes are closed.

Her head tips back a little, like she's scenting the air through her mask. Standing there, the wind at my back, in my sneak suit unwashed after three weeks of hard travel, I realize—

She *smells* me.

I bolt forward, pulse knife screaming to life.

She spins to face me, and I see the skins, the leather. They're rebels.

I hesitate in midswing—her foot lashes out as I pass. It connects with my stomach, knocking the breath out of me.

Staggering past, I trip on the gas machine and stumble down the rocky slope. In a flash, both of them are on top of me, my knife hand held fast in someone's grip. My other arm goes up to ward off blows, but they don't hit me.

They pull my sneak suit mask off.

Before I can stop myself, I suck in half a breath.

The world starts spinning. I try to yell and warn the Vics, but there's not enough air in my lungs—and if I breathe more, I'll pass out.

Both of the rebels are staring down at my bare face, wide-eyed.

"Whoops," one says, releasing me.

"Sorry, Boss," the other says. "Didn't know it was you."

REBELS

"So you aren't the boss?" Sussy says. "You're her fancy sister?"

"She's *my* fancy sister," I grumble, pressing Painless. My ribs are still pounding from the kick she landed.

"Rafia," Col says in a warning tone. "Don't be random."

He's right—I can't blow my sister's cover. I have to play my old game again.

But with my bruised ribs and shoulder, and this headache from the knockout gas, it's hard to find the impersonation inside me. Every time the world allows me to be myself, going back gets trickier.

I touch Courage to get the voice right . . .

"I'm Rafia of Shreve. Take us to my sister."

The two rebels look up from their food, uncertain.

We're in the middle of camp, feeding our uninvited guests by the bonfire. Most of the Vics are unconscious around us. Col was smart enough to slip a mask on, and Zura was on watch at the far lip of the crater, too high for the gas to reach. Her cruel, pretty face is making the rebels nervous.

But they're still managing to eat our last spagbol.

"Boss didn't say anything about you coming to visit," Dex says.

"This isn't a family reunion," Col says. "We're here to help with the Iron Mountain."

Both of them freeze.

Then Sussy tries to act casual. "Huh. Where'd you hear about that?"

"Straight from the Paz AI," I say. "Then I told my close personal friend Boss X about it—and *you* heard it from *him*."

Dex nods slowly, X's name winning me some respect.

"Okay." He turns to Col and Zura. "But who are they?"

Col looks annoyed—he's not used to having to introduce himself.

Sussy elbows Dex. "That's Col Palafox, the head Vic. Him and Boss Frey fought together at Shreve. He got captured."

"Oh, right," Dex says, but still looks a little confused. I'm guessing the rebels out here don't watch the feeds a lot.

"Zura fought there too," Col says. "We all did. We're on your side."

"Well, *now* you are," Sussy says with a laugh. "But when you were tearing up Rusty cities for metal, you didn't like us rebels much."

Col just looks away, like he still doesn't like rebels.

"If you had a choice," she goes on, "you'd be back home in your mansion. Not out here with us."

"My mansion is a bomb crater. And I do have a choice—I've been offered sanctuary in seventeen cities." Col gestures disgustedly at her spagbol. "All with decent food. But here I am, out in the wild with you."

Sussy looks down at her bowl. "Hey, I *like* spagbol."

"We're offering to help," Col explains.

"Blood is one thing," Dex says to him. "But Boss is always talking about how you Vics are useless. That's why she ran away."

Zura lets out a low growl. Col looks pleadingly at me.

I'm still not a hundred percent sure why Rafi's out here. Trin's theory, that she's always wanted to become me, has never fully settled in my head. There must have been some tension between her and the Vics—Rafi doesn't like any situation where she's not in charge.

But she won't say no to me.

"Listen," I say. "You know how my sister changes her mind, right? And how she's been asking for help from all over? If you get this wrong, she's going to be mad."

Sussy and Dex share a worried glance. Rafi may be pretending to be me, but it seems she hasn't changed *that* much.

"So why not take us to Frey?" I say. "Let her decide."

Dex gives this a thought, then looks at Sussy.

She sighs. "Guess that's what bosses are for."

The next morning, the two rebels take us all deeper into the mountains. The forest is thicker out here, with old snow lying heavy in the shadows.

More rebels join us along the way, coming to gawk at me, the boss's rich sister. Soon we have a full-fledged escort. Half a dozen crews, all gathering here to take on the Iron Mountain.

Whatever that is.

These are the rebels of the deep wild. No pretty surge—their teeth aren't even straight. Their boards are in dubious states of repair, and most of them aren't wearing crash bracelets.

I really am the fancy one, with my body armor and military hoverboard. But the rebels are more envious of our Vic backpacks—fully waterproof, their magnetic lifters making them light as feathers as we ride.

I wonder how long these rebels have lived out here. Sussy and Dex knew enough woodcraft to sneak up on Veron without suits. They were adept with Col's bow and arrow this morning, bringing down breakfast with a few shots.

Most runaways bring city tech with them—water purifiers, direction finders. But these rebels drink straight from streams and ponds, and navigate by the landmarks and the sun. A few have accents I haven't heard before, some so thick that I have to translate for the Vics.

It's logic-missing that Rafi joined a crew this far out in the wild.

How did she become their boss?

The sun is high when Sussy finally brings our party to a halt, halfway up a mountainside.

At first, I think we're just stopping to eat and pee. But the rebels spring into action, scraping away scrub and pine branches to reveal an opening the rock. It's four meters across, three high, and the rotted-away ties of an old railroad disappear into its depths.

It's absolutely black inside.

"A mine shaft?" Col asks.

Sussy nods. "The Rusties didn't just strip-mine. They also dug tunnels like you wouldn't believe."

"How deep?" I ask. The air from the mine shaft smells damp and alien to me, like it comes from another universe.

"We haven't got to the bottom yet," Dex says. "Couple klicks, at least."

A shudder goes through me. Two kilometers underground.

For a moment, I wonder if this really is my sister's crew. What if it's just a trap? A way to seal us city folk inside a mountain forever?

But that's just my claustrophobia babbling in my head, like this mine shaft is a mountain-size version of Rafi's broken elevator.

Or maybe I'm nervous about finding answers to all of the questions that have been buzzing in my head.

I reach for my wrist, just enough Calm to settle.

The rebels lead us inside. I expect them to use torches, but they just stride into the darkness. Zura switches on her body armor lights, revealing dozens of hoverboards lined up along the walls.

"Best let your eyes adjust," Dex says.

When Zura turns her lights off again, it's darker than any night in here. Even with my implants, there's nothing in infrared but the bobbing shapes of body heat.

But as we go deeper, a cool greenish glow slowly builds around us.

The walls are covered with little squiggles of light. I stop to look closer at them. This has to be city tech, but I've never seen anything like it.

"What's the power source?"

"Don't know," Dex says. "Whatever worms eat."

"Glowworms?" Col says, leaning in beside me. "They look too bright to be natural."

"Genetic engineering?" Dr. Leyva asks.

"They've always been here, far as we know," Sussy says. "Come on. Boss Frey doesn't like waiting."

Boss Frey. Something starts to pulse through me, dizzy and joyful and nervous-making all at once.

She's stolen my name and made me her heir. She's run away from our fight against my father. She's the closest person to me in the world, and I don't know why she's here or what she's up to.

I don't even know what feel to use.

But at last I'm going to see my sister again.

BOSS FREY

There are diversions along the way. A cave full of hydroponic plants, smelling of roses and latrine nanos. A colony of bats trained to swarm the enemy, in case the lair is ever attacked. A shaft that goes straight down—Dex drops a rock for us and counts to ten before we hear the clatter below.

But then a rumble of voices echoes along the stone corridors like a distant waterfall, and my skin prickles. My sister is close.

Col takes my hand. "Are you okay?"

"Yeah." My voice sounds shivery, but I decide not to reach for more Calm. Part of me wants to be ready for anything.

The narrow sides of the mineshaft open wide, out into a natural cavern. Stalactites loom like dangling knives. A mineral smell makes the cool air heavy, and glowworms cover the ceiling like a sky of green stars.

At least a hundred rebels throng the cavern. My sister has invited all the assembled crews to witness our reunion.

317

The crowd parts for us—and there she is, splayed across a chair carved from the stone of the mountain itself, a throne.

And at last I understand why she's the boss.

Same as any rebel, Rafi is wearing skins and furs. But they fit her perfectly. Her jacket glitters with baubles of amber, quartz, the bones of small animals. Feathers shimmer in her hair.

Regal and composed, she's the product of all her years of training, a lifetime spent preparing to rule.

Maybe this is why she picked a crew so deep in the wild—anyone who watched the gossip feeds would spot Rafi's style instantly. Her imperious expression, her posture, all of it screams first daughter of Shreve.

When she stands to greet us, the room falls silent all the way to its corners.

Rafi lets the tension build. I can't tell whether she's happy to see me or angry that I'm here, threatening to bring down her charade.

I reach for Steadfast. I don't know my own sister anymore.

Her face breaks into a smile.

"Rafi!" She crosses the room, wraps me in her arms.

Our embrace is hard and long, as rough as a hug from Boss X. She feels different in my arms now—leaner, stronger, like she's the bodyguard and I'm the princess.

But it's all part of her spell, an illusion.

Pulling away at last, she turns to Col, beaming again.

"Col Palafox!"

They hug like old comrades-in-arms, even though they've never met before.

It's soul-rattling. A lifetime of pretending to be Rafi hasn't prepared me for *her* pretending to be *me*.

All eyes dart back and forth between us, as if the rebels are amazed to have two copies of their boss in one room.

She lets Col go, turns to look me up and down. My shorn hair, my dusty body armor. "I've missed you, big sister."

I draw myself taller, trying to force the old impersonation to settle. I've been in my own skin for so long, the scrutiny of this crowd feels like more than I can stand.

"I've missed you too, Frey. We have a lot to talk about. Perhaps someplace private?"

"Of course." She smiles, glances at Col. "But are we planning a battle? Or a wedding?"

A murmur goes through the crowd.

A wedding? Then it clicks—if Col is still engaged to the boss's sister, he's almost as good as crew. The whole point of this performance is to build trust between the rebels and the Vics.

Rafi is still Rafi. Everything has a purpose.

And suddenly this is easy again.

"We have a city to save, little sister," I say. "But after that, a wedding out here in the wild might be . . . diverting."

Another stir passes through the cavern. Behind my sister, Sussy's eyes have gone wide in the gloom.

They may not have the feeds here, but even rebels need this—the glamour, the gossip, all the things my sister was born to bestow.

"Diverting indeed." My sister reaches out, and a young rebel hands her a flask. "The Smoke lives!"

As the cheer goes up, people start passing out bottles. Suddenly a bash is taking form around us—pure Rafi.

"Get X and Yandre," she orders the boy who gave her the flask. "The other bosses too. We'll meet in the Spider Room in half an hour."

The names hit me like a touch of Calm. Boss X is here, and Yandre, and maybe more old friends.

But then I wonder—why aren't they here now? A hundred rebels in this room, and not a single familiar face among them.

Rafia of Shreve leaves nothing to chance. So why weren't my friends invited?

And with that question comes another:

Why don't I trust my own sister anymore?

SPIDER ROOM

The Spider Room isn't full of spiders.

It's a junction with eight tunnels heading off in all directions, some climbing away, some slanted downward—like the legs of a tarantula in midstride.

My sister claps her hands. Artificial lights pop on, harsh and squint-making after the soft glow of the worms. An old wooden table fills the chamber, eight chairs around it.

The space is much smaller than the cavern, but it's just me, Col, and my sister.

At last we're face-to-face, no audience. No need to lie.

And the first thing Rafi says is—

"What *happened* to your hair?"

I stare at her. "An earthquake."

"Of course, Frey. But you're *me* now." She reaches up and fingers my ragged haircut in disbelief. "There are standards to uphold."

"Are you kidding, Rafi? I've crossed the continent to see you, and you're talking about my *hair*?"

"Frey," she says coolly, "do you even know why I'm here?"

The words make me shrink, and suddenly I'm her little sister again. Like she's scolding me for a dropped line in a speech or a fumbled introduction on a receiving line.

"To get away from me," I say, my fingers itching for more Courage. "You left me."

"*I* left *you*?" Rafi laughs bitterly. "You were the one who put on Daddy's choker. We were about to escape, together at last. There I was, the first moments of real freedom in my whole life, and you vanished! You left me with outcasts and barbarians—without a sister, when I most needed you!"

She looks at Col, her eyes flashing.

"All for some boy you'd met a few weeks before."

What she's saying hits me all at once, a stone from the sky.

The night of the battle, I was supposed to leave with the rest of them. But then Col was captured. I didn't give any warning, just let the rest of them fly off without me. I put on Rafi's dress, the bomb collar . . .

And left my sister to fend for herself. With no one to guide her but rebels, who hated everything she represents, and the rudderless Victorians.

Rafi turns away from us, staring into the darkness past our little puddle of light. "As you can see, I have adapted to your neglect. But now you're trying to wreck this. These rebels are *dangerous*, Frey. Do you want them to find out their new boss is a fraud?"

"We're here to help," Col says firmly.

"And *you*." She turns to him again. "In another week, I'll have two dozen crews here. An alliance of rebels is shaky—the last thing I need is Vics making them nervous. That's why I left you behind!"

I reach for my wrist, but I don't know what to feel.

I was raised to protect Rafi, and I disappeared when she most needed me.

Dona Oliver's voice sounds in my head.

But you threw it away for a boy.

One of the feathers in Rafi's hair has come loose and floated to the floor. I bend down to pick it up.

"I'm sorry," I say, offering her the feather. Under the artificial lights, an iridescence limns it. The colors match streaks of dye in her hair.

She takes it from my hand. "From the Amazon, little sister. As valuable as gold."

Everything that brought me to this place—the Iron Mountain, the fall of Paz, the fight against my father—fades away.

I just need to know one thing.

"You knew they were rescuing me, Rafi. Why did you run away? And why keep being *me*? All I ever wanted was my own identity, my own name. Why take that?"

A little snort comes out of her. Her hands slide down her leather dress, touching every beautiful bit of tailoring. "Do I *look* like I'm trying to be you?"

I take a step backward. "But that's what Trin . . ."

"She asked, so I gave her some psycho-babble about my identity. But you know me better than that." Rafi slides the feather back into her hair. "This masquerade has a purpose."

"What is it?" I plead.

"You have to swear not to tell anyone," she says. "Especially not your rebel pals."

"Of course. I just need to know."

"And this boy can keep a secret?"

Col draws himself up taller. "I spent a month pretending that Frey was you. Surrounded by dust, and they never realized."

"True." She gives him an approving nod. "By the way, Col, you didn't make a bad fiancé."

"Thanks," he says. "What's this all about?"

"Our family." Rafi's voice falls lower. "When I was in the jungle, there was an old rebel in Boss Smith's crew. He told me something about Seanan."

Something sparks in my chest, all on its own.

"Your kidnapped brother?" Col asks.

Rafi nods. "There was a second chapter to the story, one our family never knew. After Daddy refused to surrender power, the kidnappers couldn't give Seanan back. But they didn't want to murder a child in cold blood, it turns out."

I lean back against the cool stone wall, suddenly dizzy. "He's still alive?"

"The kidnappers gave him to rebels to raise." Rafi leans closer. "A crew way out here in the wild so Daddy would never find him."

Under my sleeve, I reach for Steadfast.

Seanan's kidnappers were rivals of my father from Shreve. But they must have fought alongside rebels after they lost power, just like Col and his Vics are now.

"These are the wildest rebels on the continent, Frey, the most secretive. Thanks to the Iron Mountain, they're all gathering in one place. What if he's one of them?"

Rafi takes a step forward and wraps her arms around me again. Gently this time, like when we were littlies, after a long day with our separate tutors. Like when she came back from my father and had to be comforted.

Steadfast floods me.

This is the big sister I know. We were born to protect each other.

"There should've been three of us," she says, "not just you and me. And Seanan's a *rebel*, Frey, raised to fight our father. He's the brother we need."

Something settles in my body, like Belong. Like there's always been a missing piece of me, and it's falling into place.

"Why didn't you wait for me in Paz?" I ask. "I would've helped you."

"For him to come to me, I have to be a *famous* rebel, little sister. It would've taken you years to become a boss. But I'm glad you're here now."

She holds me tighter, her voice a whisper.

"Seanan's out here somewhere. And we're going to find him."

BACKUP PLAN

A few minutes later, the others join us in the Spider Room.

Boss X is here, along with Yandre and two bosses I've never met before.

Col and Yandre exclaim at seeing each other again, but X greets me like a mere acquaintance.

"You look well, Rafia of Shreve."

His reserve is for the other bosses' benefit, of course, but right now the deception is too much. Despite my promise to Rafi, I want to tell him everything.

My brother's out here somewhere.

At last I know why the rebels feel like home to me.

I give him one of Rafi's arch smiles. "Hopefully this time around, we won't lose any battles."

"The Smoke lives," he says, his wolfish face unreadable.

We all repeat the words.

Boss X introduces the other bosses, Em and Zachary. They have thick local accents, and their crews live not far away, in Rusty mine shafts like this one.

That's why they're in charge of breaking into the Iron Mountain. They know all about deadly underground gasses, mapping empty chambers with sound charges, not getting killed in rockslides.

"It's about two hundred klicks from here," Yandre explains, spreading a map out on the table. "Originally it was a coal mine. But the Rusties turned it into something else."

"A tomb," Boss Em says. "Like in the saying."

I remember the meeting in Boss X's lair in Paz. *They never die who are buried in the Iron Mountain.* "Who's buried there?"

"Not who. What." Yandre leans back in their chair. "Everyone knows about the Rusties' big mistakes—the wars, the extinctions, the damage to the planet. But their most dangerous creation doesn't get taught in school. They invented a kind of artificial being, legally a person, but not human."

Col frowns. "AIs?"

"Sort of. But these were designed to have no conscience."

"So more like military cyborgs," I say.

"These didn't have bodies, or even processors. They didn't think or feel. They were built of legal contracts, algorithms, documents—so they couldn't be killed or put in jail." Yandre's voice drops a little. "They were called corps."

"Um, okay," I say. "But what were they *for*?"

"Making money," Boss X says with a low growl. "At first, the Rusties controlled them—but eventually it was the other way around.

They didn't answer to people, or even governments. They divided up the world, almost killing it in the process."

Yandre shrugs. "There's a theory that most Rusties didn't really want all those wars, the pollution, the prisons. But the corps did, and they were too powerful to stop."

"So *that's* what's buried in the Iron Mountain?" Col asks. "A bunch of Rusty algorithms?"

Boss Zachary speaks up for the first time. "Not just the code. The Rusties worshipped their corps. They backed up every transaction, every contract. And all the data they harvested. They stole people's lives—their conversations, feed channels, cam records, pings—and built ways to manipulate them based on that information."

"You mean like Shreve?" I say.

"Your father's city has only a million people," Yandre says. "There were nine billion Rusties. Imagine a present-day propaganda team getting hold of all that."

That makes my head spin a little, remembering the city of Diego trying to become my friend. What if it had a database a thousand times larger?

"They stuffed all these records into old mine shafts," Zachary says. "So a corp could be brought back to life after a disaster. A whole mountain full of undead, world-killing data. And somewhere in those stacks, the city of Paz stored a copy of itself."

"Why would it pick this place?" I ask.

Yandre taps with two fingers, zooming the map into detailed topography and schematics. "Because the Iron Mountain lives up to its name. It's a fortress, designed to withstand a nuclear attack, guarded by an army of Rusty war machines. Paz didn't want anyone messing with its backup copy."

"Someone in the city government must have had a password to get in, in case the worst ever happened," Boss X says. "But Paz didn't count on a decapitation strike following an earthquake. We'll have to use brute force."

"Are the Rusty machines still working in there?" Rafi asks.

"The local stories go way back," Boss Em says. "Rebels trying to explore the mountain and disappearing. Lights in the sky at night. Bears triggering guard drones that come out shooting. Back in the pretty regime, this whole area was off-limits."

"But you can't make copies of city AIs," Col says. "The city *is* the program—all those solar arrays and traffic patterns."

"Usually," Yandre says. "Paz was different."

"Right," I say, recalling what Diego told me. "Pazx didn't want their walls and traffic lights snooping on them, so their AI was kept separate from the city. That's why Daddy could kill it so easy—it was all in one place, buried underground."

Rafi looks at me. "Our father told you that?"

"Diego explained it all." I shrug. "It wanted to be friends."

Now they're all staring, like they think I'm kidding.

"Cities like me." I give them one of Rafi's smiles. "One day, I'm getting one of my own."

Col shakes his head. "But Paz's processors were destroyed. Even if we find this backup copy, there's nothing left to run it on."

"Shreve's virus is fixing that," X says. "The whole city's being rebuilt as one big processor—every wall, every wire. We just replace Shreve's spyware with the original."

"The city reborn overnight, with all its ethics and customs," Yandre says. "Everyone knows Paz had some kind of defense plan, a way to drive any occupier out. Shreve will never see it coming!"

My sister sighs. "This is all very interesting. But why do we care?"

Em and Zachary look surprised—I am too. If Rafi wants to find my brother, this mission is the perfect way.

"Two million people are falling to a dictator," X says. "This is their best chance to fight back."

Rafi shrugs. "Are we servants of Paz now?"

"The free cities aren't perfect," Yandre says. "But this is a chance to hurt Shreve, keep Paz free, and destroy a mountain full of Rusty world-killing code!"

"Are you having second thoughts, Boss Frey?" X asks.

"Of course not," my sister says, relenting with a smile. "Just wanted to make sure you were all committed. It's not a game, breaking into a mountain, tangling with three-century-old war machines, and stealing a city-size AI."

The meeting moves on to details then, when and how to strike against the mountain. But I start to wonder how she chose this crew in particular, so close to the Iron Mountain.

And I remind myself what I always knew growing up:

With Rafi, everything is complicated.

RUMORS

Through my field glasses, the Iron Mountain looks like all the others. There are no visible entrances, no signs that humans have ever touched it.

I suppose that's the point. Corp data was meant to be kept safe and secret, like buried treasure.

Our recon party is on a neighboring ridge, seeing our target for the first time with our own eyes. Almost a week since I arrived at Boss Frey's lair, and six days before we attack. We're just waiting for a few more crews to arrive.

Yandre says we need three hundred fighters to take the mountain.

Listening to the rebels' hushed talk, I can tell they have an almost-superstitious fear of what's inside—the strangest, most inhuman of the Rusty legacies. As the saying goes, the corps are still in there, undead algorithms of surveillance and control, waiting to be reborn.

This is a chance to save Paz but also to burn the whole place down.

The clearing around me is full of rebels. Sixty of us on hover-boards, enough to scout the entire mountain. We'll peek into every entrance, using seismic charges to map the tunnels inside.

I touch a little Focus and raise my field glasses, searching faces for any family resemblance.

What if our brother is already here?

He must've had surge, of course. He could be any gender, have any face. But it feels like I would recognize my own brother, somehow.

Rafi thinks he'll make his own way to us, once he hears that we're allies in the fight against our father. This attack will make her the most famous boss of the wildest crew—even if Seanan has sworn off our family forever, he'll be drawn to see her for himself.

She can't imagine someone not wanting to be an heir to notoriety and power. But I can.

A presence looms behind me, and I startle.

"Sorry, X," I say. "You scared me."

Too much Focus. I hit my Neutral feel.

"All this planning is making us jumpy." Boss X waves at the mountain with disgust. "Ancient, crumbling defenses. We could have done this with a dozen good rebels."

"Don't be so sure about that." I hand him the field glasses. "My father destroyed Paz with one old Rusty weapon."

He shrugs. "Overconfidence is underrated."

"That doesn't even make sense."

"Think about it harder; you'll see it does." X raises the glasses to his face, pulling them apart for his wide-set eyes. "When you wait too long for a fight, boredom breeds rumors and discontent."

I frown. "Anything specific?"

"Some of us are wondering about your sister. Why she's out here."

Something coils tighter inside me. I've wanted to explain everything to X a hundred times, but my promise to Rafi still stands.

I sneak a little touch of Calm. "What do you mean?"

He lowers the glasses, his weather-worn eyes meeting mine. "When did you tell her about the Iron Mountain?"

"I didn't. Until last week, we hadn't seen each other since the Battle of Shreve."

"And yet she arrived here two months ago—something of a coincidence." He lowers his voice. "Almost as if she was sent here to watch over it."

A familiar flicker of doubt goes through me, but I shake my head.

"Yeah, I know. But it's just a coincidence. No one thinks she's working for my father, do they?"

"No, because they think she's *you*. But if they find out she's the heir to Shreve . . ." Boss X looks around at the preparations. Scout drones are being tested, sounding charges armed. "Things will get ugly."

"That won't happen. My sister and I have been fooling people for a long time."

"True," he says. "But Boss Smith's crew joins us in a few days— they know which of you is which. They'll ask the same questions my crew has."

He waits, expecting me to tell him more.

And I realize that I have to give X at least part of the truth.

"It's not really a coincidence," I say. "Rafi chose this place for the same reason the Rusties did—it's the deep wild, the perfect place to hide something."

"What, exactly?"

I look away. The rebel son of a dictator.

Back to lies. "Herself. She was sick of being Rafi. She wanted to be me."

"And yet she's very much Rafia of Shreve. The way she dresses. Throwing the *best* parties every night. That's not hiding."

"Because she's . . ." I reach for my wrist again, needing my Calm, but X gently places a hand on my arm.

"Talk to me without those, Frey."

I swallow. "They were an accident."

"Yet you use them all the time," he says. "When you think no one's watching. Especially when you need to lie."

He turns to face me, his eyes looming, lupine and huge. Freezing me like prey.

"You have every right to lie to your own heart," X says. "But you need to stop lying to me."

Something tears in me. You don't lie to crew.

I'd thought Boss X hadn't noticed my feels. Now I wonder if everyone has, including my sister.

"There's a reasonable explanation, I swear."

"Then give it to me. I can vouch for your sister with my crew and

334

Boss Smith's, but I have to know what's going on. We're all here, ready to risk our lives, because *you* told us about the Iron Mountain."

"Of course." I take a deep breath. "She's looking for someone."

X doesn't answer. His face is unreadable.

"Someone who's been hidden a long time," I say. "Rafi thinks they must be out in the deep wild. That's why she came here."

The silence stretches between us, until there are shouts in the air. The scouting parties are heading off toward the Iron Mountain.

X nods, like he believes me at last. But his face stays grim.

"Not all that's missing is lost," he says, and turns to walk away.

I watch him go, my heart stuttering in my chest.

What did he—

Col skims up beside me on his board. "You ready? We have to get to the other side of the mountain by noon. Full body armor."

My mind is reeling. I can't speak.

Col frowns. "What were you two talking about, anyway? That little chat looked . . . intense."

I can't answer at first. Does Boss X know something about my family?

Finally I reach for my wrist—not Calm.

Steadfast.

"It was nothing," I tell Col. "Let's go."

He glances at my fingers on my wrist. "You've been using them less lately. Only when you're upset."

"The mountain makes me nervous," I say.

Not a lie at all.

335

SKELETONS

Boss Zachary has put me with the Vics' scout group—Teo and Col, Zura and Veron. There's no rebels, so I don't have to worry about giving myself away.

As we move into position, Boss X's mysterious words twist inside me. Did he actually guess what I was talking about? Or was it just one of his usual brain-spinning pronouncements?

I want to ask Rafi, to admit that I've broken my promise a little. But she's back at her lair, welcoming more crews as they arrive. Checking faces for any hint of family resemblance.

But I don't have time to think about my brother—I need to Focus.

The Vics and I approach the mountain on our boards, staying below treetop level. No one knows how far out the Rusty defenses start, so we ride slow toward the slope, pushing aside pine branches with our hands.

"Nothing pinging us," Teo says, his eyes glued to a handscreen.

Zura points down. "See those wolf tracks? I doubt this place goes to red alert every time an animal wanders by."

"Wolves?" I peer down into the shadows. "Seriously?"

"There's five of us—big predators will keep clear," Col says. "It's snakes we have to worry about."

Snakes. I add a little Vigilance to my Focus.

Near the base of the mountain, the trees grow fewer, and moss-covered scree dots the ground below.

Zura sends a recon drone ahead—it touches down lightly on the stone. Then bounds away up the slope.

The mountain doesn't care.

"See?" she says. "Nothing to worry about. But let's get off the boards. Magnetics are noisy."

Stepping off onto the stone is nervous-making, the Focus and Vigilance making me twitch. With every footfall, I expect Rusty war drones to pop up and open fire.

"Are you okay?" Col asks, his eyes on my feels.

"I'm fine."

The mountain stays silent and still as we climb the gentle slope. Our boards hover where we left them, ready to come get us.

An unworried rabbit hops by, making my nervousness feel silly.

Of course, there are wolves around . . .

"You have *no* clue, rabbit," I mutter.

Our comms crackle to life—Boss Em's voice.

"Set your seismics. Soundings begin in five minutes."

I reach into my pack, pull out my seismic wand. With a flick, it telescopes out to half a meter. I find a patch free of stone and thrust it deep into the earth.

The others do the same, spreading them out across the slope.

Minutes later, the *boom*s of sounding charges rumble in the distance, the rock trembling under my feet. Shock waves are echoing through the whole mountain, prizing out the secret spaces inside.

I draw my pulse knife. Nothing like a few explosions to wake up ancient war machines.

The rumbling lasts for long seconds, but after it fades away, nothing stirs on the mountainside.

"What if this place is dead?" I slip my knife back into its sheath. "Could be just rumors."

"Or maybe it's the wrong mountain," Col says. "All we've got is old stories."

"Not anymore!" Teo calls from higher up. He's kneeling, clearing away brush.

I climb closer—a metal plate is set into the stone. There's a triangle logo stamped onto it, and the words *Iron Mountain Corporation*.

"Huh," I say. "They put a corp in charge of making sure all the other corps would last forever."

Teo laughs. "Classic Rusty move."

"Data's coming in," Col calls, looking at his handscreen. "There's an entrance a hundred meters up!"

Zura points. "See that pattern in the slope?"

Above us, almost weathered away, are the zigzag remnants of an old switchback road. Rusty groundcars must have used the entrance to deliver their cargos.

We climb toward the entrance. As we cross the worn-away road, chunks of ancient asphalt crumble beneath my leather boots.

"Anything pinging us?" I ask Teo.

He glances at his handscreen, shakes his head.

Maybe after three hundred years, the mountain isn't so dangerous anymore.

The entrance is half-hidden behind a loose pile of stones, the result of some bygone avalanche. Past them, a huge steel door sits askew.

It's half a meter thick, partly fallen out of its frame. Torn along the bottom, the opening is maybe big enough to squeeze beneath.

Blast marks scar the metal there.

"Someone already broke in," Col says softly.

I climb over the fallen stones, kneel, and take a sniff of the black marks. No hint of explosives tickles my nose.

"A while ago."

"Decades, maybe," Col says. "Back in the pretty regime, runaway uglies used to explore Rusty places."

Zura turns to Veron. "Take point. See what's in there."

Veron climbs up to join me at the steel door. But when he tries to crawl underneath, the gap is too small for his muscle-bound Special frame. He pushes and strains but can't force the door any higher.

"Might fit if I take off my armor," he says to Zura.

"You won't," Teo says. "But I will—it pays to be small."

Col shakes his head. "Forget it."

"Try and stop me." Teo pushes past Veron and rolls through the opening, body armor and all.

Col rolls his eyes. Strange—when the two of them disagree, even on a dangerous mission like this, it seems so simple and light. Not like me and Rafi.

"I'll get him," I tell Col, crawling down into the gap beneath the door. But my armor catches on jagged steel halfway through. I can't see much inside—just Teo's suit lights flickering across the cracked concrete floor.

"Anything in there?" I call.

"Not really." Teo's voice is steady, only a hint of nerves. "Some brush has blown in over the years. The walls look shot up, like there was a firefight."

"Anything on your screen?"

"Nothing. I'm going to—"

His voice cuts off, followed by a sudden cry.

"*Teo?*" I yell. When he doesn't answer, I use a voice command on my armor. "Fire evac!"

My armor pops open, flying in all directions.

Jagged metal scrapes at my borrowed rebel skins. But I can just squeeze through into the echoey concrete tunnel. The floor is marked like a road, leading away into the darkness.

Teo stands there, staring down at his feet.

When I see what he's looking at, my fingers reach for Calm.

"It's okay. He just got startled . . ."

. . . by the bodies—half a dozen of them spread out across the concrete roadway.

They must have died a long time ago. The corpses are desiccated—their hair dry and brittle, the skin of their faces drawn tight across their skulls, all of it lit garishly by the lights on Teo's body armor.

"By what?" Col calls.

"They were rebels," I say. Their leather clothes are cracked and dry, with crew badges pinned to them.

I look around—whatever got them, it isn't coming after us. Maybe it used its last ammo to take out these unlucky intruders.

The badges are circles of crudely beaten copper, green with age. I don't recognize which crew. But someone will know who they were.

Kneeling beside one of the bodies, I take a badge and pin it onto my own chest.

"Frey," Teo whispers. "Why are they so intact?"

I turn away from the grisly sight to face him. "What do you mean?"

"Animals could get in here easy, but none of them look like they've been . . . picked at."

"Thanks for that image." I turn back to the bodies.

He's right; there are no teeth marks in the dead rebels. The only visible wounds are scatterings of bullet holes in the old leather. Low caliber, automatic fire.

Then I see something next to one of the corpses—the body of a rat. It's almost fresh, the blood in its single bullet wound still glistening.

My hand reaches for my pulse knife, and I hit my Neutral feel, flushing the Calm from my body.

"Get out of here, Teo," I say softly. "Move slowly."

The lights from his suit waver, making the shadows dance. The tunnel stretches away from us, empty as far as we can see.

"Why, Frey?"

"Whatever got them," I whisper, "it's still around. Just get—"

A rattling sound echoes from the tunnel, and I freeze.

Something rickety and squealing with age is scraping its way toward us from the darkness.

ROBOT

Ancient servos shriek and shudder.

When it emerges into the light, the machine looks vaguely humanoid, like a spindly marionette yanked along by not enough strings.

I don't move, hoping its sensors are as decrepit as its gears.

Maybe we can get out of here without waking up more of the mountain's defenses.

"Teo," I whisper. "Back out slowly. I can handle this."

"You're not wearing armor, Frey—just like those rebels!"

Good point.

I want to reach for Courage, but any movement might give me away.

Col's voice calls through the opening. "What's that sound?"

"Stay back," Teo hisses. "And keep quiet!"

The machine has lurched into the light now. It wobbles on two feet, cradling some kind of projectile weapon in its arms.

My military tutor once told me that Rusties built their drones to look like people. *Robots*, they called them, from an old word meaning *slave*.

Typical.

The thing's head has two sensors mounted on it, like eyes. The lenses look cracked and dusty, and make little whirring sounds as they try to focus.

I gently squeeze my knife, cycling it up to half pulse.

Lightning fast, the sensors twist around to point straight at me.

"Hey, drone!" Teo shouts, switching his armor lights on and off.

But the robot ignores him, swinging up the projectile weapon to aim at my hand. It only cares about the buzzing energies of the pulse knife.

Three things happen at the same time—

I throw my knife.

The robot opens fire.

Teo hurls himself in front of me.

A fusillade of bullets pounds at his armor, sending him staggering back into me, shattering his lights. We flail in the flashing darkness, projectiles whizzing all around us.

An explosion—the robot's head torn into a thousand hot fragments by my knife.

Somehow its gun keeps firing. Teo wraps his arms around me, and I curl into a ball within the shelter of his armor. Every impact travels through him into me, like I'm inside a drum that someone's beating hard and fast.

Finally the robot's weapon expends itself.

The gunfire echoes in the chamber. Smoke and the dust of shattered concrete chokes my lungs. Teo rolls from me with a groan.

My pulse knife flits back into my open hand, feverish and humming.

Col squeezes in through the gap, his armor discarded, his rifle leveled at the headless robot. When he sees his little brother, he runs to us.

Teo still lies on the ground, his armor battered, blackened. His breathing sounds wrong.

Col kneels beside him, checking for wounds. "Teo!"

I sit up painfully, staring into the darkness, knife in hand. My ears are ringing, my night-vision implants still sparking from the gunfire.

My fingers reach for a chord of Painless and Steadfast.

Deeper in the tunnel—something's moving.

The mountain isn't done with us.

Zura's trying to scramble underneath the blast door, but none of the Specials are going to fit through.

"Drag him out," I say to Col. "Quick."

He stares at me, frozen for a moment, then grabs his brother under the arms. The concrete rasps as Teo's armor slides across it.

I sheathe my knife and pick up Col's rifle.

The two Specials reach in, pulling Teo through the opening, and Col follows. I hear armor clattering to the ground outside, the hiss of compression bandages.

I back slowly toward the blast door, keeping the rifle leveled. The noises from the tunnel are growing louder, closer.

But I am Steadfast, staring into the darkness. If only I had a light.

Of course, there's one way to see what's coming—

I open fire, letting the rifle's muzzle flash ignite the dark.

Metal forms shudder into being in the bursts of light—a dozen more of the shambling, ancient robots dance as my bullets hit. Backing them up are a pair of larger drones on six legs each, like giant metal crabs.

I stumble backward, firing all the way, then roll beneath the door.

"There's more!" I shout at Zura, dropping the empty rifle. "Including two big ones. We have to shut this entrance!"

She doesn't look up from Teo. He's on the ground, the Vics gathered around him. His uniform is bloody, torn open to show a compression bandage beneath his ribs.

His breathing sounds like a drain trying to clear.

Col looks up at me, eyes glazed. "His lungs . . ."

"My board's almost here with the medkit, sir," Veron says.

"We need all the boards *now!*" I cry. "We're going to have to fly—unless we can shut this door."

Zura looks up at the giant steel plate, the piles of rocks around us. "Not without causing an avalanche."

A long, rattling breath passes Teo's lips.

"Stay with me," Col whispers at his side.

Zura kneels at the gap, peering into the darkness. A burst of gunfire echoes from inside, forcing her back.

"Fifty meters and closing," she says. "Can we move him yet?"

"Not till he's stable," Veron says. "It's a tension pneumothorax—air building up in his chest cavity. Every time he breathes, the pressure crushes his lungs a little more."

Col stares at the Special's cruel pretty face. "What do we *do about it?*"

"We let the air out, sir. Once I get my—"

The riderless boards come sliding in at head level. Veron grabs a medkit from his. He zips it open and pulls out a tube from a sterile pack.

The thing writhes in his hand—smart metal.

"Angiocatheter," he says to it. "Sixteen gauge."

It takes solid form, thin as a stiletto.

I recall my first aid classes, practicing this on a dummy in case Rafi was ever shot in the chest.

It gave me nightmares every time.

Veron douses Teo's side with medspray, just beneath his armpit. Clutching the tube like a knife, he slips it in between the ribs.

Even with the Steadfast lighting up my veins, I have to turn away.

I take Col's hand. He gasps beside me.

There's a liquid, hissing sound, like wet air escaping under pressure.

"Can we move him now?" Zura calls. She has a snake camera wrapped beneath the door. "They're almost here!"

"He needs a minute to stabilize," Veron says.

Col looks at me, his eyes wide. "Help."

I reach for Calm, and it collides with my battle frenzy, my Steadfast.

Everything slows down.

"It's going to be okay," I say to Col, searching the boards still hovering there . . .

My eyes fall on a splinter mine. Powerful enough to destroy the smaller drones, and the big ones can't fit through.

Unless they use those cannons to blow their way out—and bring the mountainside down on us.

"Get clear," I yell, twisting the mine's timer to three seconds.

I slide it through the gap.

We cover Teo with our bodies.

A moment later, a sovereign *boom* echoes through the mountain. The massive door shudders, and smoke geysers through the gap beneath, swirling around us.

For a moment, I can't see or breathe. The explosion rings in my ears.

I try to wave away the smoke, blinking dust from my eyes, coughing. The rocks piled beside the opening are peppered with splinter darts from the mine. I hear the squeal of shredded gears from inside the tunnel.

My hands find Col beside me. "Is he okay?"

His voice is ragged. "Still breathing."

Boss Zachary's voice crackles in our comms.

"Freeze right where you are, everyone. Seismics are picking up something."

"Rafia here, with the Vics," I say, still coughing. "That was us. We took fire—had to return."

"This is bigger than gunfire. It's all over the place. The whole damn mountain's waking up."

"Um, yeah," I say as the smoke begins to clear. "That was definitely us."

HAZE

"Can we move him now?" Col shouts, tears streaking his face.

"Yes, sir!" Veron yells through the smoke.

I spot Teo's board among the others and pull it to the ground. We line it up beside him and each take a limb.

"One, two . . ." Veron barks.

On *three*, we shift Teo over. He lets out a groan, but his breathing seems better now. Still pained, but without that awful gurgling sound.

I try not to look at the bubbling needle sticking from his side.

Veron kneels on his own board. "I'll tandem with him."

"I'll take the other side," Col says, locking Teo's crash bracelets in place. "You two cover us."

I grab my own board, hoist myself up and on.

Boss Zachary is in our comms again.

"Okay, rebels, I'm calling this a straight-up fiasco.

"Everyone pull out, now!"

"Way ahead of you," Zura mutters.

From behind us comes a grinding sound—the blast door shuddering in its frame. Some ancient mechanism is trying to open it.

It moves half a meter higher, then jams.

Two metal claws reach out and grip the bottom of the door, heaving at the tons of steel—another pair joins them. The big six-legged drones are still working, and trying to kill us.

I draw my knife.

"Quarter speed!" Zura shouts, and eases ahead on her board.

Col and Vernon follow, flanking Teo. I bring up the rear.

As we slip down the mountainside, a metal shrieking comes from behind us. The broken blast door is slowly rising, lifted by the two crab-shaped drones.

When they emerge into the sunlight, I get my first good look at their weapons.

Not cannons—flamethrowers. A terrifying Rusty weapon, designed for fighting in caves and tunnels.

"Faster!" I shout.

The Iron Mountain isn't going to let us leave in peace.

In my comms, dozens of rebels are shouting about the ancient defenses waking up. That splinter mine has triggered an all-out alert.

I wonder how long before the mountain goes back to sleep again.

Weeks? Months?

Or maybe it never sleeps.

"Hold up!" Zura shouts from ahead, skidding to a halt.

In front of her, the rocks at the edge of the trees are writhing.

"Smart matter," she says. "That isn't Rusty tech."

"We can't stop!" I cry, pointing at the flamethrower drones scuttling toward us down the slope.

Zura accelerates again, leading us sideways, skirting the boundary between bare mountainside and forest. But there's no gap in the swath of moving rocks.

Maybe we should risk crossing them. The Paz AI didn't seem particularly bloodthirsty. The rocks might just be to scare off rebels and non-tech tribes . . .

But then I see it—a haze springing into the air. The rocks are shedding some kind of nanos, like a thick surveillance dust. A shimmering wall rises before us, as high as I can see.

Zura waves us back up the slope, away from the haze—but the flamethrower drones are still there. We head sideways again, putting more distance between us and them.

I flinch with every swerve we take, wondering what these accelerations are doing to the fluid in Teo's chest.

Gunshots erupt ahead of us—another squad of rebel scouts, also trapped on the mountain. They're laying down fire through the haze.

The shots pass uselessly through. One of the rebels pushes forward into the shimmering wall, testing it.

Zura waves us to a halt.

I raise my field glasses to watch.

The rebel holds out some kind of handscreen before her, taking readings as she goes. Her bright tin jewelry flashes in the high sun, and she has a low-tech bow across her back, a quiver full of arrows with real feathers.

Nothing happens at first, the haze enveloping the rebel and her board. Then she looks up from her handscreen, swats at herself like she's being stung.

Her hoverboard starts to shudder in the air. Its surface is changing color, turning orangey-brown, as if rust is spreading through it.

Then everything starts to seethe—her crash bracelets, the handscreen, the field pack strapped to her board. All of it changes to the same rust color, pieces flaking away as I watch.

Her board tips, the front-end magnetics failing. It slips forward through the air, on an invisible ramp. She hits the ground hard, spilling off onto the rocks. The board shatters on impact, breaking into pieces that crumble like ash in the breeze.

I almost look away, expecting the haze to keep eating . . .

But the girl stands up, holding an injured elbow. Her hands are empty, everything gone except her fur and leather clothing. Even her metal jewelry has crumbled away.

The bow and arrows are still there, but the shiny arrowheads are gone.

"Organics," I say. "That's all it leaves behind."

The Paz AI might have been too civilized to kill anyone, but it set a trap that costs an intruder everything—a stern warning not to come again.

The other rebel scouts stare helplessly at their companion. No hoverboard, hardly any equipment left. Out here in the wild, that's a deadly loss.

"We can't go through, sir," Veron says. "Your brother . . ."

We all look at Teo.

The tube that's keeping him alive is made of smart metal. The haze would crumble it into dust.

"We have sounding charges," Col says. "Maybe we could blow a hole and fly through before it closes."

Zura shakes her head. "One speck of that stuff . . ."

I look back at the crab drones. They're still coming, scrambling at us along the slope.

"What if we had flamethrowers?" I say.

FIRE IN THE HOLE

"How, exactly?" Zura asks.

I reach for more Focus, making myself think it through carefully. Flamethrowers aren't a long-range weapon. The crab drones are at least a minute from being close enough to hit us.

These follow the usual design. Two tanks of fuel—one propellant, the other flammable.

I imagine all that fuel mixing and igniting. Sheets of fire flinging out in all directions.

"We lead the drones into the haze," I say. "Let the nanos do the rest."

"*Lead* them?" Zura says. "We can barely take a sharp turn with Teo."

"I'll do it. You three wait for the hole to open up."

Col shakes his head. "Frey. You're not even wearing body—"

"Teo got himself shot protecting me." I swing my board around to face the six-legged drones. "It's okay, Col. I promise not to die."

355

I zoom away, not waiting for an answer.

More Steadfast.

The two drones spot me headed toward them and rear back on their hind legs, like startled scorpions. The igniters spark to life in the maw of their weapons, two burning eyes staring at me.

I veer away, keeping my distance from the drones so they don't waste any fuel on me. And so I don't get cooked alive.

My pulse knife buzzes in my hand.

One of the drones opens fire, flame geysering out across the mountainside. It falls short of me, a hundred burning droplets scattered on the stone. I feel the heat of it even in the noonday sun.

The drones are charging down the slope, almost within range . . .

That's when the problem with my plan becomes clear.

For them to follow me into the nanos, *I* have to go into the nanos.

Zura and the others are upslope, ready to fly down through any opening. They're probably wondering what I'm going to do next.

Me too.

The other crab drone fires—another jet of flame that falls short. Why are they wasting their fuel at this range?

Then I feel the knife pulsing in my hand. And remember the way the robot in the tunnel keyed on it.

Of course—the mountain's drones are designed for fighting in pitch-blackness. They don't use visible light at all. But they can sense the buzzing energies of my knife.

"Sorry, X."

I squeeze the knife to full pulse and hurl it at the wall of haze.

As it roars away, I fly parallel to the haze, crouched low on my board. The flamethrower drones ignore me, following the knife.

Just before they plunge into the glimmering wall, they let off twin volleys of flame, burning away the nanos. For a moment, it looks like they'll make it through.

But the haze roils around them, spun into a vortex by the heat of the flames. Patches of rust appear on the drones' metal legs.

For a moment, they stagger on the rocky boundary, squealing as servos and gears are eaten away. Then the rust spreads to the fuel tanks on their backs . . .

Pressurized gas gushes out in all directions. A smell like the oil lamps at my father's hunting lodge fills the air.

But there's no explosion.

The drones' igniters must have failed before the tanks fell apart—there's nothing to spark the fumes.

A streak comes from the Vics behind me, a single incendiary round. It hits the billowing cloud of fuel.

Suddenly the world is on fire.

A scalding wave of heat hits, throwing me backward from my board onto stony ground. Flames pass over me in sheets. My lungs are scalded, my eyes forced shut. The sky turns red.

For a moment, I can't breathe. Then the heat passes, and I suck in the smell of singed hair and burned leather. There's a taste in my mouth like kerosene.

A shadow blots out the sun, and Col's voice fights through the ringing in my head.

"Frey! Come on!"

I stand on wobbly legs, staring at the dark mushroom cloud rising before me. The explosion has carved a huge hole in the wall of haze, clear of the nanos.

Col and the others are waiting for me.

"Just go!" I yell, clambering back onto my board, still dizzy from the blast. I lean forward on my knees, until the ground is rushing past me.

I reach for Painless, push hard.

Then I see it on my armored glove—the tiniest patch of rust.

And it's spreading.

I pull off that glove, then the other, and fling them aside.

But there are tiny colonies of rust on my field glasses. On my med-spray bottle, my handscreen . . .

My hoverboard.

I skid to a halt, staring at the spreading rust, not knowing what to do.

I haven't even crossed the rocks yet—the blast must have thrown a wave of nanos at me. I can only hope the Vics were far enough away.

"Frey!" comes Col's voice in my comms. "We're through. Where are you?"

He sounds crackly, barely audible.

The nanos are in my ears, eating away the comm implants.

"Go on," I say, not sure if he can hear. "Get Teo home."

No answer.

The board starts to waver beneath me. I barely have time to step off onto the rocks before it breaks up, cracking along a dozen fissures of rust. The metal buckles of my jacket fall away one by one.

The crew badge I took from the dead rebel is the last thing to crumble.

There's nothing left but my leather clothes and boots.

Staring down at myself, something washes over me—a wild and sudden happiness. Like all I've ever wanted was to lose everything, to have it all burned away. To stand here in the wild, shorn of all my city tech.

Alone and unencumbered. Ecstatic somehow.

That doesn't make sense. Why am I feeling . . .

Rapture, mixed with Belong, and a dozen other emotions piling on.

I look down at my feels.

The rows of little faces are turning to rust.

FEELS

All my feels hit at once.

Waves of Sadness, waves of Joy.

Grief in smothering black clouds, shot through with electric streaks of Anger.

A battering rain of Philosophical and Elucidation, my head crowded with rants and realizations, unstuck memories rattling loose.

Like the flamethrowers' fuel tanks, the little canisters of hormones in my wrist are breaking apart, spilling three dozen emotions into my blood. My feels are mingling, igniting, exploding across my heart.

My muscles flinch, my stomach twists and shudders. Cold sweat and hot tears, a broken laughter racking my chest. Every wire of nervous tissue sings and screams beneath my skin, a fathomless, Painless agony.

It's everything I've ever felt before, a thousand strange new emotions that mix and burn and flail inside me. My brain tries to protect itself, to spin away into the dark, but Vigilance and Focus force my awareness of every detail.

The moment is Relentless—and endless.

And ends all at once, a door slamming on a loud, wild party.

Suddenly I'm standing on a flame-scorched mountainside, staring at rusted faces on my wrist, feeling nothing but empty and confused.

"Col," I say, but my comms are silent.

"Frey?" someone answers.

I look up. A rebel scout group is approaching on their boards.

"Are you hit?" comes a question.

The fog of confusion starts to lift, and at last I recognize the voice.

"Boss X?" My throat is dry.

He hands me a flask. I take it and drink deep.

The cool water feels like nothing.

Yandre is with him, and three others from X's crew. People who know my real name.

That's handy. I've got nothing left to lie with.

"You okay?" Yandre asks. "Anything burned besides your hair?"

I run a hand across my scalp. It's patched and bristly, like dry grass.

"Lost my comms to the haze . . . and my feels." I blink for heat vision. It's still there, my implants too deep inside my eyes to be infected. "You shouldn't touch me, though. I'm covered with nanos."

Yandre lifts a handscreen, sweeps it across my body. "They're already breaking down, chica. They're designed to fade quick, or they'd eat the whole mountain."

"Oh." The dirt beneath my feet hasn't disintegrated. The Paz AI was too smart to let loose some all-consuming goo.

I guess that's good, the world not ending.

Down toward the forest, the smart-matter rocks are blackened from the explosion, but the wall of haze has formed again.

"Still trapped," I murmur.

"Who says we want to leave?" Boss X says, his eyes sparkling.

Yandre lets out a sigh. "Here's the situation, Frey. We're breaking into the Iron Mountain, getting this done now."

I stare at them. "The five of you?"

"Six, if you want to join," X says. "And another dozen gathering above. More than enough."

I should be astonished, and terrified for them. But my body isn't ready for more emotions.

"That's brain-missing," I manage.

"But necessary." X looks up at the mushroom cloud still half blotting out the sky, its edges shearing in the breeze. "That blast was big enough for satellites to see. The city governments will wonder what's happening. They'll send recon forces. Now may be our last chance."

"My fault," I say, tying to feel a shard of guilt, and failing. "We had to get Teo out."

Boss X lets out a low growl. "The 'Foxes. Typical."

"He took a bullet for me," I say, trying to remember which feeling goes with that.

Thankful? Cherish? They're all dulled inside me.

One of the others speaks up. "They're ready for us, Boss."

X reaches out, a heavy hand on my shoulder. "Coming, Frey?"

For a second, I don't know.

But then I feel it, a hint of battle in my veins. That frenzy that was born in me the first time I saved my sister.

The feel that's all mine.

"Sure. But I don't have anything to fight with." A flicker of shame goes through me. "Sorry, X, but the haze ate your gift."

He waves my apology away. "Even at half pulse, nanos would burn before they got close. Have you tried calling it?"

I raise my hand, holding up two fingers.

A moment later, the knife flits into my grip, cool and steady.

Something like Calm goes through me then, mixed with Relief—pulse knives still give me feels.

"Not lost, just missing." X takes a battery from his belt, tosses it to me. "Now all we need is a way inside."

I feed the battery to my knife, looking up at the ancient switchback half-covered in stones.

"That part's easy, Boss. We found an opening."

"What kind of defenses?" Yandre asks.

My battle ecstasy starts to tremble, like water about to boil.

"All kinds." I smile. "But we blew them up."

CAVES

We stand at the open blast door, nineteen rebels and me.

"A fraction of the force Em and Zach wanted," Yandre says.

X's eyes gleam in the darkness. "And twice what we need."

His lance buzzes to life, and I put my hand on his shoulder.

"No pulse weapons till absolutely necessary, Boss. They make the drones in the mountain angry." My own knife is in its sheath. "But they're perfect if we need a distraction."

"I'll do more than distract them," he grumbles.

We head deeper into the tunnel, climbing over the shredded remains of the robots. Metal spikes from Zura's splinter mine jut from the walls, like we're inside some medieval torture device.

As we leave the opening behind, darkness envelops us.

I blink for night vision, and the rebels shift into shimmering heat blobs, like dull red planets orbiting the hot sun of X's animal metabolism.

I keep waiting for a twinge of fear to hit me, here in the dark. But nothing stirs my blood except a readiness for battle. Not my usual frenzy, but smoothed out by my explosion of feels into something cold and steely.

And only a glimmer so far.

The tunnel slopes downward, deeper into the cool stone. I can sense the crushing weight of the mountain above us, but claustrophobia doesn't settle in. Maybe it's been burned away along with my feels.

It will take Col and the Vics hours to reach Rafi's base—a long time for a field dressing to hold.

I reach for Hope.

It's gone.

"The seismics found a big chamber." Yandre's face is ghostly in the light of their handscreen. "About a klick from here. It's the deepest part of the whole complex. All the tunnels lead there, like a traffic junction."

"At least this isn't a game of hide-and-seek," Boss X rumbles in the dark.

No, but what kind of game is it?

We'll find more Rusty defenses, of course—crude, brutal, still deadly after three hundred years. But also whatever tricks the city of Paz left behind.

The darkness seems alive around us.

I reach for Focus, but nothing's there.

Before the feels, how did I force my brain to concentrate? These shadows are just a blur of darkness around me. My brain refuses to catch hold of anything.

We walk for five minutes. Nothing happens.

My feels itch like a phantom limb, and I'm not even sure which one I need.

"Why's it so quiet?" I mutter in the dark. "Boss Zach said the whole mountain was waking up."

"Licking its wounds," Yandre says. "A lot of the mountain's drones went into those nanos."

Helpful, but it also means a lot of good rebels have lost their boards, their equipment, which is everything a rebel owns.

That should make me sad.

Beside me, Boss X is scenting the air.

"Anything?" I ask.

He doesn't answer, just raises a fist. We halt.

He stands there, motionless for ten long seconds—then suddenly leaps into the air, his pulse lance buzzing to life, sweeping across the ceiling. Sparks and stone-dust swirl around us.

A drone the size of a house cat falls from above, sliced in two.

I kneel to look at it. "That thing was quiet."

"In sleep mode," X says. "But it had a definite scent."

The machine is covered with tiny arms, each with a different tool.

"Just a repair drone," Yandre says. "But that means there's something around for it to fix."

X kneels beside me, his sharp eyes staring at each of the tools. Finally he pries one free and sniffs it.

"Kerosene," he says.

I nod. "Could've been fixing one of the flamethrower drones we—"

X grabs my arm, and I hear it too.

A scraping sound, like an ancient door opening. Then the clank of mechanical legs.

"Take cover!" X cries.

My frenzy stirs at last.

A tongue of flame leaps from the darkness, fills the corridor with sudden heat and light, bouncing off the walls, coiling around us.

We scatter, spilling cries of pain and shock. The flames flow like liquid into every space. The smell of burned hair and skin and clothing fills the air.

Flamethrowers are deadly in closed spaces.

Boss X's pulse lance ignites again, roaring through the burning dark. Before I can even draw my knife, I hear the flamethrower being cut to pieces.

"Careful!" I shout. "Don't hit . . ."

The lance cycles down, and X stands there among the scattered pieces of the drone. All six legs lie on the ground, nothing moving except shadows. A last dribble of fire trails from the drone's body to the amputated maw of the thrower.

". . . the fuel tanks," I say.

X gives me a disdainful look in the flickering light. Behind him, the tanks are perfectly intact.

"Everyone okay?" Yandre asks.

The answer is a rueful laugh or two, and the hiss of medspray.

I become aware of something pulsing through me. A burned patch on skin on my shoulder. My fingers reach for Painless . . .

I've forgotten how *annoying* pain can be. But at least it keeps my heart going. My battle frenzy is real now.

Yandre hits my shoulder with medspray. It's not as good as Painless.

"Where'd that thing come from?" I ask.

X points. Behind the fallen six-legged machine is an opening. Perfectly flush with the tunnel wall, the door is engineered to disappear when closed.

"Still half a klick to go," I say. "How many more of these hidden doors, you think?"

"They won't use fire near the center," he says. "Not if that's where the data's stored."

I squint in the flickering light—his fur is singed away along his left arm, right where feels would be. The bare skin is red and mottled.

"You should spray that."

He smiles, all wolf. "Why? It focuses the mind."

A thought flashes through me—what did he look like before the surge? Maybe his desire came from some part of him, something lupine in his eyes, his brow.

Or did he look normal and boring?

Maybe it came from who he was, not what he looked like.

I've been avoiding these questions since his strange words this morning. But somehow it's easier to have these thoughts with my feels burned away. Nothing rushes up to push them down.

Before his wolf surge, he might have looked like my sister and me.

"Boss—" I start.

He holds up a hand for silence. His ears are twitching.

"Small things on legs. From all directions."

"Your pulse lance," I say. "They spotted it."

"Boss!" Yandre shouts, eyes on their handscreen. "Motion sensors are giving me hundreds of pings . . . thousands!"

X and I stare at each other. The Iron Mountain is still awake.

"How much ammo do you all have left?" I ask.

X shakes his head.

Both of us turn to the flamethrower.

"Yandre," I say, "do you have any bombs?"

CORPS

We run, two sounding charges ticking behind us, nestled between the fuel tanks of the flamethrower drone.

We have two minutes to get away.

There's no point in being stealthy. The tunnel dances with our flashlights as we run. I can see the traffic markings on the roadway clearly now—stop signs and speed limits, booths for security guards. A whole Rusty city once existed down here, a network of machines and people.

But there's no time to stop and look.

We're halfway to the central chamber, when we see them coming at us—small spindly-legged drones, like spiders.

They swarm the walls and ceiling of the tunnel, the mountain's last line of defense, ready to overwhelm us with sheer numbers.

We can't let them slow us down.

The rebels open fire with their autorifles, blasting spiders into parts. Those that get through, X sweeps away, and my darting knife protects him from any that skitter inside the reach of his lance.

The little drones aren't quick or smart—definitely Rusty tech—but they keep coming.

"I'm out!" one of the rebels shouts. She swings her rifle by its shoulder stock, flailing at the little machines.

"Me too!" another yells.

A rebel beside me cries out in pain. One of the spiders has grabbed his arm, squeezing with all eight of its metal legs.

A moment later he drops, out cold from an injection of knockout juice—or worse.

But we can't stop for the wounded. The bombs behind us are still ticking.

"Thirty seconds!" Yandre cries.

More of our guns fall silent, out of ammo, or rebels bitten by the spiders. We fight with flares, stun grenades, and shock wands stolen from wardens long ago.

Without Boss X, we'd be overwhelmed, but his pulse lance flails and buzzes.

The ranks of the little drones are thinning. For a moment, it seems like we're in the clear . . .

Until I look over my shoulder.

Another horde of spiders is on its way, filling the tunnel behind us, drawn from every quarter of the mountain.

"Five, four . . ." Yandre's voice rings out. *"Down!"*

We drop to the ground, piling into a heap, those with body armor on top. They empty their water bottles onto themselves, like rain leaking down to the rest of us.

Boss X is beside me, breathless and slicked with sweat.

"My brothers and sisters," he pants. "You are all . . . very heavy."

A grim laugh bubbles through us.

The conflagration comes then—a flash of light, then a roar and shock wave at the tardy speed of sound. All that burning fuel channeling down the tunnels, flowing along walls and ceilings.

It hits us in a swell of heat, burning the air in our lungs, scalding bare skin. The noise and fury, the reek of kerosene and burned hair all too familiar.

Then it travels past, leaving us behind.

The pile of rebels shifts atop me. With muttered curses, whimpers of pain, and coughing, we sort ourselves. More medspray, but no one is critically hurt.

There are still a handful of spiders coming toward us down the tunnel, but they wobble drunkenly, their small metal bodies covered with sticky burning goo.

One by one, they shudder to a halt.

"I'll go back, Boss," Yandre says, pulling out their medkit.

X nods. "Take two with you."

All those fallen rebels—they were defenseless in the path of the flame. Only twelve of us still stand.

There's nothing but battle frenzy in my veins. No grief, no anguish. Like the rest of me was burned away with my feels.

I can worry about the fallen later. About X.

"Let's finish this," I say.

The central chamber is bigger than a soccer stadium.

The entrance is wide enough to drive a construction drone through. An ancient Rusty ground truck sits stalled halfway in, its cargo never delivered.

It all just ended one day. A whole civilization.

As we cross the threshold, lights flicker on around us. The rebels draw what weapons they have, and X's lance roars back to life.

But nothing comes at us.

I sheathe my knife. "Maybe the Rusties didn't want any firefights in here with their precious data."

"There are still Paz's tricks to worry about," X says, but his pulse lance falls silent.

Thousands of giant cabinets fill the room, four meters high. We spread across the chamber, searching.

X and I fall in together, walking down the corridors between the cabinets, staring at the strange markings on their doors. The logos of ancient corps are simple shapes and bold colors, like magic glyphs signifying power and permanence.

The floor is covered with unreadable markings, nav symbols for the drones that once scurried here, filing and retrieving. A few sit rusting at intersections on fat rubber wheels, their batteries forever spent.

"How do we find Paz in all this?" I ask.

X grumbles, then pulls at one of the cabinet doors. When it resists, he cuts it open with his lance, to reveal . . .

Paper.

Stacks of it, binders and boxes. More than in my father's collection of Rusty-era books. More paper than I've ever seen in one place.

Boss X pulls out a handful. It's covered in tiny print, rows of numbers and names. List of transactions, deals, promises, all incomprehensible now.

The paper is ancient and dry, and crumbles in his hand when he makes a fist.

He looks more confused than I've ever seen him. "*This* was what had them trying to kill the planet? Pieces of *paper?*"

I can only stare. I thought we'd find data and code, machines that threatened to resurrect the corps, ancient demons brought back to life.

But this is just dead trees.

"Looks like the old saying about this mountain was wrong," I say. "The corps aren't coming back, are they?"

X slides a fresh battery into his pulse lance. "Maybe they only existed in the Rusties' heads."

He hands me a battery pack for my knife. Something about the gesture—the unthinking, easy sharing—makes me realize we're alone.

"Can I ask a question, Boss?"

"You just did. Ask a more interesting one."

I groan. "Earlier today, you said something weird. 'Not all that's missing is lost.'"

"I did. And your question?"

"What did you *mean* by that?"

His lupine eyes meet mine at last. "Anything that's truly yours is still with you, even if you can't see it."

"I feel like you could be more specific."

He shrugs. "Not just things—people. The connections are still there."

"X. *What* connections?"

"Love, family," he says. "But this isn't the time, Frey."

I open my mouth to keep pressing him, and nothing comes out. My hand takes my wrist, where Elucidation used to be—but the little face is burned away.

And yet my heart is beating hard and fast. My feelings aren't gone. They've simply found a new place, deeper inside me. And they won't let me speak.

If X is my brother, I have to tell him what I did.

Who I killed.

"Boss!" comes a cry from across the chamber.

We linger a moment, until I nod my okay. Then we turn and run.

The other rebels are already gathered when we arrive, around a pile of data bricks in Paz orange, sitting in the corner of the chamber. The backed-up city is smaller than I expected, all of it on a single, fully charged hoverpallet.

But a warning perimeter is painted on the floor around it—jagged stripes with lightning bolts.

Everyone stays well back.

"Boss," one of the rebels says. "This might be the power supply."

A set of cables leads from the pallet to the chamber wall.

"Too easy," I say, inspecting the pallet from every side. The backup would need a link to the surface for new data to come in, and for solar power. But beating the defenses has to be trickier than simply unplugging them.

The warning stripes look lethal, but the Paz AI wasn't a killer at heart. And there aren't any dead rats piled up on the perimeter.

"Don't cut the cable," I say. "I'm going to wake it up."

X shakes his head. "Frey, let's discuss this."

"If the other cities are on their way here, we don't have time."

I step past the perimeter.

A siren shrieks to life—red lights fill the chamber. A dozen weapons spring from the wall, their laser sights playing across my body.

I freeze, hands up.

"I'm not here to mess with you."

No answer. The weapons splay out, taking aim at the rest of X's crew. But one stays focused on my forehead, its sighting laser a halo in my vision.

A whisper of fear feathers in my chest. I'm almost grateful for it.

"There's been a disaster in Paz," I say. "We need you."

An endless pause drags out, but finally the sirens cut off.

The machine speaks.

"Ah, Frey. I've been expecting you."

PAZ

"You know who I am?" I ask.

"My last full backup was seven hours before the disaster," Paz says. "But during the quake, a block of data arrived—detailed readings from the earthquake, and a message that you might come."

I stare at the pile of cubes. "How much of you is in there?"

"All of my memories, in compressed form, but only a fraction of my intelligence. My only connection to the outside world was severed by the quake, except a few sensors on my solar panels. May I ask you something?"

I nod, ready for the AI to test me, to make sure I'm really here to bring it back to life.

"How many dead?" it asks.

That sends a leftover spark of Grief through my veins. Suddenly the pile of cubes looks forlorn, lonely in this cavern of dead trees and crumbling corps.

"A hundred thousand," I tell it.

Another pause, nothing but the hum of the room around us, the air passing through all those empty tunnels.

Finally Paz says, "I lack the capacity to process that."

"Yeah, me too."

"You tried to warn me," Paz says. "The earthquake wasn't natural—it was murder. But I failed to listen."

And I didn't scream my warning from the rooftops, because I was busy looking for my sister. The thought makes me reach for my wrist. But there was nothing there that could've fixed this, even before I lost my feels.

The lights in the chamber shift from red to white again. The weapons pull back into the walls.

"Take me home," the city says.

The backup data lifts into the air on its hoverpallet, weightless but still massive. It takes some pushing to get it moving, but then momentum carries the pallet along.

Yandre and the others join us at the entrance to the central chamber, bringing two of the wounded rebels back. Their burns are awful—charred hands, leather melted into skin. Full medclamps are wrapped around their arms, delivering doses of painkiller. But horror still shows in their eyes.

The other six are lost.

I reach for Grief . . . and nothing is there.

Or maybe not nothing. A dull ache that won't go away, that I wish there was a way to sharpen.

Climbing away from the central chamber, we pass them one by one. Yandre takes their crew badges, blackened and twisted by the flames. We add their weight to the backup's pallet, an echo of the city's countless dead.

The burned remains of spider drones crunch underfoot.

"How sturdy are you?" Yandre asks the city backup. "If there's a firefight."

"There won't be any shooting. I have the shutdown codes for every drone in the mountain."

I sigh. "We could've used those."

"There was only time for a few words, Frey," the city says. "The quake was hitting me as we spoke. But I'm sorry for those you've lost."

"Pay us back by retaking your city," X says. "And hitting Shreve any way you can."

"That I will guarantee."

I glance at the data blocks. At least Paz's confidence has been faithfully preserved.

As we draw closer to the entrance, we hear drones scuttling in the darkness around us. True to its word, Paz sends them away.

Soon the opening is in sight, bright sunlight lancing through.

"Wait," the city says. "There's something out there."

We drag the pallet to a halt, readying our weapons.

"My topside sensors detect two hovercraft. What origin, I can't tell."

Yandre pulls out their handscreen. "Less than an hour since the blast. Whoever it is got here quick."

They all look at me.

"Could be Shreve," I admit. "But when the Vics rescued me, other cities came in with orbital forces. Could be anyone."

Yandre looks up from their screen. "Can't tell from here, Boss. Someone has to go out and look."

X gestures to me. "Come on."

The two of us climb toward the light. We cross the long-dead rebels, the bodies of the robots destroyed by the splinter mine, weapons still gripped in their metal hands. The giant blast door still stands, half raised, our hoverboards stacked outside.

We creep out into the stones from the long-ago avalanche. After the darkness inside the mountain, the sun is punishingly bright.

I can't see anything at first, but the hum of lifting fans fills the air.

X points down at the tree line. Two heavy orbital drones linger there, fully armored, investigating the spot where the flamethrowers exploded.

Their livery is the black and gray of Shreve.

"He's here," I whisper.

That familiar tremor goes through me. Being watched, followed, trapped. He'll never leave me alone. That feel isn't gone at all.

It won't be until he's dead.

X's ears twitch, and he looks up—a flash crosses the bright sky. Then another, followed by the *huff* of drogue chutes opening.

My father is coming in force.

"What do we do?" I ask. "We can't let him kill Paz again."

X squints in the daylight, looking down at the tree line.

"Is that a wrecked drone?" he asks.

The Shreve orbitals are hovering over something in the rocks. The ceramic spine of an airframe, picked clean, the rest of it crumbling into orange-brown rust in the wall of haze.

"Yeah," I say. "Looks like it got eaten."

X looks at me, and smiles. "That gives me an idea."

"Lure the other two into the nanos?"

"It's that or wait for Shreve to come in and get us."

"We're out of ammo, Boss. And no rebels are coming to help us with that haze still there."

"Those old robots at the tunnel entrance," X says. "Do their weapons still work?"

"Well enough to shoot Teo. But there's only a dozen of us!"

"Ten," he says. "You and Yandre have to fly the backup out."

"That pallet barely—" I begin, but X gestures at the hoverboards stacked behind us. Six extra, thanks to the dead rebels inside.

Four of them could carry the data, two each in tandem mode with me and Yandre. X's plan is almost workable, except . . .

"One speck of that haze gets on you, Boss, you'll be defenseless."

He shrugs. "Not if it gets on them first."

Another streak crosses the sky, another reentry *boom*. Black-and-gray Shreve livery on the chute.

Every minute we argue only makes the situation worse.

"Okay," I say. "Might as well try. But I'm sticking with you, Boss. Let someone take the backup out."

X hesitates, his hands falling heavy on my shoulders.

"Frey. I have something to tell you."

I flinch. This moment had to come.

"Me first," I say. "Something I should've told you along time ago."

He cocks his head a little. "Quickly, then."

It takes long seconds for me to start talking, seconds wasted. But then another Shreve orbital streaks the sky, forcing the words from me.

"The assassin last year. The boy you loved . . . he was trying to kill my sister."

"No. Your father was the target."

"Right," I say. "But Rafi took his place at the last moment. All we knew was that someone was shooting at everyone, at Rafi. I did my job."

"You protected your sister."

"Yes . . . with my knife." A gulf opens in me, an emptiness. "I killed the boy you loved. I'm sorry, X."

He doesn't move.

"It was my job," I say.

I know this isn't my fault. The assassin could've killed my sister. But emotions have no logic.

I killed X's love.

The worst part—it was ecstasy for me, the moment in which I first found my battle frenzy. Every fight since is just an echo of that rapture.

It's the only feel I'm certain about, and I found it in killing some-one. By turning him into a spray of red mist with my first pulse knife.

Another boom rumbles the sky. X still hasn't moved. His dark eyes are silvering with tears.

"It was what I was created to do." My voice breaks at last. "Save my sister."

Finally he nods, like the meaning of my words has penetrated.

"The assassin," Boss X says. "His name was Seanan."

SEANAN

I killed my brother.

With a pulse knife, leaving almost nothing of him.

The first person I ever killed. The day I found my ecstasy.

My father's security must have known within a few hours. They would've checked the assassin's DNA, those little fragments of him that I scattered across the room.

From that moment on, my father hated me.

It was logic-missing of him—protecting my sister was what I was born to do. It was why he made me. But emotions have no logic, especially not his.

Seanan was his real child, not a body double. His first heir, not a spare.

This all storms in my head as Yandre and I fly hard across the Iron Mountain's spine, two hoverboards on either side of us. Taking the Paz backup away from the thunder and flames of battle. Saving a city from—

I killed my brother.

It keeps hitting me, pounding like a headache. Like the ghost of my feels hammering on the inside of their tomb.

That's why my father had a painting of me in his trophy room. Why he sent me to Victoria as a hostage. From the day I turned Seanan into red mist, he was searching for an excuse to throw away his murderous daughter.

The Palafoxes had to die so that my father had an excuse to end me too.

The war, the conquest of Victoria, a hundred thousand Pazx dead—what if all of it was one vast ritual, a sacrifice, a way to cleanse himself of *me*?

As we fly down the mountain's other side, the Paz backup sends a signal to the nanos in our way. The haze shimmers before us, then falls like sudden rain. We pass over the rocks, and our boards don't disintegrate beneath our feet.

But the battle spills down behind us—the orbital drones giving chase. Two people with six hoverboards, laden with bright orange cargo, we stand out.

They must know the rebels' attack is only a distraction.

A deadly one. X's board roars up to meet the drones, and the flicker of his pulse lance takes two of them down.

I killed his love, my brother, as I was born to do.

The rebels are falling, overmatched. Their ancient Rusty guns, taken from the robots, do almost nothing against heavy drones. And now a wave of Shreve soldiers is coming down, in powered armor, each streaking from orbit on their own glider wings.

But the haze springs up behind us again, catching another of our pursuers.

The orbital drone writhes against the bright sky, tumbling as the nanos tear through its lifting fans. By the time it hits the ground, nothing's left but an airframe.

Just behind it, X tries to veer from the wall of haze—too late.

"Paz!" I cry. "Turn the nanos off again!"

"Frey," it says. "My city needs saving."

X's board shudders, skidding in the air. He tries to bring it to a halt, but it's crumbling beneath his feet. He's thrown forward, rolling in the dirt.

More drones are coming across the mountain, and glider soldiers behind them. The wall of nanos grows taller, Paz's defenses set to full to save itself.

Anything else would be logic-missing.

I watch Boss X spring to his feet, defiant, his lance flaring for a moment. Just like my knife, the nanos can't get past the rampant energies surrounding it.

But there's only him left, tiny in the distance, against the might of Shreve.

Yandre and I plunge into the trees.

Ride hard, ride fast.

Don't look back.

Feel nothing.

I killed my brother. I killed my brother.

And X is taken or dead.

PARTY

My sister throws a bash.

We won, after all. We took the Iron Mountain. The ancient Rusty ghosts buried there are dead at last. We rescued the mind—maybe the soul—of Paz.

Everyone shows up. The crews that scouted the mountain, even those who lost their boards and had to walk back. The two hundred unlucky rebels who came all this way, only to miss the battle. Those who never cared about saving some city AI, but who wouldn't miss a Boss Frey bash. One crew arrives in a vertical-takeoff jet, splitting the sky with a sonic boom before it circles around and lands on a tendril of fire.

The Victorians are here too, all of them alive and well. After a two-hundred-klick ride with a tube sticking out of Teo's chest, the autodoc had him patched up inside an hour. Yandre and I arrived to find him and Col waiting at the entrance of the mine.

We kept waiting, but none of the other rebels who went into the Iron Mountain came home after us.

Not one.

Rafi's cavernous throne room isn't big enough, so the party spills across the mountainside. Food, noise, drink, bonfires, the night sky peppered with safety fireworks—even a few explosions of the old-fashioned, unsafe kind.

It's not like the stately summer festivals in Shreve, those measured, choreographed, color-themed displays. Rebel fireworks shows are mock battles—flares split open and lit, sent skittering along the ground at each other, homemade rockets sputtering at the sky.

I watch from the ridgeline, alone with my bubbly, letting myself feel the celebration without it asking too much of me. All that joy is too much to bear, when the Joy inside me is burned away.

Yandre and I are the heroes of the hour, the only people to emerge from the heart of the Iron Mountain alive and free. There's talk of Yandre becoming a boss—and maybe me too.

I'd be Boss Rafia, of course. My greatest victory, and my sister gets the credit.

I lost my strongest ally. X, my friend.

Somewhere deep in my heart is languish, grief, and torn.

I killed my brother.

"Frey?" someone calls through the darkness. I can't quite place the voice, so Rafi's balletic posture fills me.

"Wrong sister," I say, gesturing at the party. "Frey's down there."

"I'm not looking for a boss."

My eyes search the darkness. Then a weeping willow of flame

388

bursts in the sky, shimmering blue and gold across a bland, familiar face.

A freshly minted avatar of the sovereign city of Diego.

The bubbly in my stomach goes sour. It's nervous-making, meeting someone you recently chopped in half.

But nervous is better than feeling nothing.

"You're looking well," I say. "Compared to last time."

That uninflected smile. "Can't say the same for you."

I rub a hand over the fuzz on my scalp. After two close encounters with exploding flamethrowers, I'm basically hair-missing. Though maybe the city means my sadness.

"Taking a page from Tally's book," I say. "Letting the scars heal naturally."

"Nature is overrated," Diego says.

"Spoken like a city. Speaking of scars, sorry about cutting you in half. It wasn't personal."

The avatar shrugs. "I'm not a person."

I turn away. Something about that shrug has never looked quite human.

"You're not a rebel either," I say. "And this is a rebel bash—so why are you here? If you think you can lock me up again, I have several hundred heavily armed friends who beg to differ."

"We detained you for your own safety." They sit on the rocks beside me, straightening their dress with small, precise motions. "And you seem safe enough."

"So this is a social call?"

"We're assisting in the transfer of the Paz backup. We'll take it back tonight and load it straight into the walls. In a few days, the city will start coming back to consciousness."

I frown. "And erase my father's spyware? I thought you wanted to let him think his conquest was on schedule."

"A change of plan—we can't let a fellow AI drift without a city. Besides, the Paz backup has proof that the earthquake was unnatural. That should make your father's existence difficult enough."

"Won't it just make everyone more afraid of him?"

"A little of both." They smile. "In any case, the occupation of Paz will fail."

Those last six words send something through me. My feels may have crumbled, but I can still recognize a win. The rebels at the mountain didn't die for nothing.

Shatter City might finally start to become whole again.

But the feeling doesn't quite reach my heart.

"My father still killed a hundred thousand people," I say.

"Who must be avenged. That's the reason for our visit. To tell you that our deal remains in place, Frey of Shreve."

I shake my head. "Rafi's the better choice."

"We just met her down there, pretending to be you. We do not concur."

I stare down at the bash. "She's a born leader. Look at all these rebels wrapped around her finger."

"A city is not a crew, Frey."

"Maybe not. But I don't know anything about running either!"

The avatar waves its hand at the night around us. "Frey, this is all *your* doing. Paz whispered two words in your ear, and this peculiar web of alliances formed around you. You saved a city."

"Not me. It was Yandre, Rafi, X, the Vics. A whole bunch of other crews."

"But you linked them." The avatar stands, still looking down at the bash. "The heirs of two first families, a dozen free cities, and the largest gathering of rebels since Tally Youngblood disappeared—all allied against your father. Only you could've made those connections."

"I didn't *connect* anything. You had me locked up when all this got started!"

"And your friends rescued you—allies are a strength."

"Not mine," I say with a sigh. "The Vics are coming apart at the seams."

"Dysfunctional, yet they freed you from our custody, and we are very resourceful. And didn't Teo Palafox take a bullet for you? That's what he told us, anyway. Several times."

I feel a smile on my face, then remind myself not to be charmed by this machine. They are not my friend, just the enemy of my enemy.

"Fine, I have lots of allies. But the rebels only want chaos, and their best leader's just fallen. And my father still has that earthquake weapon. No one's safe from him."

"Agreed. That's why our deal still stands."

I take a long swig from my bubbly. "The Pazx will hate it, having their walls watching them. Even if it's their own AI instead of Shreve."

Diego gives an inhuman shrug. "They'll get used to it. My people did."

Essa won't, and neither will Primero. But rather than give their names to this machine, I change the subject.

"Do you really think you can kill my father?"

The sovereign city of Diego turns and walks away, for a moment ignoring the question. But then that vast, empty smile glitters from the edge of the darkness.

"One of us will have to, Frey."

NAME

Half an hour later, the vertical-takeoff jet lifts into the sky again. Not a rebel craft after all, but Diego taking Paz's backup away. Maybe to the same building where they kept me.

I'm alone for a while, letting the bash flow over me. That distant happy noise is like my feels trying to sputter to life again—as weak as watered-down bubbly.

A hoverboard climbs the hill toward me. I'd recognize the rider's stance anywhere, because it's my own.

A muted pulse of dread goes through my body. I haven't told her yet.

I don't even have Calm to help me.

"Avoiding the bash, little sister?" Rafi steps off her board, the feathers in her hair silhouetted against fireworks.

"I lost crew today."

"So did our friends down there." She sweeps her arm across the party. "Some lost every scrap of tech they own. That's why they need this. You do too."

"I don't have to go to parties for you anymore," I say.

"This isn't for me—it's for you." She sits, puts an arm around me. "What if you *made* yourself happy?"

So Rafi knew about my feels too.

I show her my wrist. "Not an option anymore."

She stares closely, until a rattle of fireworks lights up the burned-away faces.

"Oh, right. The nanos." Rafi takes my hand gently. "I'm so sorry, little sister. I really thought they'd help."

I turn to face her, frowning.

"Wait. You requested the surge in Paz. Did you *want* them to wind up on me?"

She gives me her sweetest smile, the one I've never managed to get right.

"Seriously?" I yell. "How did you even know I'd wind up in an autodoc?"

"This is *you* we're talking about, silly." Rafi laughs. "You've been injured once a week since we were seven years old."

I can't argue that one.

"And you needed help, Frey. You put a bomb collar on—willingly!"

"To save Col."

She rolls her eyes—and in that moment, the difference between the two of us cuts through me, as cool and sharp as a touch of Philosophical.

Rafia will never risk herself for someone else.

Except maybe me.

I hand her the half-empty bottle. "If you thought I needed help, why not stick around in Paz? Why not *be there* for me?"

"News flash, Frey: Your big sister is not a paragon of stability." She takes a swig from the bottle. "And I was furious at you for leaving me alone. Also this bubbly is warm."

She throws it away. The bottle doesn't smash, just rolls, wobbling out into the darkness.

Rafi looks disappointed. "Didn't the feels work *at all*? Didn't they make you happy sometimes? Fill you with Joy? Paz told me they'd help."

"They did, for a while. You should try them sometime."

I expect her to argue, but she only says, "If you think I should."

We're silent for a while, and I realize it's time.

"Rafi, I have something to tell you."

She groans. "Don't tell me you're going away again. Even when I'm furious at you, I hate us being apart! We can go wherever you want now. To the jungle with Col. Or somewhere with hot and cold running water, like Diego . . ."

"It's about our brother."

That silences Rafia of Shreve.

The sky crackles again, filling with the glitter of a thousand small explosions while I choose my words.

Not carefully, it turns out.

"Boss X knew him."

"*Knew* him?" Her hand squeezes mine tight. "Frey, no . . ."

"He was the assassin, when we were fifteen. I killed him."

The words leave me like a shudder, tearing something along the way.

I turn to face her.

Other than my name, Rafi is all that I have that stretches back to my childhood. My sister is still half of who I am, even when she's on the other side of the continent. If she decides to hate me, I'm not sure what happens.

She stares at me for a while, then turns to watch the bash.

The empty space where my feels used to be burns, and I imagine all the chords of emotions I could play now. Manic and Elucidation to tell her everything. Cherish to think what might have been if there were three of us.

Or maybe just a straight touch of Grief.

The only trace of Seanan left in the world was on Boss X's pendant, and that was taken with him.

Finally Rafi sighs and puts an arm around me.

"So we're alone again."

My mouth is dry. "You're not mad at me?"

She laughs.

"At you, little sister? You were just protecting me, like always." A shrug. "Besides, the little fool might've shot us."

"He was our *brother*, Rafi."

"Exactly—our father's son." And just like that, the sadness leaves her face, as if drained by a long touch of Philosophical. She starts pulling off her rings one by one, throwing them into the darkness.

The metal strikes the stones out there with little *ping*s.

I can only watch, dumbfounded. When X was angry at me for killing Seanan, it made sense, even if it was logic-missing.

This is the other way around.

Maybe I won't ever understand my sister.

"It really *felt* like there were three of us." She takes off the last ring. Drops it on the ground. "But I suppose you can't always trust your feels."

"I'm sorry, Rafi."

"It was supposed to be a surprise for you," she says softly. "The best present I could ever give. A way to make you happy. You're always so sad."

Languish moves in me, muted, but as vast as the fall of Paz.

"Oh, Rafi." I take her hand.

"At least I can stop being a rebel now." My sister pulls a feather from her hair, holds it up to my face. "Do you want my crew, little sister?"

"Your crew?"

"Yes, take them all."

She's right—I could become Boss Frey, with my own loyal rebels to fight against our father. Flush with this victory, all the assembled crews down there would follow me.

With the resources of a dozen free cities behind us.

"Maybe that's a better present," Rafi says. "Instead of one rebel sibling—hundreds."

She slides the shiny feather behind my ear. Exactly where she was wearing it.

"We'll need a wig," she says. "Or I can shave my head in solidarity, just before we switch. I'd do that for you, little sister."

Of course—to pass as Boss Frey, I'd have to become my sister again. Walk like her, talk like her. Play the dark queen on Rafi's underground throne, full of charm and guile.

I shake my head. "All I want is my name back. Just stop being me."

"Really?" She rolls her eyes. "I offer you an army, and you want your *name*?"

"It's the only thing I have that's really mine."

She groans a little. "You don't even remember where *Frey* came from, do you?"

I look at her. "It's what they called me. Same as any name."

"Oh, Frey." My big sister stands up, straightens, like she's giving a speech. "All right, let this be my present for you—the story of *Frey*."

I stare up at her, confused.

"You had some other name until we were four," she says. "I can't recall what. Just some word Security came up with."

"You mean Mirror. That was my code name, like you were Gemstone."

"Of course! Except Mirror was your *name*, little sister. At least until Sensei Noriko started to teach me the ancient art of handwriting."

My fingers reach for Focus, but it's not there.

"I don't understand."

"The first thing Noriko taught me to write was *Rafia*. I tried to teach you too, under the covers that night. Only you weren't very good at it."

I frown. "My handwriting's still terrible."

"True. But at least you can get the letters in the right order now."

Something passes through me. "Stop, Rafi. This isn't true."

"It's not only true, it's wonderful," she says, her eyes wide. "You named yourself, little sister—even if it's just *my* name, sideways and misspelled. I can't believe you forgot. It was your first victory."

I stare at her, uncertain if she's lying.

I remember being called *Mirror*. But at some point they stopped, even though they still called my sister *Gemstone* during lockdowns and emergencies.

There's no way to find out if she's lying. Everyone who would know the truth is my enemy now, in a fortified city half a continent away.

"I love you no matter what you call yourself, little sister." Rafi turns to face the party. "But this is my last rebel bash—you should enjoy it. Please, for me?"

"I don't want to."

I am Frey.

"Suit yourself." Rafia lets out a frustrated sigh. "By the way, Diego was looking for you, just before they left. Seemed important. Did they find you?"

As I open my mouth, the smallest tremor of warning goes through me.

"No," I say.

SPY

It's lonely up on the ridge, but I still don't go to my sister's bash.

There's only room for one Frey down there.

With my feels missing, melancholy comes stalking—the certainty that I'll always be here on the outside, looking in. Like when I was little, watching recordings of my sister's private birthday parties to memorize the faces of her friends. I knew their names, but they weren't supposed to ever know mine.

Maybe someday I'll get my feels put back in, for nights like these.

Just when gloom is about to hit, he finds me.

"*There* you are" comes Col's voice from the dark. "I was starting to think Rafi was kidding about you being up here."

I hold out my hand, waiting for him to take it.

He's warm from the climb, and a little wobbly as he sits beside me. He smells like bubbly and dancing and bonfires.

The Vics got their win, after all.

But he's too good an ally to crash his good mood against mine—my war didn't go well today.

X is dead or taken.

Col wraps an arm around me. Same as he did after I told him about Seanan this afternoon. And, same as then, he lets me keep my silence for a while.

I try to feel something simple with him—like in the first days of the war. But so much is burned away now.

My feels. My brother.

Even my name feels flimsy now.

Col is here, but my heart itches for a long touch of Cherish. That warm, full completeness in my chest, while I lean against this boy beside me.

Maybe that feeling is out there somewhere, and I can get to it again.

"How's Teo?" I ask.

"In bed, bored. The autodoc says he shouldn't breathe bonfire smoke with patched lungs."

"It's my fault he got shot. He was shielding me."

Col squeezes me. "You went in and saved him. He knows that."

That makes me smile.

I keep worrying that the Vics aren't strong enough to fight beside me. That there are fewer of them every time we meet. That not all of them trust me.

But they keep sticking around. Allies to the last.

More silence. Maybe this is everything I need right now—Col's steady presence next to me.

Maybe I don't always have to feel so much.

But when the next big volley of fireworks lifts our eyes, he says something nerve-rattling.

"There's good news from Shreve."

I turn to him. Diego can't have struck at my father already.

"That's a contradiction in terms," I say. "What happened?"

Col hesitates. "I have to confess something first. Remember Bossier Fountain?"

"Where we got rescued by butterflies and knockout gas? That may seem like a hundred years ago, Col, but it's a hard thing to forget."

He nods. "It was a surprise appearance."

I cast my mind back. My father wanted me and Col together in public, to prove to the world that our love was real. And Dona Oliver only told me the day before . . .

"A late addition to the schedule," I murmur.

But the rebels and Vics showed up with gas, antiaircraft, those flying masks. They even had time to get Yandre an invitation to our engagement ball.

"I see what you mean. How'd they find out before we did?"

"Someone made contact with Teo three months ago, a few days after we were captured."

"Someone . . ." It starts to come clear in my bubbly-addled head. "Someone in Shreve?"

Col nods. "A spy, close to your father, who wants him taken down."

My brain spins for a moment, wondering who it could be. One of my trainers? Dr. Orteg? Someone in Security?

Definitely not Dona Oliver. She loved having a new, compliant Rafi.

"When did you hear about this?"

"That meeting on the Cobra, the one you weren't invited to."

I pull away a little. "You never told me."

"There wasn't time. And the truth is . . ." He takes a long breath. "You could've been captured in Paz, interrogated by Shreve. It was better for everyone if you didn't know."

"Col, your secret meeting was *before* I decided to stay in Paz. You can't use that . . ." My voice fades—and I see at last that the Vics were right.

I was someone who *could* leave Col. Someone who would run off to find her own sister, fight her own war, expose herself to capture, even with the dictator of Shreve searching everywhere for her.

Like X said, I am chaos.

Leyva and Zura knew me too well, and Col listened to them.

"Okay," I say. But it stings.

Even in victory, here we are again, fighting different wars.

Allies, but never perfectly aligned.

"Frey . . ." Col runs his fingers across my bristly head. With my hair this short, his touch shimmers on my scalp. "We're going to be happy again. We just have to fix the world."

A little shiver goes through me. But his words . . .

I've been Jubilant, Ecstatic, Sublime, and all of them are burned away.

How am I supposed to be *happy* again?

"No more secrets from each other," he says. "No more separations."

"How can you know that, Col?"

"Because that's what we both want, right?" His touch lingers on the back of my neck.

"Well, the city of Diego *did* admit you Vics are pretty good allies."

"You are too." He leans forward to kiss me, the scent of fireworks on his clothes, of bubbly on his lips.

And I feel safe. Like happiness is out there somewhere.

Our lips part, but only for a moment—the next kiss is slow and buzzing, the distant chaos of the rebel bash washing over us like rain.

Like the missing feels on my arm are just another scar.

"So what was the news?" I murmur.

Col pulls back a little, his dark eyes reflecting the fireworks crackling in the sky.

"The spy," he says. "They contacted us again. Boss X is alive."

MISSION

I'm not waiting for Diego to strike against my father.

There isn't time.

I'm getting ready, using all my connections, all my allies in this fight. Every piece of tech that Yandre can beg, borrow, or fabricate. Every scrap of intelligence the free cities have gathered. Every rebel and Vic willing to come along.

Only the *best* commandoes.

We're going back to Shreve, but not in force this time.

In stealth.

Bone implants to fool the scanners. Skinsuits that fleck off borrowed DNA. Shoes to alter our gaits. Larynx chips that change our voices.

And face-shifting surgery, of course, like the pretties of old.

We'll walk into Shreve as different people, random citizens. Impostors.

Because X is our brother-in-arms.

And there's another reason—if I'm going to rule my father's city one day, I have to see what it's like for his people, living in the shadow of his tower, breathing his dust, watching every word.

Don't say what you think. Don't move the wrong way.

Don't dream too loudly.

Don't have the wrong feels.

Spending a month in my father's tower, pretending to be Rafi every minute—it almost erased who I was. But the citizens of Shreve have spent a decade hiding themselves, living as impostors every day.

What if something's missing in them now? Lost to the dust?

There has to be a way to give it back to them.

As X told me . . . *Not all that's missing is gone.*

Maybe I can save my city.

ABOUT THE AUTHOR

Scott Westerfeld is the author of the Uglies series, the Leviathan trilogy, the Zeroes series, as well as the Spill Zone graphic novels, the novel *Afterworlds*, and the first book in the Horizon series. He has also written books for adults. Born in Texas, he and his wife now split their time between Sydney, Australia and New York City. You can find him online at scottwesterfeld.com.